I0526663

Until We Say Goodbye

by

Jane Drager

This is a work of fiction. Names, characters, places, and incidents are either the product of the author's imagination or are used fictitiously, and any resemblance to actual persons living or dead, business establishments, events, or locales, is entirely coincidental.

Until We Say Goodbye

COPYRIGHT © 2018 by Jane Drager

All rights reserved. No part of this book may be used or reproduced in any manner whatsoever without written permission of the author or The Wild Rose Press, Inc. except in the case of brief quotations embodied in critical articles or reviews.
Contact Information: info@thewildrosepress.com

Cover Art by *RJMorris*

The Wild Rose Press, Inc.
PO Box 708
Adams Basin, NY 14410-0708
Visit us at www.thewildrosepress.com

Publishing History
First Crimson Rose Edition, 2018
Print ISBN 978-1-5092-2314-5
Digital ISBN 978-1-5092-2315-2

Published in the United States of America

"We'll go to the bedroom together. Otherwise, I'll blow off your head." He yanked on her arm.

Gun or no gun, she wasn't one to be pushed around. *I'm dead anyway.* Lauren swung a fist toward his head while simultaneously lifting a knee to his groin.

He released a loud oomph and buckled but recovered to swing the gun at her head.

Metal impacted. Bone cracked. The room whirled.

Eric clutched her throat and jammed the gun between her eyes.

The metal felt cold against her skin, and the distinct smell of gun oil hit her nose. Images of her father and brother hunting groundhogs passed through her mind. Strange to think of something so silly when the hand gripping her throat tightened against her airway. Her father would never forgive her if she didn't fight. Pain ignored, she again kneed Eric's groin and buckled him enough to loosen his hold. But she hit the floor, too dizzy to escape. Nausea churned her stomach. She crawled along the floor, struggling to clear her vision. Blood dripped onto the white carpet. Oh, my God, Mrs. Stewart's rug!

Eric released a harsh laugh, jerked her to her feet, and struck her jaw with the pistol.

Her head snapped, and a gray glaze covered her vision. She lost all sense of place and time. No sounds registered. No one rushed to the rescue. Eric forced her onto feet that refused to move. *So, this is what it's like to die.*

Praise for Jane Drager

THE RIDDLE KEY is an interesting story. The characters were rich in life and realistic. The descriptions were great, they left you feeling like someone might be looking over your shoulder.

~ Candy B.

ASK NOTHING IN RETURN is a great read. The story is well laid out with lots of clues and twists to keep one reading. Several players add to the mystery and how it all works out is a surprise. Loved this story from start to finish!

~ Leanne D.

THE RIDDLE KEY was quite gripping. The book completely kept me hooked. The author made the plot interesting and kept the story flowing smoothly.

~ Krithika S.

SECRETS AND ASSUMPTIONS was such a great book, I couldn't put it down. Nothing pleases me more than a woman who takes charge of her own destiny.

~ Elizabeth J.

Dedication

To Betty, my sister and best bud.

Chapter One

Deems Lambert grumbled like a disgruntled orangutan as he trudged up the stairs to his sister's third floor apartment. He was too old to be reprimanded by a mother living a thousand miles away, but to calm her before she stroked, he'd agreed to check on his little sister while he had the mid-morning free.

He hadn't seen Jan in months and rarely bothered to call her on the phone. Consequently, he hardly knew what was going on in her young life. She kept busy with college, and he with work—both in different sections of Manhattan. Two worlds apart in age and lifestyle.

The staircase creaked underfoot, drawing the attention of a second floor tenant who peeked through a chain-secured door. The old woman's gaze cut him in two. To keep the peace, he smiled politely, even though he hadn't the slightest inclination to make her acquaintance.

Thin, cheap carpet, worn in the center by years of foot traffic, covered the steps. The building was one of the city's many brownstones, converted into an apartment occupying each floor, which helped the landlord pay for the high cost of living in New York. Before the start of the new school year, Jan moved from her dinky dorm room and found this place on East Sixty-Eighth Street, close enough to Hunter College, her school of choice. He helped her move what few possessions she owned but hadn't taken the time afterward to see what she'd done with the place.

Truthfully, he never expected her to last this long. Two years under her belt and still no declared major or plans for a future. Big deal, a bunch of liberal art courses. "Until I decide what I want to do," she'd said. He'd be old and gray before she made a decision. But she was his little sister, and he'd help her in any way possible. If she wanted to live here, fine. The place was decent enough. At least, no odoriferous smells assaulted his nose, like decomposing garbage.

Deems paused midway up the third flight, because a lion blocked his path. Not an actual lion, more like an over-sized tomcat fed too many snacks. He glared at the creature, willing it to move, but the furry ball lay spread on the step like a rolled-up rug, eyeing him through one open slit, his purr more like a growl. "Shoo!"

Did one say shoo to a cat? What other word applied? Scat? Scram? The damn beast hardly twitched a muscle except to yawn. Since an important part of his anatomy was in danger of being clawed from his body, Deems cupped a hand around his testicles and stepped over the feline.

The stuffiness worsened as he climbed. Too cool for air conditioning and too warm for a heater. No windows either. Hence, no air flow. The higher he climbed, the hotter the air, and he loosened his tie enough to relieve the strangling effect of limited oxygen.

When Jan first chose this old place and called to tell him, she bubbled with the enthusiasm of a young woman finally on her own. Even though he'd agreed to pay her rent, he'd gladly dole out more for a better apartment. Unfortunately, she loved the layout the second she crossed the threshold.

Slightly breathless and with leg muscles complaining, he stood before door number three, hesitant. Maybe he should have called. What if she wasn't home or still asleep? He had so much to do at the office. He checked his watch. Twelve twenty-three. *Too late now.* He raised a fist to knock when the door flew open. A woman stopped in her tracks, mouth agape, a pair of gorgeous green eyes wide. Her hair was a mane of dark brown, long and wavy, that floated around her shoulders.

Gripping the doorknob, she retreated a step. "Oh!"

His heart slammed against his rib cage. He attributed the sensation to the suddenness of her appearance, but wow, what a beauty! Swallowing hard and forcing a scowl, he dropped his hand. "You're supposed to look through the peephole before you open the door. This is New York, you know, not the safest city on Earth." She scowled right back, not in a mad sort of way since her sparkling gaze nearly bowled him over.

She scanned him from head to toe. "We don't receive too many well-dressed men at our door. What do you want?"

"I'm looking for Janice Lambert."

"Jan, for you!" She rushed past him. "Behave yourself. I'm only running to the first floor for the mail."

A vanilla scent drifted to his nose, and he snapped his head in a quick double-take. Although a familiar fragrance, she somehow made it truly intoxicating.

Clearing his throat, he cupped a hand near his mouth. "Watch out for the lion on the steps!"

She glanced over her shoulder and grinned. "That's King George. He's harmless." Within a second, she disappeared down the stairs.

Without question, she had a strong-looking appearance with broad shoulders tapering to a slim waist, definitely not the pampered type with delicate bones and painted fingernails, but not a muscle-bound Goliath either. If he had to pick a word, he'd use healthy with meat in all the right places, filling her blue jeans and T-shirt nicely.

"Hey!"

Startled, he turned to see his sister standing in the doorway. Jan was a small woman, five foot if that, and fit his definition of delicate, except he knew her to be a feisty little devil. Her light brown hair, cut Afro style, was frizzier than ever, and combined with her tie-dyed clothes, she resembled a throwback to the 1960s flower-child era. As with most city dwellers, her skin had a milky-white appearance since the only way to obtain a tan was from spending time on a rooftop. She was younger by ten years, and because of their age spread, they were never close.

She gave him a quick hug. "Well, this is a treat, especially for a guy who has to schedule a time to pee." Hands on hips, she stepped back. "What brings you here?"

Scrunching his face at her comment about his busy work schedule, he crossed the threshold and sucked in a whiff of her familiar citrus scent. "Mom called. She yelled at me for not checking on you." He and Jan weren't blessed with the same mother. Only four at the time, his mother had died after a short illness. A few years passed before his father remarried. Then, along came Jan. At ten years old, he was in no mood to have a baby sister, but he grew to love her and would do anything to make her happy—short of spoiling her to death.

Looking around, he stood in the living room where nothing matched. Different size end tables, different colored lamps. A comfy sofa of red, a stiff side chair of purple. On the wall, a flat-screen TV faced the sofa along with posters of rock stars, none of whom he recognized.

The living room led to the two bedrooms and one bath while a small eat-in kitchen sat off to the side in its own tight cubbyhole. A typical New York City apartment demanding exorbitant rent for scant amenities. At least, the place had a few windows—one in the kitchen, one in each bedroom, and a skylight in the bathroom since Jan had the top floor. "Nice job with decorating." What else could he say...that the place was as colorful as her clothes? He had offered her money to buy furniture, but she stubbornly refused.

Jan patted an orange pillow and positioned it in the corner of the sofa. "Thanks. I saved a bundle by shopping at yard sales."

More like something left at curbside for trash pickup. He motioned with his thumb toward the door. "Who was the woman I passed?"

"My roommate. She'll be back."

This was news. His brow cocked. "You never told me about a roommate."

Patting a blue pillow, she placed it in the opposite sofa corner. "She's short term. She needed a place to stay for five months, and I wanted some company." As she waved him to follow into the kitchen, Jan threw a furtive glance toward the open front door. "Hurry."

She shoved him through the archway and toward the stove. Leaning forward, she shot a quick glance over her shoulder. "I know you're paying my monthly rent, but Lauren doesn't know, and our agreement is for her to pay half. I use the money for the utilities and groceries." She jutted her small chin and grinned. "You must have noticed I haven't asked for any extra money."

When necessary, Jan never hesitated to call or text her big brother for a handout. She received an allowance but also had a credit card for emergencies. Sometimes, her *emergencies* created quite a bill. He nodded at his sister with a satisfied smile. "Not a bad arrangement. I commend your initiative." He gave a slight bow.

Jan's face beamed. "A chip off the old block?"

"Undoubtedly." He suppressed a smile.

"The arrangement's been great, too. Lauren's like an older sister. She's closer to your age and has this maturity that I can only hope to achieve. We've become great friends, and I'll miss her when she leaves." She dragged out a kitchen chair from under the table and gestured for him to sit. "Did Mom really call you?"

Wow, the two chairs and table matched! "'fraid so. She had every right to yell. I've been neglecting my little sister." Applying pressure, he checked the chair's sturdiness but wasn't ready to sit. Curiosity about Jan's roommate kept him on his feet, and he slowly inched toward the kitchen entrance. "Mom's threatening to drag Dad back to Chicago so they can entice you to leave New York."

Her small mouth fell open. "Leave Florida for Chicago? Are they crazy? Maybe they're getting too much sun." She pulled out the other chair but didn't sit. "Besides, Chicago isn't that much different from New York. Like you, I'm used to city life." She pointed toward the doorway. "Now, Lauren, she's a fish out of water here. She comes from some small town in Pennsylvania."

The front door closed. Ever so casually, Deems leaned against the archway to see Jan's roommate sorting the mail. Her hair fell forward in gentle waves but not enough to hide her soft profile with the cute chin and slightly upturned nose. No alabaster skin on this woman. Her face and forearms glowed with the tan of outdoor living.

"Want some coffee?"

Jan's voice jerked his attention to the kitchen. "Sure."

"Sit and have a cookie." She opened a tin and slid the container onto the table. "Lauren's a fantastic cook. I can buy anything, and she'll make something mouth-watering."

He settled at the small table and grabbed a cookie. Chocolate chip, one of his favorites.

Eyeing his suit, Jan frowned. "You can take off your suit jacket, Deems."

Sacrilege in his book. A true violation of his dress code. Instead, he undid all three buttons.

As Jan grabbed the coffee carafe and filled the glass with tap water, she rotated her head and smirked. "And the tie, dear brother. You don't always have to dress so formally."

Irritation swept through him. "I just came from the office, Jan, and have every intention of returning. You should know that." A suit and tie were a part of him, like a symbol of the man within. He never wore anything less. "How's school?" Best to avoid the subject of a wardrobe he wouldn't change for anyone.

She sighed heavily. "Boring. I don't know why I'm going." She poured the water into the machine and then opened a can of coffee, sprinkling the grounds into the filter instead of measuring.

After her high school graduation, he had encouraged her to spend a year working in either several service jobs or an office to see what captured her interest. Disregarding his advice, she entered college with no vocation in mind, accumulating credits for subjects that held no value to the outside world. She wasn't building a career. Instead, she majored in wasting time and money. "Is your roommate in one of your classes?" He popped another cookie into his mouth. The combination of butter and chocolate reminded him of his favorite bake shop in Chicago, and he just might wolf down the entire batch.

"Oh, no. She's studying with a well-known Italian artist and is only here for a few more months." With her finger on the start switch, she paused. "I wish I had her focus."

Well, she admits the fault. A plus.

Jan flipped on the appliance and turned, her thin face bright. "Do you want to meet her?"

He'd been wondering how to broach the subject of a formal introduction without sounding interested. The last item on his agenda was for Jan to play matchmaker for her older brother. "Okay, but before you make introductions, what does she know about me?"

She shrugged a set of small shoulders. "That we both have brothers. Other than that, nothing."

No bragging? No big-brother-is-the-best-in-the-world speech? He wasn't sure whether to feel disappointed or relieved.

"I know how private you are, Deems. We only talked about brothers in general." She stepped toward the doorway. "Lauren!"

Jan's roommate wandered in while reading a letter. She glanced up with a jolt to meet Deems' gaze.

His breath hitched. He'd met a lot of beautiful women over the years but never one with such a down-to-earth look. She wore no jewelry, just a plain watch on her left wrist. A trace of mascara accented her eyes, which, in his opinion, needed no enhancement, but her face appeared natural with her cheeks slightly flushed.

Jan grabbed Lauren's arm and edged her toward the table. "Lauren Howell, meet my brother, Deems."

Two perfectly arched eyebrows rose. "Jan mentioned you once or twice." She extended her hand. "Hi."

He stood to take her hand, and sparks shot up his arm on contact. She had a firm grip, stronger than some men on his payroll. Her mouth dropped open slightly as her gaze scanned his face but gave no impression if the spark was mutual. She was of average height, possibly five-six to his six-one, and even had biceps showing from below her T-shirt sleeve. The strong urge to hold onto her hand forever collided with common sense until she tugged a bit to break the spell. Clearing his throat, he released her before she labeled him as some sex-starved New Yorker. "Jan tells me you're an artist."

Jan stepped forward. "Actually, Lauren has a Master's in Education. She's smart."

Smiling, Lauren rolled her eyes. "Not that smart. Look, I'm sure you two want to visit. I'm late for an afternoon class." She grabbed a green apple from the fruit basket on the counter. "I'll be late tonight, Jan, probably after six. Nice to meet you, Mr. Lambert."

Deems watched her from the kitchen entrance as she slipped on a jacket, hoisted a backpack onto one shoulder, and headed for the front door.

She paused to meet his gaze, hand on the doorknob, and a curl of a smile touched her lips that immediately radiated from her eyes. She lifted a hand for a small wave and left, closing the door behind her.

Suddenly, the apartment felt empty. Lauren had a presence about her that he couldn't understand. Maturity certainly. A woman who understood her place in the world. Definitely a far cry from any of Jan's regular friends. He reclaimed his seat at the table while Jan poured two cups of coffee. "She seems nice."

"I like her." Jan extracted the milk carton from the refrigerator and placed the container in front of him.

He pointed to the fruit basket full of red, green, and yellow apples. "Aren't the green ones bitter?"

"Yes, the Granny Smith. Great for cooking, but Lauren likes them as is. The more bitter, the better, she says. I tried one." Crinkling her nose, she shuddered. "Real pucker power."

Deems poured a hefty amount of milk into his cup until the coffee changed to pale beige, the way he drank it. He wasn't sure he should ask the question, but he had to know. "Is Lauren seeing anyone?"

Jan sat and wrapped her hands around the mug.

"No, and she won't either. Her ex-fiancé burned her big time. She won't even look at another man."

But she looked at me. For some reason, that minor fact caused his chest to swell. Hiding a grin, he sipped his coffee. "She's very beautiful."

"She's got the looks to stop a freight train. Guys are constantly asking about her." She spooned three teaspoons of sugar into her coffee and stirred. "I wish I was that pretty."

How many men? Two? Twenty? Far too much testosterone floated around a college campus, and Jan's apartment was definitely too close. With little else to say except squelch his annoyance, he reached across the table and squeezed Jan's hand. "You're pretty in your own way. Like me. I'm not one of those drop-dead gorgeous guys that women chase." He released her hand to grab another cookie with thoughts drifting to other possible delights on Lauren's bake list.

"If women knew more about you, they'd chase."

"For all the wrong reasons." He shoved the entire cookie into his mouth and crunched on the buttery sweet goodness.

She wagged a finger. "Not necessarily, big brother. You're always a little too shy around women. I don't understand how you can be such a successful businessman and yet get all tongue-tied around women."

Chewing before he choked to death, he swallowed his mouthful with a sip of coffee. "Not tongue-tied, Jan. Cautious. You know how some women play games."

"All right, cautious." She dipped the edge of a cookie into her coffee. "How often do you meet a woman with a face like hers?"

Beautiful women were a dime a dozen in New York. Most were frivolous and wandered from day to day without a real purpose to their lives. Far too many hoped to attract the attention of a rich man, and Manhattan had quite a few wealthy men, many already married.

Deems grabbed another cookie. Dear Lord, how many had he eaten? Maybe he should stop before strangling his waistline. "What happened with Lauren's fiancé?"

Staring into her cup, Jan stirred her coffee. "She'll tell you in her own time—provided you come around more often." Glancing up, she grinned, her hazel eyes twinkling. "I assume you're interested?"

More than interested. Wild horses couldn't keep him away after one glimpse of Jan's extremely attractive roommate.

Chapter Two

With a heavy sigh, Lauren Howell stared at the staircase leading to her third floor apartment. On days like this, she really wished for an elevator. Even a bucket on a rope would do. Anything to hoist her up to avoid the long climb. Either that or take a nap here on the first floor with King George. *The lion.* At the memory of Deems' words, she chuckled and plodded up the stairs.

Although a week and a half had passed since she met Jan's brother, she squelched her curiosity by concentrating on her purpose in New York. Yes, she'd experienced an electrical jolt when their hands touched, but so what? She had absolutely no interest in dating, no matter how attractive the prospect.

Right now, her objective was to climb these stairs before collapsing in an exhausted heap. From seven this morning until six in the evening, she'd spent a long day in art class and arrived at the brownstone barely able to keep her eyes open. A full thirteen-hour session.

Antonio scheduled a special day for the students, which included cutting, mounting, and soldering glass art too heavy to move. All six students participated, each working on a section before joining the pieces to complete a grandiose masterpiece that she swore could never fit anywhere. Then, as a team, they each lifted a corner for placement against the wall, being oh-so careful, inching their feet across the room, and hardly breathing. Naturally, the glass snapped straight down the middle and shattered onto the concrete floor. Disheartened, she stared at the shards, waiting for the colors to meld together like special effects in a movie.

Antonio laughed so hard he almost tipped from his chair, all the while declaring the project as a valuable lesson learned. "Never rush the soldering," he said. A mantra he repeated over and over. Obviously, someone hadn't listened.

She yawned as her foot touched the third floor landing only to discover the door to her apartment wide open. Male voices flowed from within, one angry and the others subdued. Her grip tightened on the handrail. Had something happened to Jan? Were they robbed?

Heart thumping, she hurried to the doorway to see four men standing in the middle of the living room. Two were uniformed NYPD officers, the third, her landlord, Mr. O'Reilly, and the fourth, Deems Lambert, who looked red-faced and furious. Simultaneously, they turned toward her, as if some invisible force yanked on a string. She raised a brow. "What's going on?"

Mr. O'Reilly, with his gray, wispy hair standing straight up from the top of his head, approached first. "I'm sorry, Ms. Howell, but this man claims to be Ms. Lambert's brother. I ain't never seen him before, and since I'm no spring chicken to handle a guy this size, I called the cops. He demanded to be let into the apartment."

With a gaze cutting her in two, Deems stepped forward, his neck veins straining against his skin. "Where's Jan?"

Lauren jumped at his harsh tone. The man stood

like a bull ready to charge with nostrils flaring and hands rolled into tight fists. She hadn't seen a man this angry since her father burned the starter coil on his tractor. Sucking in a breath to steady her nerves, she turned to Mr. O'Reilly. "You could have called me."

O'Reilly shook his head. "He's too belligerent."

A cop positioned himself between her and Deems. "Do you know this gentleman?"

"Huh?" Despite Deems' bull-in-a-china-shop look, he was still a handsome man, and she had to force away her gaze to focus on the officer. "Yes, he's Jan's brother."

Deems stepped around the cop. "Then, where the hell is she? I've been calling her all day with no answer." Gaze narrowed, he pointed an accusing finger in her face. "Even your landlord said he hasn't seen her. Why wasn't she reported missing?"

Fatigue swept through her body with her feet and back complaining the loudest. Could she help it if brother and sister rarely communicated? But she'd better say something before the man blew a gasket. Shaking her head, Lauren dropped her backpack onto the floor and faced Deems. "Because she's not missing. She's still in the Bahamas with Eric."

Squinting, Deems scowled. "Who's Eric?"

"Her boyfriend. Didn't she tell you?"

"Obviously not." His jaw twitched, and he glanced from one man to the next until returning his gaze to her. "How long has she been going with him?"

With a hand over her mouth, she stifled a yawn. "I don't know. A couple of months maybe. You want me to go to the precinct for a lie-detector test?"

Whoa! His head snapped so fast she swore a neck

15

vertebrae cracked. *Geez, mister, chill out.*

The officer, who had been standing between them, cleared his throat. "Is there any way you can reach Ms. Lambert to reassure her brother?"

She checked her wristwatch. "She agreed to turn on her phone at eight every night. That was ten minutes ago. Let's see if she remembered." *Hell, I wouldn't.* She slipped her cell phone from her jeans back pocket and typed a text message. *Call me. Urgent.* She showed the officer before hitting the Send button.

A long two minutes later, her phone rang. "Will you please talk to your brother before he has me thrown in jail? No, no, he'll explain." She thrust the phone into Deems' face.

He promptly responded with an annoyed glare.

Of all days for such excitement. Any other evening would be run-of-the-mill boring, but after hours on her feet, she had a kink in her neck, a cramp in her right calf, and the beginnings of a headache. She needed food and quiet. Besides, regardless what Deems Lambert believed, Jan was old enough to do as she pleased. Granted at age twenty-two, she wasn't the most mature woman to deal with a man like Eric, but Lauren had no business to judge.

For her, Jan had turned into a godsend. Money was tight, and Lauren desperately needed an inexpensive place to live. Rooming with Jan proved a hell of a lot cheaper than all other options. Food and lodging cost far too much in Manhattan, and with transportation factored in, Lauren barely had two dimes to rub together. Consequently, she walked the fifteen blocks to her class every day and only occasionally rode the subway home. Like tonight when she'd been too exhausted to walk.

While conversing with his sister, Deems paced, yelling mostly, his aggravation at her unannounced trip apparent.

Mr. O'Reilly raised both hands in the air and left while the two officers waited by the front door, conversing between themselves.

Lauren dropped onto the sofa and rubbed her eyes. The whole scene was comical in a way, reminiscent of a sit-com where big brother overreacted to his little sister's lah-de-dah ways. Deems probably thought Lauren had done away with her roommate to have the apartment all to herself. Little did he know she'd rather stay in a flophouse than pay the full exorbitant rent.

Finished with his tirade, Deems disconnected and walked to the officers.

Her gaze followed him. He wasn't a drop-dead gorgeous guy but definitely an attractive one who wore a business suit like he popped out of his mother's womb fully dressed. Dark brown hair fell loosely over one brow, partially hiding the pale brown hue of his eyes. He was a lot older than Jan, maybe closer to Lauren's age of twenty-nine, and looked every bit the successful businessman with a slim build on a tall frame. No wedding band but that meant nothing in this day and age. Still, his sheer physical presence was impressive enough for anyone to take notice. Including her.

Deems shook hands with the officers.

One cop turned to her with a semi-salute. "Shall we escort him to the street, ma'am?"

She would like nothing more than to be left alone, but Deems had such a deep grimace on his face, she almost felt sorry for him. "I think he's tamed, officer.

Thank you."

They tipped their hats and left.

Deems closed the door and shot her a quick glance. "I overreacted." After crossing the room, he handed her the phone.

"I'll say." She took the phone, and their fingers brushed ever so slightly. Such a simple touch caused another spark that bolted straight to her core. Her breath hitched, but she avoided eye contract. More than likely, the sudden arc could be attributed to fatigue or, better yet, a static shock from the rug. She slid the phone onto the end table. "You caused quite a ruckus, Mr. Lambert."

The grimace intensified. "I should apologize to Mr. O'Reilly. I scared him—and you. Jan never mentioned a boyfriend." He stuffed his hands into his trouser pockets and tilted his head. "Is he a decent fellow?"

Leaning back, she shrugged and rested her head on the sofa's cushion. "He's not a man I'd date." She wasn't about to influence his opinion merely because she detested the air Eric Drummer breathed. Jan's boyfriend had a way of raising the hairs on the back of Lauren's neck, and she avoided him as much as possible. "For the record, your sister went on a spur-of-the-moment trip. Eric called, said he had two tickets to the Bahamas, and off they went. I'm hoping Jan hasn't put the rest of the trip on her charge card." *Oops.* She inwardly winced. So much for not influencing his opinion.

With a frown, Deems jingled the change in his pocket and walked around to the front of the sofa to face her, his gaze guarded. "She's allowed to charge anything she wants."

"Good, because I didn't mean to let that slip." She ran her fingers through her hair. "Sometimes, I worry about her. Jan's a grown woman if, however, a tad naïve."

"She's never been anything *but* naïve. That's why I panicked." His gaze relaxed, and a smile spread onto his lips. "I'm glad you're here."

His warm smile nearly liquefied her bones. Even without showing teeth, he conveyed a sexiness she hadn't seen in a long time. *I must be too tired.* Why else would she want to wrestle him to the floor and have her way with him? She stifled a yawn. "My time in New York is almost over, Mr. Lambert. Jan will be on her own soon enough."

His smile disappeared.

Hopefully, he hadn't expected her to be Jan's chaperone. Lauren Howell had her own problems, and the majority involved money. She met his gaze. "She'll be fine, Mr. Lambert."

He grunted then shifted his gaze from one rock star poster to the next. "Jan and I were never close, Lauren. We have a ten-year spread between our ages, and I moved from Chicago to New York before she finished high school." He turned from the posters and settled onto the other end of the sofa. "We had different mothers. Mine died when I was four."

That explained the age difference and dissimilar appearance. Jan had a washed-out look with her pale skin and light hair and compensated with flowery clothes. On the other hand, Deems had a deeper skin tone and dark hair. He also had height, which Jan desperately needed.

Without lifting her head from the backrest, Lauren

shifted on the seat to study him. The man definitely had exquisite taste in clothes. The charcoal gray suit fit his shoulders perfectly and tapered to his waist. His shoes were Italian, and a gold watch covered his left wrist. Whether he had money or not wasn't her concern since many men—and women—pretended to be upper crust when, in fact, they scraped the bottom of a barrel and ate hot dogs every night. Her family was lower middle class and bursting with pride, and even though her Masters in Education raised her to a different level, she stood just as proud by her family's side.

Sleep crept over her. She should shoo him out since he picked the most inopportune time to rant and rave about his sister, but he had a nice voice, deep and masculine, the kind that gave a woman chills. Plus, he was easy on the eyes. He'd also filled the apartment with his musk scent. Nice. Enticing. Better than Eric's eau de motor oil.

"Is Jan serious with this guy?"

Who? Blinking fast, she shook herself and met his gaze. "He's all she talks about."

He unbuttoned his suit jacket and leaned back, relaxing an arm on the sofa's armrest. "Is Eric living here?"

Her gaze snapped up to his face. She had been staring at the sparkling diamond embedded in his tie tack. "Not yet. I'd say the move's inevitable. I'm praying she holds off inviting him until I'm gone." She used both hands to stifle a yawn.

He sat forward and slapped his knees. "You're tired. I should go."

Yes, he should but made no attempt to stand. He looked at her with a quizzical lift to his brow, as if he wanted permission to move.

She inwardly smiled because she wasn't about to dismiss him. Which surprised her. Fatigue had swept over her like a blanket, and all her limbs turned into lead. Yet, for the life of her, she refused to speak up. One word from her, and he'd be out the door, so why not say goodnight?

Because she wanted a chance to talk with a man who had two feet firmly planted on the ground. Jan was okay for conversation, but she had the mentality of a high school senior, and Lauren passed that stage a long time ago. And of the five students in her art class, three were so friggin' competitive, they created stressful sessions which she hurried to escape.

Sitting forward, she gave Deems a slight smile. "Yes, I'm tired, Mr. Lambert, but I'm also hungry. Care for some leftover chicken casserole?" She stood, and he joined her. This time, she let her gaze linger on his face, at his square jaw with barely a hint of a stubble, on his full lips, and the trimmed sideburns near his ears. Definitely a man who took pride in his appearance.

"Do I pass?"

She jerked then widened her eyes. "Huh?" *Oh, my God, I am blatantly staring*! Heat rose into her cheeks. "Sorry. I didn't mean to be rude."

His gaze sparkled. "No problem. You gave me a chance to return the scrutiny."

Oh, hell, and she hadn't noticed. With a wave, she gestured toward the kitchen. "Nothing fancy, Mr. Lambert. Just casserole and iced tea."

"That sounds perfect." He walked behind her but stopped in the archway to the kitchen.

She grabbed plates from an overhead cabinet, took

the casserole from the refrigerator, and spooned a healthy portion onto each. After sliding one dish into the microwave and hitting the Start button, she then reached for tea glasses and set them on the table. While taking dinnerware from the drawer, she glanced over her shoulder. He had stepped into the kitchen but watched her with a guarded gaze. Since he'd already suspected her of doing away with Jan, maybe he contemplated a poisoning of his food. The idea almost made her laugh. She replaced the lid on the casserole and returned the dish to the refrigerator. "Deems is unusual for a first name."

Pulling out a chair, he lowered onto the thin cushion. "The name belongs to my great-grandfather on my mother's side. The name is old English, but my mother's family is actually from Dublin."

Jan had mentioned her brother on several occasions but hardly said anything worth retaining. Now, she understood why. Their ten-year age spread created too wide of a rift. Jan was still a little girl while he dated or worked, and from what Jan said, Deems mainly worked. Lauren and her brother, Bill, were only three years apart and always had a close relationship.

After placing the hot plate in front of Deems, Lauren slipped in the second dish for reheating and punched in numbers for time. Facing him, she waited by leaning against the counter, arms folded across her chest.

Deems sniffed the steam rising from his food. "Smells good."

"My mother's recipe." The timer dinged. She placed her plate on the table and settled at the table while he poured the tea from a large pitcher. She stifled another yawn with a quick glance in his direction. "Sorry, long day."

"You didn't have to invite me to eat." He forked in a mouthful, and his eyes widened. "Wow, this is great!" He shoveled in more and chewed, eyes closed. "I haven't had food this good since I lived with my parents in Chicago. Marry me."

What? She started, met the twinkle in his gaze, then leaned back and laughed.

Grinning, he waved his fork toward her. "That's better. Your whole face brightens when you laugh."

She gave him a long, quiet look. "What would you do if I said yes?"

"I'd stutter and stammer and wonder how the hell to take back the words." He winked. "I'm glad to see you have a sense of humor. I'd like to know a little about you, Lauren Howell."

She took two napkins from the holder on the table and handed him one. "I teach creative art, high school level. Once I'm done with this special class, I'd like to include stained glass in my course." She forked in a mouthful and chewed. "I'm studying with Antonio Giovanni Cartilano, the most famous stained glass artist in the country."

His gaze focused on her face. "But school is in session. Why are you here and not teaching?"

"Because the State of Pennsylvania is in a budget crisis. Schools in every county were closed and consolidated." Her mouth twisted to the side. "I lost my job last June along with dozens of others. So, I enrolled in Antonio's class before applying for a new position." She should be careful giving her life history to a stranger, but the man had a way of relaxing her. A

23

combination of his voice and gentle smile, along with the kindness that passed onto his face, left her with a warm tingle. These days, most men gave her a cold chill.

"Jan mentioned you were strapped for cash."

Whew, touchy subject. Avoiding eye contact, she toyed with her food. "I'm collecting unemployment, but New York is far too pricey to live here on Pennsylvania's monthly allotment. Once I return home, I'll find a temporary job as a food server." She met his gaze. "I worked my way through college doing three-D murals for businesses and developed quite a reputation in Harrisburg."

A smile tugged on the corner of his mouth. "Sounds impressive. You can probably do the same in New York."

Dear Lord, never! Such a statement made her skin crawl. She waved her fork. "This city is not where I want to be." She sipped her tea. "My biggest dream is to open my own studio if and whenever I buy my own house."

"To teach?"

"Teach and create." Which wouldn't happen for a long time given her current lack of funds.

He forked in a mouthful, chewed, then swallowed. "I wish Jan had more focus. I'm hoping you influence her in some way."

"We've talked, but she hasn't a clue about her future." With the napkin, she wiped the corner of her lips. "Jan's young, even at twenty-two. Most kids her age think college is a big party."

"I suppose that's how she met Eric." Cringing, he met her gaze. "Drugs?"

Her brows furrowed. "I'm not sure. That's why I'm hoping she holds off with their live-in arrangement." His mouth opened to speak, but she extended a finger to stop him. "Yes, I talked to her about protection." She shrugged and smiled. "Big sister stuff."

His shoulders relaxed. "Thank you, provided she follows your advice. I promised Mom and Dad I'd watch out for Jan, but so far, I've done a lousy job. Truthfully, I'm surprised she applied to a New York college and not one in Chicago."

She held up a finger. "I can answer that. She wanted her parents to move to Florida without worrying about her. By coming to New York, she'd at least have you nearby."

A brow lifted, and he shot her a quick glance. "I didn't realize she'd be so considerate." He finished the food on his plate, wiped the napkin over his mouth, and leaned back. "I shouldn't complain about her lack of focus. I barely passed a year of college before I quit." He finished his tea in three gulps and stood. With his empty plate in hand, he walked to the sink. "Since you fed me, I'll wash up."

She almost choked on her casserole. When was the last time she heard a man volunteer for kitchen detail, especially one dressed in a silk shirt and tie? Suppressing a smile, she stood. "No, I'll take care of the dishes, Mr. Lambert. Come on, I'll walk you to the door."

Deems was a nice change from his chatterbox sister. And he seemed comfortable enough sitting at their small kitchen table. But truth be told, she had enough experience with men to know when one showed more than a casual interest. Sure, he hadn't said a word, but his gaze spoke volumes. Best to push him out of the apartment before his musk cologne weakened her resolve.

At the front door, he paused with his hand on the knob, his smile gentle. "I'm sorry I frightened you. With Jan not answering her phone and you not at home, I honestly believed something happened to her."

"And when I walked in alone, I was suspected of dastardly deeds?"

His gaze twinkled. "Something like that." He opened the door. "Thanks for dinner."

The breeze of the moving door blew his cologne past her, and the fragrance assaulted her senses in a way that stirred something deep inside her gut. Since the breakup of her engagement, she hadn't had a good round of sex, and she'd love to be in a man's arms again. But to start a relationship while in New York would be asinine. Even with a man as tempting as Jan's brother. What if he kissed her, today, this second? *Hell, I won't even stop him.*

But he simply smiled.

A gesture that displayed beautiful white teeth bright enough to weaken her knees.

Narrowing his gaze, he leaned close. "Don't call me Mr. Lambert anymore. You make me feel old."

Because she couldn't help herself, she smiled right back.

Chapter Three

Before popping the cake pan into the preheated oven, Lauren licked the spicy batter off her fingers. Apple cake, a specialty from her hometown in apple country. Jan and Eric were due home tonight, and she'd prepared a scrumptious meal to welcome them. Oven-baked chicken, mashed potatoes with tons of butter and garlic, peas, a salad with homemade dressing, and an inexpensive bottle of white wine. She'd gotten the chicken and potatoes on sale, a lucky break considering her budget. Of course, a sale in Manhattan was a far cry from one at home, but she'd take what she could, even though New York prices bordered on highway robbery.

Today was Wednesday, and as a lucky break, Antonio cut their class short to attend an art show somewhere in Massachusetts. Lauren had ample time to shop for bargains, but why she bothered to feed two lovebirds perpetually in la-la land was unclear. To be nice, she supposed. Just because she detested Eric's presence didn't mean she had to make her feelings known to Jan. Besides, they were originally scheduled to fly in on Saturday, but for some reason, they cut their vacation three days short. Hopefully, neither caught a bug on the trip.

"Lauren, we're home!"

Tossing her apron onto the counter, Lauren hurried to the living room as Jan swung several bags and boxes onto the sofa. Eric clunked the suitcases on the floor like he hadn't an ounce of strength left to carry them. They were both red from a short week on the beach…well, Jan was red with her frizzy hair frizzier than ever. She resembled a cooked beet with fuzz. Eric Drummer showed more tan than red since he spent the majority of his time working on his beat-up sedan. After such a trip, he should have lost the motor oil clogging his pores—assuming he'd taken a bath or a dip in the ocean.

What those two saw in each other remained a mystery. Janice Lambert was a cute, little woman, five foot and not an inch taller. At twenty-two, she barely had a shape, definitely no breasts so she saved on bra purchases. She wore only flowery or tie-dyed clothes, which hung loose to the point of flowing, but they gave her desperately needed color.

Eric Drummer, however, wasn't a man who caught a woman's eye. Tall, lanky, and slightly slumped at the shoulders, he was six years older than Jan with stringy brown hair, shoulder-length and untrimmed. He had a habit of pushing the strands behind his ears with both hands in a feminine gesture that annoyed the hell out of Lauren. He wasn't handsome in any way with too long a nose, brown eyes squeezed too close, and an untrimmed goatee. His entire wardrobe consisted of faded jeans with multiple rips and worn T-shirts overdue for the rag pile. He claimed his poor-man attire helped his case at the unemployment office.

Lauren hugged Jan but merely nodded at Eric. The repulsion of that man touching her was beyond her tolerance. Jan might be all ga-ga over him, but Lauren considered him a freeloader, a man taking advantage of

Jan's innocence.

Stepping back with a smile, Lauren placed her hands on her hips, her gaze sweeping from Jan to Eric. "So, how was the trip?"

Jan beamed. "We had a smashing time. And I've got great news." She wrapped an arm around Eric's waist. "Eric's moving in!"

Aw, shit. Couldn't they wait two more months? Hiding a grimace, Lauren shot a glance from one face to the other. "Here? Now?"

"Sure, what better time than now?" Tilting her head, Jan stared lovingly at her boyfriend, sighed, and then returned her gaze to Lauren. "We discussed the arrangement and decided we'd save a lot of money if he lived with us. Great news, huh?"

Yeah, just wonderful. Her chest tightened. "Shouldn't we talk to Mr. O'Reilly? He may not like the idea of three people in this place." *Dear Lord, how can I possibly dissuade her?*

Jan waved aside the comment. "We'll be three people for a couple of months. After you leave, we'll be back to two. He shouldn't complain." She gave Eric's waist a squeeze. "The best part of the whole deal is now we'll split the rent in three."

Eric released himself from Jan's arm wrap and leaned toward Lauren. "We definitely don't want you to leave. I may be on unemployment, but I can help with the rent."

His unemployment allotment should be substantially higher than hers. That was the only pleasant news arising from Jan's announcement. Lauren needed all the breaks available. But good Lord, Eric? How could she possibly live in the same apartment and share the same bathroom with such a scumbag? She'd rather poke out her eye with a stick.

With no other recourse in the foreseeable future, Lauren swallowed her concerns and let out a sigh. "All right." Nothing else to do but accept the change. She hugged Jan a second time. "I'm happy for you, honey." *May as well make the best of the situation.*

Ever since she moved in, Lauren had acted like a mother hen to Jan, and they discussed an abundance of issues. One of which included Eric's age. Since Jan had an obvious lack of maturity, she risked being stepped on by Eric. Actually, the word might be trampled, and Jan's invitation to Eric smacked of impulsiveness, a subject not well conceived as far as privacy issues and space. The apartment had two bedrooms but only one full bath, one television in the living room, and a two-seater kitchen table. The idea of sharing close quarters with a man like Eric made Lauren's skin crawl.

I'll tolerate him. To look for another place with only two months before her classes ended would be a lesson in futility. She was a big girl and had taken care of herself since the start of college. Eric was just another bump in the road.

The oven timer buzzed. She clapped her hands and waved Jan toward the kitchen. "We'll have more room if we eat in the living room. Eric, clear off the sofa." Hurrying, she grabbed her oven mitts and removed the cake pan as Eric's cell phone shrilled.

After several minutes, he joined Jan and Lauren in the kitchen. "I'm running out for a few minutes. You two start without me." He kissed Jan on the top of her head. "I'm taking your backpack."

"Why?" Jan reached for his arm but grabbed only

air. "The bag's full of dirty laundry."

Scratching his head, he stopped in the archway. "Oh, right. I'll dump the clothes on the bed. Be back in a jiff." He gave a quick wave and left.

Both women stared at the empty archway until the front door slammed.

Shaking herself, Jan frowned. "I guess we may as well eat in here. Who knows when he'll return." She took wine glasses from the cabinet and set them on the table. "He's been acting weird lately."

"Weirder than normal?" Lauren hooked her arm through Jan's and urged her to sit at the table. "Maybe this is a good time to explain why you cut three days from your vacation."

"Oh—" Jan shot Lauren a pained look but quickly broke eye contact. "Eric said an old friend is in town, and he wants to see him before he leaves." She shrugged her small shoulders. "He said it's important."

More important than a trip to the Bahamas with a girlfriend? Talk about an ego-buster. "Who paid for this trip, Jan?"

Jan lowered her gaze even further and shuffled her feet on the linoleum floor. "Me. He'd made all the plans but admitted to his lack of cash." She shot her a sideways glance. "He bought the plane tickets, though."

Whoop de do. Typical male. Working his own agenda…like her ex.

The days passed. Lauren fell into a routine of avoiding the lovebirds who kissed and cuddled at every opportunity. Always feeling like a third wheel, she spent a lot of time in Central Park since the location wasn't far from the studio. She'd munch on a sandwich or an apple, killing time before walking home. She rarely cooked except for herself in the morning and hadn't eaten dinner with them since she took no great pleasure sitting near Eric. Anyway, Jan wanted to impress him with her culinary skills. Too bad his table manners bordered on Neanderthal. He wolfed food like garbage being shoved into a disposal.

Since the beginning of the semester, on every Tuesday and Thursday, Jan attended an early morning class while Lauren's five-day-a-week class began promptly at ten unless specifically ordered to arrive earlier. Eric stumbled from bed when the mood hit him and flicked on the TV where he lounged on the sofa for the majority of the day. He was never fully dressed, always shirtless to show a chest with no muscles, no hair, and absolutely no stimulus to a woman's libido. With his stringy hair and the chronic odor of motor oil, the man was about as appealing as a used tissue. But Jan loved him, and that was all that mattered...to her.

One night, while reading a magazine in bed, Lauren let her thoughts drift and immediately conjured images of Deems. She wasn't sure why he popped into her head. He hadn't come around since their dinner together and only talked to Jan once after her return from the Bahamas. Since she ate alone most of the time, Lauren longed for another casual conversation with a man far better than slovenly Eric. Every once in a while, she'd come home and sit on the outside step with Mr. O'Reilly, but he was in his seventies and of no comparison to a man like Deems.

If truth be told, the thought of seeking Deems' company was dangerous. She attributed her bit of mind wandering to the intense loneliness of being in New York without family or friends. Sure, she'd call her mother or a few close girlfriends, but nothing beat having a face-to-face talk with a live human. These days, Jan centered most of her attention on Eric, so she and Lauren rarely spent time together. If anything, Eric had caused a rift in their friendship wider than the Grand Canyon.

One morning, to Lauren's surprise, Eric strolled into the kitchen while she ate breakfast at the table. He wore no shirt, no socks, and his jeans had the snap loose, revealing the unmistakable absence of underwear.

He scrunched his face at her scrambled eggs and spinach and yawned loudly. "Any coffee left?"

Suppressing a shudder, she fully expected him to scratch himself, or worse, stretch until his pants fell. "Help yourself." She bit into her toast and glanced at the wall clock. "The time is barely eight o'clock. Why are you awake so early?" A job interview? A chance to contribute rather than take? *Yeah, right. Dream on.*

"I wanted to talk to you without Jan home." He poured coffee into a cup and spooned in his usual six teaspoons of sugar.

Lauren wiped the last of her eggs with the toast, not in the least willing to have a private conversation with the man. "What do you want to talk about?"

"You, in particular." He leaned against the counter and crossed his legs. As usual, his gaze lingered on her chest. "When will you let me try you out?"

Her gut clenched. She stopped chewing and scrutinized him. "Meaning?" Like she hadn't a clue to his indecent implication.

Lifting his gaze to her face, he grinned. "You're not dating and gotta have some need building. I'd like to help you with that."

He'd given her subtle hints over the past several days, but this was a direct proposition. She leaned back, wide-eyed. "If you're suggesting a sexual dalliance, no thanks."

"Why not? We have a lot of time in the morning after Jan leaves. She'll never know."

Ah, isn't loyalty wonderful. Her stomach churned. Lowering her fork, she crossed her arms over her chest. "I'll know, Eric. You should be ashamed for suggesting such a thing."

Lauren wasn't ignorant to Eric being closer to her age than Jan's. With his gutter mentality, he probably considered Lauren more sexually experienced and worth coercing into bed. But, God forbid, the man was repulsive.

Eric eyed her over the steam of his cup. "I'm in an apartment with two women, one naïve and cute, the other sexy as hell. I'm here for the asking." He sipped his coffee. "Let's say I'm offering a payback for your kindness."

Oh, puke, puke. She swallowed hard. "Don't hold your breath, Eric. I'd never do anything to hurt Jan. She's like a younger sister."

"Well, unfortunately for you, Jan's counting the days to when you leave. I'd rather keep us as a threesome."

With one hand under the table, she gripped her knee and squeezed hard. Jan didn't deserve this damn man, but to keep the peace, Lauren bit her tongue. Otherwise, he could find her fist in his face.

Her cell phone rang. Grateful for the interruption, she grabbed the device from the table and answered.

The caller ID showed Mr. O'Reilly. "Hi."

"Ms. Howell, will you tell Drummer he still owes me twenty bucks?"

"Sure, but why call me? He has his own phone."

"Because the dimwit gave me a non-working number. Just tell him to pay up, or I break the lock and haul his junk to the curb." He disconnected.

Lauren slipped her phone into her jeans pocket. "Mr. O'Reilly wants his twenty bucks, or your stuff goes to the curb." She grabbed her plate and mug then hurried to the sink. Whirling, she glared and pointed a finger. "Make sure you give him your correct phone number so I won't hear about your business."

While sipping, he waved a hand in the air. "Yeah, yeah, I'll take care of him. He wants a lousy twenty bucks a month for storage. No biggie." He placed his cup on the counter and raised his brows. "You got a spare twenty bucks?"

"Nope." She quickly washed her dish, mug and fry pan. Best to hurry and get the hell out of the apartment.

"Ten bucks then."

Damn, what a friggin' loser. "Forget it."

"Look, Lauren, about us."

Grabbing a dishtowel for her hands, she faced him with a steady gaze. "There is no *us*, Eric. Never gonna happen." She glanced at the wall clock. Still plenty of time before class but better to leave early to avoid any more conversation. "Time to go." She snatched a Granny Smith apple from the fruit basket and rushed past him.

Eric followed her into the living room. "How about I drive you?"

"No, thanks. I like to walk."

"Or maybe you'd rather I not know where your class is. I can find out from Jan."

Yeah, right. Smirking, she grabbed her jacket from the coat rack. "Good luck with that. She doesn't know because she never asked." After slipping her arms through the sleeves, she lifted her hair away from the collar then, as was her habit, slid her wallet into the inside pocket.

"I'll follow you in my car."

She grunted. "That bucket of bolts leaves a smoke trail for two blocks, Eric. If you care to remain unseen, buy yourself a better car." Reaching over the sofa, she zipped up her backpack then hoisted the bag onto her shoulder.

"Wait a minute." Eyes wide, Eric stepped forward, pointing. "That pack belongs to Jan."

Pausing by the front door, she tugged on the strap. "Not anymore. She needs a pack with wider side pockets. Since mine was bigger, we swapped last night."

"Why doesn't she go out and buy one?"

This damn guy must think Jan rolled in dough. Lauren pursed her lips. "Maybe because her credit card is maxed from your impromptu vacation." She opened the door.

"Lauren, wait." Eyeing the pack, he hurried toward her and gripped the door. "You're coming home tonight, right?"

An odd question. She raised a brow. "You want me to stay away?"

"No—no, come home like normal." Still staring at the pack, he licked his lips while rubbing a palm against his hip. Then, he pasted on a smile.

The gesture looked about as phony as a fifteen dollar bill. *At least, he isn't staring at my boobs.*

Dropping his hand from the door, he cleared his throat and stepped back. "Jan loves you, but she loves me more. She won't believe you."

Gut clenching, she faced him. "You mean if I tell her you hit on me?" She'd already figured out that tidbit, especially after Eric's news about Jan counting the days. Jan was hopelessly infatuated with Eric. To her, the man could do no wrong.

One and a half months to go. I've got to keep him at bay before I break every bone in his face.

Chapter Four

While knocking on his sister's door, Deems prayed he wouldn't have a repeat of his last visit. What a mess that night. After calling Jan all afternoon and leaving voicemails with no answers, he'd arrived to pound on her door, frightening the old woman on the second floor, who promptly notified the landlord. O'Reilly, in turn, took one look at Deems and called the police. Then, Lauren walked into an apartment full of men and him shouting at the top of his lungs. So much ruckus only to discover Jan took a trip to the Bahamas with a boyfriend.

His sister hadn't said a word about a love in her life nor called to tell him where she was going or who with. Hell, she hadn't bothered to answer her phone until Lauren's message, and that hurt. Suppose he had something important to convey, like Mom was sick and on her death bed? Just because Jan was old enough to do as she pleased didn't make her behavior right.

And Lauren... *Oh, God.* The color had drained from her face the second she stepped across the threshold. He swore up and down that her paleness indicated guilt, but her cheeks flushed pink after a few explanations. He made a complete fool of himself. Jan was fine. With a simple phone number search for Lauren Howell, he could have saved himself a lot of embarrassment.

Despite the whole fiasco, Lauren invited him to stay. That, more than any gesture, eased his over-reactive emotional state, and *she* was the reason he now stood at Jan's door. He loved his sister, but Lauren was the woman on his mind. Why, he wasn't sure. He certainly had no interest in another relationship and, from what Jan said, neither did Lauren.

Still, the woman aroused his curiosity. She appeared unlike any female ever to cross his path. Calm yet assertive. Confident but with ego in check. A woman capable of taking care of herself in one of the biggest cities in the world. Jan described Lauren as a fish out of water, but Lauren definitely fell into a category all her own. He'd like to know her better, even for the short duration of her stay.

The door flew open.

A man stood with his hand on the door frame, his nostrils flaring like a dragon defending his domain. He wore faded jeans with ripped knees, a T-shirt stained and full of holes, and long brown hair matted with grease. He gave the overall appearance of a man in desperate need of a bath. A whale of a bruise colored his left jaw, but his hands were too dirty to see if his knuckles matched. They scrutinized each other for several long seconds until Deems shook himself. "Who are you?"

The man stretched to his full height. "Who's asking?"

Deems bristled. He wasn't in the mood to be challenged by some scumbag in his sister's apartment, especially one smelling of motor oil. "I'm looking for Jan. I'm her brother."

The guy's posture relaxed, and his face broke into

a smile that showed a missing eye tooth, yellow enamel, and a distinct lack of dental care. How any woman could kiss a mouth like that without vomiting should be given a medal.

Face brightening, the man extended his hand. "Hey, pleased to meet you, dude. I'm Eric, Jan's fiancé. Come in."

His gut clenched. *Fiancé?* Jan kissed *that* mouth? He shook the strong grip then checked his hand for any residual grease before stepping into the apartment.

"Yo, Jan, your brother's here!" Eric slapped Deems on the shoulder. "Nice to meet you, man. Deems, right? Jan told me a lot about you."

Too much probably. Scanning the room for a mirror, he wondered if Eric had left a hand print on his gray suit jacket.

Jan hurried from the bedroom, her smile wide. "Hi. I see you two have met."

Deems gestured with his thumb at Eric. "Fiancé?"

She wrapped her arm around Eric's waist. "Yesterday, in fact. I was about to call you, but we're still celebrating." She gave Eric an affectionate squeeze. "I think Mom and Dad will be pleased."

Pissed is the word, not pleased.

His sister and the grease guy made an oddly out-of-place couple, like neither belonged in the twenty-first century. Eric resembled a throwback to an era when men shunned baths, and Jan to a time when hippies engaged in carefree sex and organized protests. Scumbag and flower-child. *Oh, yeah, Mom and Dad will be real thrilled.*

He inwardly groaned. His sister's choice of men over the years had been questionable. Some women attracted stray animals. For Jan, stray men. Every single one never possessed a job or skill, as if she simply found them on a street corner. To date, Eric topped the list, and Deems struggled to swallow the sour tang in his mouth. He had no right to interfere—yet. He gave a slight nod in Eric's direction but spoke directly to Jan. "Does he live here?"

"Sure, ever since the Bahamas. It's been great."

Every muscle in his body tightened. Bad enough the man slept with his sister, but he lived too close to Lauren. *That* arrangement would never do. With a direct glare at Jan, Deems nodded toward the kitchen. "We need to talk privately."

Her shoulders quirked, and she clutched Eric's waist tighter to her body. "Eric's part of my life now. You can talk in front of him." She thrust out her lower lip.

Commendable to see his sister with a little backbone, but this wasn't the time for comment. "I won't talk in front of him, Jan. What you say later is not my concern, but for the moment, I want a word with you alone." He glowered at Eric.

The lanky man forced Jan's arm from his waist then retreated with his hands raised in surrender. "Yeah, okay, a family affair. I get it. I'll be outside working on my car."

After the door closed, Jan folded her arms across her chest and scowled. "That attitude was extremely rude."

Her opinion of his manners wasn't up for debate. With Jan's history, she'd fight tooth and nail for Eric no matter what argument her brother presented. Before speaking, he took a calming breath. "I don't appreciate paying your rent when Eric should take over."

Her scowl disappeared to be replaced by wide eyes and open mouth. Stepping toward him, she dropped her arms to her sides. "He doesn't have a job, Deems."

Somehow, that came as no surprise. He sighed heavily. "He should find one, and soon."

"But without Lauren, we'll never make the rent."

Without Lauren? Narrowing his gaze, he studied his sister. "Where's Lauren?"

"I threw her out."

"What?" Dear Lord, his voice rose an octave. Clearing his throat, he stared. "You said you were good friends."

Chin high, she met his stare. "We were before she made a move on Eric. She lunged at him. He told me everything."

His mouth fell. More likely, the other way around, and the thought tensed every muscle in his body. "And you believe him?"

Again, she folded her arms across her chest, stepped back, and pouted. "Of course, I believe him. Eric's the most faithful man I know. He won't lie."

Deems' impression of Eric was a man who'd sell his mother for a loaf of bread. But really, Lauren and Eric? The whole scenario sucked, and he silently cursed. Although... He gave his sister a one-eyed gaze. "How'd Eric get the bruise on his jaw?"

"Car hood."

"Damn good right hook for a car hood. You sure he's telling the truth?"

Her lips tightened. "I trust him, okay? Ask him yourself."

Deems refused to waste his breath. What he needed

was Lauren's side of the story.

Jan gripped his arm. "You won't stop paying the rent, right?"

Never had such a strong sense of frustration swept over him so fast. All he wanted was to see Lauren's beautiful smile, not Eric's bad teeth, and certainly not the news of Jan's engagement to a man with hardly a dime to his name.

His gaze intense, he tightened his jaw in an effort to remain calm. "You told Eric about me, and how I'm paying your rent?"

"Well, sure." She toyed with the edging on the sofa back. "He worried about how we'd do without Lauren."

Of all the stupid... With one hand, he gripped his forehead and rubbed the throb building in his temples. He'd warned her so many times about men out for a free ride. When would she learn? He dropped his hand and gave her a long look. "And how much *have* you told him?"

She kicked the bottom of the sofa with a bare foot. "Not everything, Deems, but enough to ease his mind."

Heat flushed through him, and he fought like mad to control an explosion. Where the hell had Jan put her brain? Enough meant too much. He turned away from his sister and counted to ten. The ten stretched to twenty, and he again rubbed his forehead before facing her. "Where's Lauren?" He'd used as steady a voice as possible, but even to his ears, the words sounded strained.

Her gaze flashed. "I don't know and don't care. She has no right to go after my boyfriend."

Either he misjudged Lauren, or Jan had her head buried in sand. Drawing in slow, steady breaths, he met his sister's gaze. "Sorry, Jan, I don't believe she went after Eric."

Jan slammed her fist into the sofa's back cushion. "I'm telling the truth! She's jealous of my good fortune and paraded naked in front of him."

That was the most ridiculous statement he'd ever heard. Lauren had too much class for a scumbag like Eric, but he kept the opinion to himself. Jan was being led along some golden path with blinders. "When did all this occur?"

"Three days ago."

And Eric proposed yesterday after he discovered Jan's brother had money. *My poor naïve sister.* His expression stern, Deems shook his finger in Jan's face. "I'll pay the rent for two more months. After that, job or no job, Eric takes over. I won't support a freeloader, Jan." He dropped his hand and glared at his little sister. "I'll continue with your tuition, but I want you to pick a major. If you don't, you'll pay for your own classes. Since you want to act all mature by living with a boyfriend, then you should take responsibility for your own support. Now—" He took out his cell phone and tapped the Contacts icon. "What's Lauren's number?"

"Why?"

"A successful businessman always likes to hear both sides of an argument."

She shook her frizzy head. "She'll feed you lies just like she fed them to me."

With his blood pressure about to burst out his ears, Deems sucked in a deep breath in an effort not to crush the phone in his hand. He hated to cut off her monetary support, but hell, her engagement to a worthless piece of shit smacked of impulsiveness. He gritted his teeth.

"I'm after answers, Jan. What's her number?"

Jan told him.

He punched the numbers into his contact list and then returned the phone to his pocket. "How long since Eric moved in? Two weeks?"

Pulling at a thread on the sofa back, she fidgeted. "About that. Why?"

"If I hadn't been away on business, maybe I could have diffused the situation. I'd like to think you and Lauren had a big misunderstanding."

She broke the thread and tossed it to the floor. "No misunderstanding." Stepping close, she glared upward. "Stop treating me like a child."

But Jan was a child, naïve and gullible enough to believe Eric. Lauren, as her roommate, had been a blessing in disguise. But she was gone, and damned if he'd believe a word out of Eric's mouth.

Chapter Five

Too curious to wait, Deems dialed Lauren's phone as soon as he descended the stairs. Voicemail kicked in, and simply hearing her voice caused a surge in his heart rate. "Hi. It's Deems Lambert. If you're game for a free dinner, give me a call."

What else could he say? *I want to know what really happened because I don't believe Jan?* He prided himself on being a good judge of character, and Lauren had impressed him with her focus. She'd also expressed her dislike for Eric, so Jan's accusation hardly made sense. Unless Lauren's objective was to have Eric evicted, and the plan backfired. Somehow, that assumption seemed preposterous, too. While slipping his phone into his suit jacket, he descended the brownstone's steps.

"Yo, Deems!" Eric slammed the trunk of a dark blue sedan that had seen better days.

Dents covered every fender with rust forming over exposed metal—which was about everywhere. The sedan emblem on the grill was half-broken, and paint peeled into curls on the roof. The car was as dilapidated as his clothes. *Hard to believe Jan wants to marry this loser.*

While wiping his hands on a greasy rag, Eric meandered toward him. "Jan tell you about Lauren?"

He bristled. "Of course."

Frowning, Eric shook his head. "Shocked the hell out of me, man, but I'd like Lauren to know I've got no hard feelings."

How nice of him. Stepping to the side, Deems positioned himself downwind of Eric's motor smell. "What exactly happened?"

"Don't rightly know 'cause I was half-asleep at the time." He averted his gaze to somewhere up the street. "She came onto me strong, man." Grinning, he cocked his head. "I'll admit, she's a beautiful woman, but Jan's my girl." He met Deems' gaze. "I won't do anything to hurt your sister."

"Uh-huh." In daylight, Eric's bruised jaw took on a multitude of colors. A touch of red, green, and purple. A regular rainbow. *Car hood, my ass.* With a nod, he motioned toward Eric's face. "Nasty bruise. Looks like a right hook."

With a greasy palm, Eric rubbed his jaw. "A beauty, eh?" He nodded toward his car. "The hood support slipped. Knocked my face smack onto the radiator." After spitting onto the sidewalk, Eric tucked the dirty rag into his back pocket. "I hate to see Lauren and Jan split like this. I'd like to find her."

I'm sure you would. His throat tightened, but he forced himself to remain nonchalant. "Lauren can be anywhere in the city."

"What about this art class she's taking? You remember the guy's name or where he's at?"

If alarm bells weren't clanging inside his head, he'd be a little more civil with the man. But he didn't trust Eric. He'd confronted far too many men with ulterior motives, and Jan's fiancé fit the bill. Deems scowled. "I've only met Lauren twice, Eric. I don't know much about her." Which was true—except for a gut feeling that Lauren had been wronged.

"Well, if you can help me out, I'd appreciate a call." He nodded toward Deems' suit jacket. "I'll give you my number."

Obviously, Eric saw him slip his phone into his pocket as he walked down the steps. So, for the second time within an hour, Deems entered another number into his contact list. He had no intention of telling Eric anything, but to keep the peace, he obliged. After all, the man could soon be his brother-in-law. He inwardly shuddered at the thought.

Finished relaying his number, Eric let his gaze wander upward toward Jan's third-floor apartment. "Keep this hush-hush between us, man."

Devious fellow. Another fine, upstanding citizen. Did he really expect Deems to keep secrets from his sister? Deems replaced his phone to his pocket and studied Eric. "You intend to approach Lauren without telling Jan?"

A sly grin curled the corner of Eric's lips. "Let's say I want to keep Jan happy. She won't admit it, but she misses Lauren."

Deems hadn't gotten that impression. Jan adamantly defended Eric and expressed no desire to reconcile with Lauren. On the other hand, Eric showed more interest in Lauren's return, and Deems had a pretty good idea why.

Eric pointed to the silver limo across the street. "That yours?"

Were those dollar signs flashing in Eric's brown eyes? *Jan, you are a fool.*

Chest tight, Deems stuffed his hands into his

trouser pockets and snorted. "Company car, Eric. No biggie."

"Are you kidding, man?" He twisted his mouth to the side. "You're probably near the top of the ladder for such a privilege."

All right, Jan hadn't told him everything. That fact eased his gut a little, and he dropped his arms to his sides. "I'm a high-end salesman, Eric. I work for a living—which reminds me." Frowning, he faced him. "Jan tells me you're unemployed. How can you propose marriage when you have no means of support?"

"Aw, man." Eric kicked at a patch of weeds growing between the sidewalk and curb cracks, his gaze darting to a passing car. "After Lauren left, the poor girl was heartbroken. Proposing helped cheer her up." Moving away, he leaned against somebody's dust-covered car while slipping his hands into his jeans front pockets. "I have some prospects developing, but I need to find Lauren first. I gotta set things straight." He shot Deems a quick glance. "You *are* gonna look for her, right?"

The vision of Eric even remotely close to Lauren turned his stomach. His back stiffened. "Jan made her feelings about Lauren perfectly clear, Eric. If you're attempting to restore their friendship, then you should call Lauren first."

Eric scratched his head. "I tried. Left several messages, text and voicemail." Simultaneously, he crossed his arms and legs. "She probably doesn't recognize my number."

More likely, Lauren wanted nothing to do with Eric Drummer. *Smart woman*. She recognized a loser better than Jan. Feeling the urge to escape, he glanced at his watch. "Gotta go, Eric." Without waiting for a response, Deems crossed the street to his limo.

Like many neighborhoods in New York, parking was at a premium, and most cars stayed permanently in their spot at curbside, gathering dust. Others had the expense of a multi-level garage with its guaranteed parking slot. Public transportation and taxis were the norm, but gridlock happened every single day. For that reason, his company provided a limo and driver.

Seeing Deems approach, Lou Zane jumped from the driver's seat to open the rear door. In the eyes of women, Lou could only be described as big, black, and beautiful. Because of his size, he often doubled as a bodyguard. With women, the three B's. With men, an imposing figure implying caution.

"You look troubled, Mr. Lambert."

At the sound of Lou's deep voice, Deems jerked his gaze from the asphalt street to his chauffeur. "I am." He turned to look at Eric who kept his gaze in his direction, still leaning against the car. "That guy is my sister's fiancé." Merely saying the words revolted him.

Lou's gaze snapped to Eric. A brow lifted. "Oh." He shrugged broad shoulders under a tailored black suit. "He might be a nice guy."

"Yeah, I'm forcing myself to keep an open mind." Damn near impossible. The situation was awkward with Jan being of legal age and capable of her own decisions. He just wished she made better ones.

Leaning forward, Lou's gaze twinkled. "Someone landed a good right hook on his jaw."

Suppressing a smile, Deems patted Lou's broad shoulder. "I have a feeling I know who that someone is."

His cell phone rang. He slipped the device from his pocket, recognized the caller ID, and experienced a brief pitter-patter in the center of his chest to see Lauren's name on the screen. So odd how that beautiful woman affected him, but maybe for a change, he'd receive some straight answers. He stepped into the limo for privacy. "Hi."

"Hi, yourself. I'm surprised to hear from you. Does your invitation still stand?"

"Absolutely." Her voice had a smooth tone, mature and downright sexy with a slight hint of a Pennsylvania accent. She probably mesmerized her high school students, because she sure as hell caught his attention. All his anger at Jan and Eric flew out the window. "Where are you? I'll swing by to pick you up."

"I have a half hour of class left, and I'm not dressed for anything fancy."

"That's fine. I know a great deli that serves the best sandwiches. The shop's at Seventy-First and Park. Are you close?" Silence. Was she having second thoughts? "Lauren?"

"How about I meet you?"

Caution laced her words. Of him or men in general? Hell, whatever happened between her and Eric made him even more curious.

"I'll meet you, Deems. One hour, okay?"

"All right, I'll see you then." His mind racing, he disconnected and stared at his phone. She purposely hid her location. Was she afraid he might tell Jan? Or worse, tell Eric?

Lou opened the partition window. "Where to, Mr. Lambert?"

Deems checked his watch. An hour to kill. Any

other time, he'd return to the office, do a few things, and then head out. But his concentration sucked...especially for business. "Take a slow drive to Seventieth and Park, Lou. You can drop me off then head home. I'll take a cab when I'm done."

And the short walk would ease some of the doubts about Lauren's hesitation.

****

I shouldn't do this.

Mumbling like some dimwit who hadn't enough sense to keep the words to herself, Lauren repeated the mantra with every step along the sidewalk. She almost called Deems to cancel, but her heart, mind, and stomach complained. Yes, she wanted to see him, and her heart flipped to hear his voice, but the man proved way too tempting for any woman. She lacked the time and inclination to start anything, whether an affair or a simple fling, and especially, with a man from New York. *So, why accept? Is the prospect of a free meal overriding common sense?*

Money was so tight the bills squealed whenever she slipped one from her wallet. More than once, Lauren regretted signing up for Antonio's class. Then, she learned something new and thanked the Lord for coming. If her home life had remained status quo, she'd have the money to be comfortable and wouldn't need an invitation to dinner. As with her luck, her world turned upside down prior to her class's start date, and she could only make the best of a lousy situation. Deems' offer for a free meal notched up her oh-woe-is-me mood to a tolerable level.

She stopped at a crosswalk and waited for the green light. Her stay with Jan had made for a welcomed stability. At present, Lauren faced the limbo of her early arrival—not knowing who to trust. Antonio and the other five students helped break the loneliness, but they stayed within their own circles. Naturally, pride prevented her from discussing her lack of funds.

Once the light changed, Lauren crossed with the crowd and headed along Seventy-Fifth Street before turning onto Park Avenue and toward Seventy-First.

I hate New York. People and cars everywhere. No privacy except behind a closed and locked door. The constant noise of blaring car horns, crowds at every corner, and the piercing wail of emergency vehicles surrounded the people of Manhattan, causing throbs to develop within her sinuses. She missed her hometown of Arendtsville with its acres of apple orchards, fresh air, and above all, the silence. Neighbors stopped to chat, and news circulated faster than a radio broadcast. Here in New York, with its millions of people, she had often experienced a profound loneliness, a stranger among so many—even though with her outgoing nature, she could strike up a conversation with anyone. New Yorkers were too damn aloof and preferred to avoid eye contact for fear of having to say hello. Maybe her loneliness was why she accepted Deems' invitation. She thoroughly enjoyed his company during their impromptu dinner together. Nothing would please her more than to have a friend to call while in this forsaken city.

She waited at the Seventy-Third Street cross light when a tug on her backpack forced her to turn. Recognizing the Hispanic male with the broad grin on his face, she scowled. "Not you again. Why don't you buy a pack from a store?"

He stepped alongside. "Because I like yours more. The offer stands at fifty bucks for the pack and its contents."

Was this typical big-city behavior, or could this guy be a nut on the loose? Crossing hurriedly with the green light, she glanced over her shoulder. "Look, buddy, I don't have time to find replacements for my supplies. The answer is still no."

Whatever was his obsession with her pack proved beyond her comprehension. He could easily buy a good bag for less at any discount store. The man had approached her twice already with his offer, and evidently, "no" wasn't an option. He wore the same clothes as yesterday—blue jeans and gray T-shirt covered by a black leather jacket. He stood at her height and had short, black curly hair with a black mustache. No scumbag-look thankfully, but he gave her the creeps just the same. She hopped onto the opposite curb and quickened her pace.

He followed, staying one step ahead. "Why'd you leave your Sixty-Eighth Street apartment? Don't you know a decent pad is hard to come by in this city?"

Her throat tightened, and not breaking her stride, she shot him a glare. "How'd you know where I lived?"

He grinned in answer.

Damn him. "Leave me alone." She scooted around a slow walker.

"A hundred bucks then." He collided into a light pole, recovered quickly, and then hurried to catch up.

Too bad the damn metal didn't break his neck. "Same story. Scram before I call the cops."

He stopped while she continued. "We'll meet again, doll."

I'm sure we will. She glanced over her shoulder, but he had disappeared. The man was a bona fide mental case. *All right, calm down.* She'd rather not have Deems see her aggravated over some asshole. Nothing ruined a dinner more than to bitch and moan over something as ridiculous as a guy wanting her backpack.

She neared Seventy-First and Park and sucked in a breath at the sight of Deems waiting. Dressed in a light gray business suit with a matching tie, he stood on the corner under Irving's Deli sign, his dark hair gently blowing with the slight spring breeze. They'd met three times already, and on each occasion, he'd worn a suit. Different colors but, nonetheless, expensive. Her wardrobe consisted of blue jeans, T-shirts, and a lightweight jacket, hardly a match for his well-tailored look.

He turned, and her heart thumped wildly. His pale brown eyes locked onto her while his lips stretched into a smile. Dear Lord, he was perhaps the most attractive man she'd ever met, and her emotions slammed together. Happy to see him, but afraid for the same reason. Caution collided with guilt. *Without question, I'm making a big mistake.*

The closer she came, the broader his smile grew. Her knees turned into butter, and she swore up and down she'd melt into a puddle of cream, but she somehow stopped in front of him without tripping over her own feet.

Without a second of hesitation, he placed both hands on her cheeks, lifted her face upward, and pressed his lips onto hers.

Chapter Six

Lauren's heart just stopped. He'd caught her so off-guard, she couldn't respond. But she loved every second. She'd forgotten the Hispanic, Jan, Eric—hell, even her dislike for New York. His lips tasted so good, and she reveled in their softness, even though she stood with both hands clutching the pack's shoulder straps like they were her only means of support. She wanted so much to wrap her arms around him but dared not. Otherwise, she'd lose herself in his musk scent and never forgive her weakness.

After he suckled without a care that they stood in the middle of the sidewalk, he brushed his lips across hers and lifted his head. His gaze lingered on her lips while both thumbs stroked her cheeks. She almost melted right into his palms.

A gentle smile curled the corners of his mouth. "Sorry. I don't often act impulsively, but in your case, I couldn't resist." His gaze twinkled. "If you had dropped the backpack, you'd be in my arms."

Damn, I should have sold the bag to the Hispanic pest.

With a feather touch, he swept his palms along her jawline, and a shiver shot straight down her spine. She silently cursed the betrayal of her body. Right or wrong, she wanted him. The man was absolutely intoxicating. And that revelation scared her big time.

Yep, I shouldn't have come.

He dropped his hands. "I see you found the place okay."

She stared at his mouth, willing his lips to return. Her brain urged her to say something, but her tongue felt tied into a knot. How could one man cause such an instantaneous reaction? Hell, even her heart rate threatened to take off for the stratosphere. She swallowed hard. "Hi." Somehow, she managed to roll out that one word.

He pointed to the deli sign over the corner shop door, a gaudy display of bright orange and black lettering with paintings of deli sandwiches in every corner. "Hope you're hungry." He opened the door and ushered her inside.

The place was packed. Customers lined the front of the glass display case, either placing an order or waiting for one. Six people worked behind the counter—one on the cash register, two on the griddle, and three hustling with sandwiches. The shop was long and narrow with two rows of small tables and chairs stretching from the front window to a restroom door at the rear of the store. Surprisingly, half of the tables were unoccupied.

The abundance of aromas reminded her of home, from the richness of fresh bread to the complexity of fried onions—all familiar scents from her mother's kitchen. Add the hominess of fresh, brewed coffee, and the dead would rise from the grave. Given a choice, she'd stand in the middle of the store for hours and sniff.

After studying the overhead menu, she and Deems placed their orders at the register. While Deems waited, she grabbed napkins, straws, and plastic utensils then chose a table by the windows. Slipping the pack from her shoulders, she hooked the straps onto her chair's backrest and settled on the seat.

She hadn't tasted very much of New York's cuisine. With Jan, she ate well enough, but without a kitchen at her current residence, a fast-food burger became her diet along with peanut butter and jelly sandwiches. Most establishments wanted a king's ransom for a decent-size salad, and even the cost for a bottle of water was obscene.

Deems joined her a few minutes later with a tray full of food. His order was roast beef on rye and hers a turkey and BLT combo.

Her mouth dropped at the size of her meal with its sides of chips, pickle, and cole slaw. "How do you eat such a sandwich? It's five inches high!"

"Like this." With both hands, he gripped half of his sandwich and took a bite on the edge. His cheeks bulged. "You eat in layers unless your mouth is big enough to swallow it whole." He leaned across the table and gave a quick jerk of his head. "Like the man against the wall."

Following his gaze, she gasped. The man had indeed widened his mouth to bite from top to bottom. Following Deems' instructions, she bit into her BLT combo and rolled her eyes. The taste of roasted turkey breast combined with crispy bacon burst on her tongue. Plus, a delectable cucumber and dill spread added a whole new world of flavor. *Definitely not a sandwich from back home.*

She chewed before speaking. "This combo is good, and I've enough here for tomorrow night's dinner. Thank you for asking me."

"Don't mention it. I usually eat alone so having a companion is a welcomed change."

Alone? How could any woman leave him alone? Flattered that he'd chosen her, she smiled. "I'd expect a man like you to have a busy social calendar. You know, business dinners and hot dates."

He wagged a finger. "Business dinners, yes. Tons of those, but only an occasional date, and I won't call them hot either. None are as enjoyable as this." Gaze sparkling, he swept a napkin over his mouth. "Not to dispel your image of me, but I'm lousy with women on a social level. Put them in a business environment, and I'm fine. You, for some reason, are easy to talk to, and I don't feel so tongue-tied."

The comment warmed her. "Why, thank you, kind sir. Must be my country upbringing." Wow, a man *not* full of himself. She bit into a strong garlic pickle and pointed the remainder his way. "But I'm a stranger in these parts and only passing through. You'll need to practice your hang-up on someone else."

His lip twitched. "Don't you like our city?"

She cringed. "Not to be insulting, Deems, but I haven't found too many things to like. Living here is expensive, and you have too much traffic and not enough open space. As enormous as this city is, I feel closed in." She pointed the pickle upward. "You can't even see the stars at night with all the light pollution and tall buildings in the way."

"Central Park is our open space."

She gave him a one-eyed look. "That's not what I call open space. Where I come from, I can stare at miles of rolling hills."

With a simple flick of his brow in answer, he bit

into his sandwich.

Typical city-slicker, and one with no idea of the beauty of open countryside. Even though she worked in Harrisburg and experienced the trials and tribulations of city life, she'd never felt as closed in as here. Manhattan was just too…tight.

Deems reached across the table to lift her chin. "You seem far away. I hope I'm not souring your mood." He dropped his hand.

"You'll never sour my mood, Deems." How could she tell him he had no equal, and that he was the kindest man she'd ever met? Sitting opposite her, he looked relaxed, as if they'd eaten together a hundred times. A far cry from the nervous fidgeting of her ex-fiancé, a man she dated from high school. She had a pretty good idea why Deems called but best to wait for him to bring up the subject.

With a faint smile tugging on the corner of his mouth, he licked the mustard oozing from his sandwich. "I've never come right out and kissed a woman on the street. I'd say my inner fear of the opposite sex is well on its way to being cured." He bit the sandwich and shoved the food to one side of his mouth. "How am I doing?"

She narrowed her gaze. "Personally, I think you're full of shit. A man as nice and as good-looking as you can't possibly have trouble with women." Men had fooled her before, and judging from his kiss, he had lots of practice. If he kissed all his women with such depth, he'd have a line of panting females on his tail.

Finished with one half of his meal, he gathered the other half and prepared to bite. "I'd say you need a friend right about now, Lauren. I'm offering my services."

A friend she could use. A handsome one, she wasn't so sure about. The man was so friggin' tempting. Although, now that she had garlic breath from the pickle, she wouldn't be tasting his lips any time soon.

"Tell me about yourself, Lauren Howell." He took a large bite of his roast beef.

She had no way of getting out of this without being rude. Of course, he needn't know everything. The last thing she wanted was to have the man feel sorry for her.

"I'm asking for a chance to be your friend, Lauren. No strings attached."

She considered Jan a friend and look what happened. Twisting her mouth to the side, she met his steady gaze. "I don't know where to begin."

"How about where you're from?"

Oh, that was easy enough. She relaxed and leaned back. "I'm from a small town called Arendtsville in Pennsylvania. We're between Harrisburg and Gettysburg." Finger wagging, she gave him a one-eyed gaze. "If you're telling me you've never been to Gettysburg, then shame on you. The town is part of our country's history." She sipped her soda.

Gaze twinkling, he chuckled. "Guilty as charged. I've been to a lot of places but not Gettysburg."

"Well, my dad is a Civil War fanatic." She rolled her eyes. "I love him dearly, but he drags the whole family to all the re-enactments."

"And you taught in Arendtsville?"

She shook her head. "Harrisburg. I had an apartment not far from my school." She forked some cole slaw. "My parents and brother, along with his wife and two kids, live on the Howell homestead in Arendtsville. We're in apple-growing country, and last winter, my parents signed over the three-hundred acre business to my brother. From here on, he'll handle the orchards."

Picking up his pickle, he waved it toward her. "What about you? Don't you deserve part of the farm?" He crunched into the pickle.

Uh-oh. His garlic breath would match hers. She munched on a few chips before answering. "I've known from day one my brother would inherit the property." She met his gaze. "Don't misunderstand. My parents love me equally but encouraged me to continue my education and pursue my art. My engagement prompted them to make my brother the official owner."

"Engagement?" Eyes wide, he hastily chewed and swallowed. "You never told me." He pointed to her left hand. "No ring."

With both hands holding her sandwich, she wagged a pinkie. "We're done, and I sold the ring, but let's not talk about that part of my life yet. The memories will give me acid reflux." She bit into her sandwich while nodding toward his near-empty plate. "Since you're way ahead of me, how about you talk for a while?" Best excuse in the world to avoid a heartbreaking memory.

"Fair enough." After swallowing the last of his sandwich, he wiped his mouth. "I was born and raised in Chicago before I moved to New York—oh, maybe five or six years ago." He sat back. "I work for a company called High-Rise International. Basically, we buy and sell high-rise properties, new or old." He leaned forward and crossed his arms on the table. "I'm the North American agent, one of several representatives based around the world. Our job is to acquire properties and establish a central office for condo fee collection and maintenance." With his straw, he stirred the ice in his soda cup. "Our strictest criteria is to acquire properties ten or more stories high. Price ranges vary from country to country."

"Sounds interesting." *Wow. A bona fide globetrotter.* Her limited finances confined her to the State of Pennsylvania with an occasional trip into Maryland. In her entire life, she hadn't flown on an airplane. She strained a smile. "You've been with them long?"

"Since inception. Close to five years." He munched on a few chips. "I like the job and make a good salary. Of course, I travel all over the country." He wiped his mouth one last time before tossing the napkin onto his paper plate. He gave her a long look. "Now, what happened at Jan's?"

She wondered when he'd get around to the subject. He'd obviously gotten her phone number from Jan and probably learned her side of the story. Eric's, too. Lauren took a large bite of her sandwich and chewed.

Jaw tight, he tapped a finger on the table. "You're avoiding my question."

She swallowed. "No, I'm not. I don't want to choke to death." She sipped her soda before making eye contact. "What did Jan tell you?"

"That she threw you out because you hit on Eric." Without breaking eye contact, he sat back. "Frankly, I found the news hard to swallow."

After her heated argument with Jan, she'd left in a huff, friendless and alone with no one willing to hear her side. Even though Jan was his sister, Deems expressed doubts, and his words encouraged her more than she cared to admit. She might have a friend after all in this blessed city.

A deli worker from behind the counter strolled among the occupied tables, handing take-out containers to those who asked.

Lauren took one and piled in the other half of her meal.

Stretching across the table, Deems slipped his fingers under Lauren's right hand. His thumb stroked across her bruised knuckles. "You hit Eric with a right hook, didn't you? And Jan is wrong about who tried what. Eric attacked you, and Jan refuses to believe."

The simple stroke of his thumb caused a surge of need to rise. She wanted someone to hold her and say everything would be all right. Her world had been in turmoil since Jo-Jo left and not once had she felt close to any man...until now.

"Lauren?" He cocked his head.

While staring at his hand holding hers, she desperately avoided eye contact, but the man was too damn compelling...and kind. Glancing up, she gave him a weak smile. "You're right on both counts. Eric's tried several times to nail me, always after Jan left for class. The clincher was the evening Jan had a lecture to attend. By then, we weren't talking much because I hid in my room, but that evening, my instructor said to catch a PBS special about stained glass art. We only have one TV, so I tuned in and was halfway through the show when Eric strolled in naked. I nearly lost my dinner."

With heat rising into her cheeks, she shifted on the seat and forced herself to continue. "He jumped me, and I swung. Then, I ran from the apartment and called Jan. Since she was in class, she couldn't answer, so I left a voicemail. But, so did Eric. Of course, she listened to his message first and believed his cockamamie story about me going after him. Jan and I had a big blow-up so I packed and left the next morning."

"To where?"

Inwardly cringing, she met his curious gaze. "Not far."

His eyebrow arched. "You're not telling me?"

"No, you're Jan's brother, and I won't blame you for taking her side."

Shaking his head, he smirked. "You're afraid I'll tell Jan, and she'll slip the address to Eric."

She'd had men after her before, but Eric entered a class all his own. Butt naked with his penis high in the sky. Licking his lips like a hungry wolf. Despite his lack of muscles, he still had strength. If she hadn't spent a childhood wrestling with her brother, she'd have lost to Eric's assault. She covered Deems' hand. "Please don't be offended. I have only a month and a half left in New York and don't want to spend my free time avoiding Eric."

"I understand." He grabbed her hand and gave a gentle squeeze. "That's why you agreed to meet me here so I wouldn't know where you're staying."

She tapped the tip of her nose and winked. "The less he knows of my whereabouts, the safer I'll feel." She returned his gentle squeeze, experienced a sudden lurch of her heart, and then quickly retracted her hand. *Mustn't get too friendly.* She stared out the window.

A steady stream of foot traffic passed along the

sidewalk. People of all ages hurried about their business, some wearing suits, some in rags, and still others in clothes tight enough to restrict blood flow. While scanning the crowds, she caught sight of a man standing in the shadows across the street. Immediately, she recognized him and wasn't sure if anger or annoyance constricted her throat.

"Something wrong?"

She sighed. "At times, I find the people of New York a bit unnerving." Meeting his gaze, she motioned with her head. "Do you see that Hispanic man across the street? He wants to buy my backpack."

With one brow cocked, he shifted his gaze out the window. "That's a little weird."

"I agree. Twice, he confronted me then again this evening on my way here." Rotating her head, she glared at the man. "He's following me." Saying the words out loud caused a flood of irritability. She wanted to rush out and crack open his skull.

Deems glanced at the pack hanging on her chair. "What's in your bag?"

"Nothing worth anything. My sketchbook and some class materials." She sipped her drink. "He offered me fifty bucks. Then a hundred. And he wants the pack *and* its contents."

Brows high, he straightened in his chair. "Why?"

"If I had the answer, I'd be a genius." She checked her watch. With each passing spring day, daylight stretched into the evening. But dusk came early in the city. Too many tall buildings to block the sunlight. She'd rather be in her room before dark, and with the Hispanic on her tail…

Deems distracted her thoughts by taking her right

hand into both of his. He seemed mesmerized by the bruised knuckles so she wiggled her fingers.

His lips curled with a smile. "You have a strong hand."

She showed him the other one by placing it alongside. "I have two strong hands from hauling bushels of apples."

He patted both hands then sat back, reached into his suit's inner pocket, and extracted a business card. "Here. You already have my cell number, but this has the office. If I'm in a meeting, I keep my phone off, and my assistant can take your call. Anytime you need to talk or want a free meal, call me, okay?"

Gingerly taking the gold-embossed card, she eyed him warily. Why was he doing this? After her experience with Eric and the Hispanic guy, she wasn't sure she trusted anyone in New York. She slipped the stiff paper into her jacket pocket.

Not long after, Lauren and Deems stepped from the deli where Deems raised his arm to hail a taxi. One immediately rolled to the curb. "The cab is for you." He opened the rear door. "Since your friend is still across the street, you're riding home even if you live two blocks away. There's no sense me offering to ride along. You'll refuse." He handed two twenties to the driver. "That should cover the fare." Then to Lauren, he waved a hand. "Get inside."

She stammered for words. "Deems—"

"Don't you dare refuse."

His generosity activated alarms in her head. Why? Because deep down, she envisioned him as much more than a friend.

Chapter Seven

Deems held the cab door for Lauren, but she made no attempt to step in. Her gaze scanned his face, as if searching. For what, he wasn't sure, but her hesitation gave him a chance to do the same. She created sensations deep inside his core that were totally foreign yet wonderful...no, breathtaking. Her touch tingled, her smile dazzled, and he loved how her gaze lingered on his lips. More than anything, he'd like to extend their time together, but he offered himself as a friend. A first in his book. Somehow, he understood those words were the ones she wanted to hear. Any other woman in her financial situation would latch onto him and never let go, take advantage of his bank account, and give him tears to weaken his resolve. But not Lauren Howell. If truth be told, he'd like to assist her in whatever way she desired. Convincing her to accept his help was the problem. "Can I call you?"

Her emerald eyes brightened. "Absolutely, as long as you remember—"

"Yes, I won't forget."

Smiling, she held out her hand. "Thanks for the free meal."

He frowned at such a formal gesture.

"Best buds have limitations, you know." She cocked her head and grinned.

He smiled at the comment. The woman presented

him with a challenge, but for now, he'd follow her rules. "I already kissed you so I guess a return kiss is out of the question?"

The grin disappeared. "Let's call us just friends, Deems…for now."

Instead of shaking her hand, he slipped his palm under hers and raised her sore knuckles to his lips. A gasp escaped from her throat, and he secretly patted himself on the back. One way or the other, he got his kiss.

She stepped into the taxi and, with a wave, drove off.

His gaze wandered across the street. The Hispanic man had disappeared.

What bothered him about this beautiful woman? Far too often, a hint of worry clouded her face and kept the smile from reaching those beautiful eyes. Without question, the episode with Eric unnerved her, and her concern with the Hispanic bordered on frustration and not fear. But she'd refused to talk about her ex-fiancé. What happened that made her so cautious?

Answers. I need answers.

In business, he considered himself an astute man, always reading his clients as if they were an open book. On a social level, he struggled with women, primarily because he couldn't read them at all. Some had crossed his path and displayed body language as plain as a neon sign. *That* message he understood. He had money. They wanted it and connived all sorts of ways to entice him into bed. The game grew old fast, and he longed for a meaningful relationship with a woman of substance. And hell, he'd finally met a worthwhile candidate, and all she wanted was to remain friends. *Just my luck.* But he hadn't made a success of himself by ceding defeat.

After a sleepless night with visions of her lovely face floating into his mind, he'd arrived at the office, ready to conquer a full morning's work but only shuffled papers without getting anywhere. Normally a workaholic, he could barely concentrate and spent most of his time staring out the window. She distracted him too much, and he *had* to uncover why. *Enough already.* He picked up his cell phone and called Lauren. Just hearing her voice brightened his day, but she refused his offer of another free meal. Instead, she suggested they meet in Central Park after her class.

He agreed to rendezvous at four-thirty near the hundred-year-old oak off Fifth Avenue and Seventy-Fifth Street. Since he hadn't the foggiest idea what an oak looked like, he concentrated on a tall tree with Lauren nearby.

The park was a flurry of activity. Walkers and joggers crowded the asphalt path. Proud parents played with toddlers on the grass. Everyone came out of the woodwork to enjoy the beautiful April afternoon. Sad to say, this morning, as in every morning, he'd stepped into his limo and then into his office building without noticing anything about the weather. Yes, the sun shined overhead but other than that…

Five minutes later, he found Lauren stretched onto the grass with her backpack as a headrest, ankles crossed, and eyes closed. She looked peaceful, a woman at ease with nature. He stood no more than a hundred feet away in the shadows of a bush, unwilling to destroy the vision of a beauty lying in wait. The idea of waking beside her every morning caused a surge of warmth to rise. She was so different from the women in his circle. Simplistic and practical, a lover of art. A teacher and farmer's daughter, one who understood hard work. Any man would be proud to have her by his side.

Bushes rustling to the right startled him. A man in a black leather jacket darted into the open and sped toward Lauren, not pausing for a second while he bent to scoop up her backpack. The Hispanic! Lauren shrieked, and he yanked harder, cursing audibly at the loop still strapped to her shoulder.

A switchblade gleamed in the sunlight.

Holy shit! Gut wrenching, Deems charged after him. "Hey!"

The man whirled and flashed his knife. Gaze wild, the Hispanic bared his teeth, released the pack, and bolted toward Seventy-Fifth Street.

With a chest tighter than a vise grip, Deems slid to a stop alongside Lauren as she struggled into a sitting position. He squatted and clutched her shoulders. "You okay?"

"Yes, I'm fine." She righted herself with a huff. "Now, the jackass wants to steal the bag." She glanced at the hands on her shoulders then shifted her gaze to his. "I'm okay, Deems…really."

He wasn't. The damn assault unnerved him, and he sucked in a calming breath. If she had gotten hurt…

"Deems?"

"Huh?" Since he stared at her face as if waiting for bruises to rise, he cleared his throat and dropped his hands. "Sorry."

A smile quirked her lips. "Don't be sorry. You came to my rescue." Pulling on her jacket sleeve, she inspected the damage. "Look at these grass stains! I'll never scrub them out."

The woman was assaulted in broad daylight, and all she worried about was grass stains? She should at least cry on his shoulder and make him feel all manly by holding her close. Hell, he almost had a heart attack.

Seeing a police officer on horseback gallop toward them, Deems helped Lauren to her feet.

The officer halted his horse. "A woman reported an attempted robbery. Are you the victim, ma'am?"

"That's me." She brushed grass and dirt from her clothes.

"Can you describe him?"

Deems stepped forward and gave the officer a full description, including the direction of his flight.

The cop repeated the words into his shoulder mike then dismounted and slipped a small notebook from his breast pocket. Clicking a ballpoint pen, the officer poised the tip over his opened notebook. "A team of officers will patrol the area around Seventy-Fifth, ma'am. In the meantime, I'll need some personal information."

Deems listened with half an ear since an uncontrollable urge to strangle someone had surfaced. He was so hot under the collar, he almost loosened his necktie. Why would this Hispanic man go after Lauren—who could clearly defend herself—when so many easy targets walked along the path? The cell phone addicts, for example, those constantly texting or talking, oblivious to the world around them. Why such persistence to obtain Lauren's pack?

He studied the bag still draped over her shoulder. A typical style—not very big, a combination of nylon and leather, common enough to buy—worn by half the student population in the entire country.

The officer closed his notebook and handed Lauren a business card. "I'll put in this report and see what develops. In the meantime, if he shows again, don't hesitate to call 911 and mention my name for reference."

His shoulder mike crackled. "Fist fight off Seventy-Third. Two females."

The officer mounted his horse and tipped his hat. "I'll be in touch, ma'am." He galloped off.

Deems silently cursed. As part of the official police report, the officer needed Lauren's New York address of which Deems heard nothing. Aggravation closed his ears. *Dammit to hell.*

Lauren turned toward him while pulling the sleeve of her jacket to expose the green smear. Her brows furrowed. "All these months of walking to class, nothing happened. Why now all of a sudden?"

He brushed grass from the back of her jacket. "The world is full of strange people, Lauren." She had loose grass on her blue jeans, but he resisted touching her so low. "You handled that well. Most women scream at the top of their lungs. Hold still." He picked a piece of dry grass from her hair.

She bent at the waist, and with two hands, ruffled her hair. Straightening, she faced him. "Any more?"

"Just one." He lied as an excuse to feel the strands' silkiness. What he wanted was to run all ten fingers through her hair and sniff. With her vanilla scent swirling around him, he barely kept temptation at bay. And now that her hair was ruffled, she looked sexy as hell.

A pair of wide eyes searched his face. "You okay?"

Oh, damn. He'd held her strand a tad too long. Dropping his hand, he frowned. "Of course, I'm okay. Nothing happened to me." Except for the growing frustration of events spiraling out of control. Helplessness threatened to overwhelm him. She could have been hurt, and he, like a jackass, took forever to unglue his feet and move. Regrettably, robberies and assaults happened every day in a big city, and the news media inundated the viewers with unnecessary coverage, often over-sensationalizing, and creating a non-reactive mindset. He wasn't immune to their subtle brainwash and sighed heavily. "Want to walk? We don't have to, of course."

"We'll walk. I won't let him...oops!"

Her foot had fallen into a hole. With one arm, he swooped her against him to hold her steady. "Easy there. You don't need to break a leg to top your day." The woman was too damn intoxicating, and to clutch her so close nearly wobbled his knees. He couldn't breathe or think, except to wonder what she looked like without clothes.

Gripping onto his shoulder for support, she shook off the dirt covering her sneaker. "Gopher hole. Nice to see you have some wildlife in Manhattan." A smile tugging on her lips, she glanced up. "Besides men, I mean."

Frowning, he stared down at the hole. "I don't know what a gopher is."

"In my opinion, nothing but a large rat." Finished, she stamped her foot then glanced up at him with a smirk. "You need to leave the city more often."

Whether she just noticed his arm around her, he wasn't sure, but she stiffened, and a wide-eyed gaze roamed over his face. Seconds later, she stretched her lips into a slow smile. Her face brightened, and he mustered every ounce of self-control not to kiss her. Friends had boundaries. He could only stare at the softness of her lips.

After a pause in space and time where the world and every movement skidded to a complete standstill, Lauren stood on tiptoe and brushed her lips against his.

Stunned by such a tantalizing maneuver, he held her and took whatever she gave while repeating over and over his promise to remain a friend.

But isn't she breaking her own rules?

The realization motivated him to react. Wrapping both arms around her to draw her close, he seized her lips, half-expecting a cry of protest. When none came, he sank in his tongue while savoring the faint hint of apple on her breath. She tasted wonderful, and if she would just slip her hands around his neck... But she kept her palms flat against his suit jacket, as if wary to give in completely. Even so, the woman had an erotic touch that sent shivers down his spine. Too bad they were standing in the middle of a public park.

A dog bark returned them to their surroundings. After giving a gentle bite on his lower lip, she pushed away and stretched her lips into a dazzling smile.

Teeth and eyes sparkled at once and damn near blinded him. He refused to release her and merely loosened his arms. "You gave me more than a friendly kiss."

Her lips pouted. "I'm sorry. I shouldn't have done that, but I couldn't resist." She fingered his tie. "Do you always wear suits?"

"Not to bed."

"What do you wear during leisure activities?"

"No tie."

Shaking her head, she broke free of his arms, snapped her fingers, and opened her palm. "I suggest you remove your tie."

He'd strip naked if she asked but obeyed, wrapped the tie into a ball, and placed it into her palm.

Chuckling, she stuffed the ball into his jacket pocket. Then, she unbuttoned his dress shirt at the collar and stood back, smiling. "That's better." She adjusted her backpack, hooked her arm through his, and urged him onto the asphalt path. "That jerk spoiled my mood. I felt pretty good about the weather and the ultimate sense of freedom until he interrupted."

"And kissing me helped?"

Her cheeks dimpled. "Oh, yeah. Thank you."

"Happy to oblige. Kiss me anytime." Hopefully soon, and in the privacy of a bedroom.

A woman pushing a stroller jogged by, her ponytail flapping. Another woman power-walked with weights in her hands. Six years living in New York and never once had he taken a stroll through Central Park.

"Do you ever feel good being outdoors, Deems, that great-to-be-alive feeling because the weather is so gorgeous?"

"Can't say I have." No sense lying. His high derived from business, not the weather, but Lauren had opened his eyes to the possibility.

She tugged on his arm to draw his gaze to hers. "Let me guess. You're one of those type A personalities who never stops to smell the roses."

"Only if I buy a dozen for a date." Which hadn't happened in a long time. That quick, her expression lost its glow. Her gaze became distant. The arm hooked in his loosened, and they walked for quite a distance in silence.

She nudged his arm. "I guess you never longed for wide-open spaces."

Uh-oh. The comment slashed too close to the quick. He was no more a country boy than she was a city slicker. He cleared his throat. "Since my job involves high-rises in big cities, I have no need to venture into the country."

She tugged on his arm. "What about vacations? Do you go anywhere?"

"I rarely take a vacation."

Her gaze snapped toward him. "Why not? You can't work all the time."

Evidently, he could, and a wave of depression swept over him. Lauren was so vibrant and full of life. His world included business and the accumulation of assets. Hers was a classroom full of eager faces. She liked green grass and open country. He'd be happy for weeks in the confines of his office. Vacations were trips to acquire new properties, and sightseeing added up to a total waste of time. Perhaps he should cut his losses and let her go before he sank too deep.

But he couldn't. Lauren Howell intrigued him, and curiosity compelled him to find out why. Her calm demeanor, for example. Minutes earlier, the woman had been mugged, yet she wasn't upset. Granted, her gaze scanned the area every several hundred feet, as would any city dweller absorbing her environment, but she showed no fear.

And with that thought…

"Jan mentioned you got burned by your fiancé." He

77

used his arm to squeeze hers. "Want to talk about him?"

They arrived at a junction where several paths converged. She pointed to the right. "Will this route take us back to Fifth Avenue?"

She probably knew the park better than anyone. Certainly better than him. "I think so." He glanced in her direction. "If the breakup with your fiancé is too personal, I'll understand."

"What do you smell in the air, Deems?"

His mind went blank, and he stared. Then, shaking himself, he sniffed. "You. Vanilla."

She squeezed his arm. "I'm serious. Concentrate on the strong fragrance in the air. Try to identify the scent."

Avoidance of the fiancé question. He wasn't surprised. Again, he sniffed. Something flowery. "I haven't the foggiest idea."

"Forsythias." She pointed to the left. "Over there behind the bench. They bloom bright yellow in spring and are probably the major trigger for allergies. You can smell their fragrance without seeing them."

"I like yours better."

She patted his arm. "You're sweet." Avoiding eye contact, she focused her gaze straight ahead. "Is there a reason you called?"

Yeah, he'd become like a useless blob behind his desk because her face would not go away. Unable to verbalize *that* particular comment, he shrugged. "I wanted to make sure you were okay. Someone needs to watch out for you while you're here, and considering what just happened, I arrived in time." Barely. If he had answered one more phone call… *Mustn't think about that.* He squeezed her arm. "You don't frighten easily."

A soft smile touched her lips, and she stared down at the path. "I'm not a poor country girl lost in the big city, Deems. I lived and worked in Harrisburg for many years before coming here." She kicked a stone onto the grass then stared off into the distance.

"You already know about my job layoff." She paused, her jaw tight. "On the day I had a meeting scheduled at the unemployment office, I arrived home to an empty apartment." She glanced his way. "Totally empty. My ex cleaned out everything, even my clothes. My only possessions were the clothes on my back, my car, and my engagement ring." Sighing, she glanced skyward. "He emptied our twenty-five thousand dollar bank account and disappeared, leaving me high and dry. The only visible evidence of occupation—besides dust balls—was the eviction notice on the kitchen counter." She again stared at the ground. "I found out Jo-Jo hadn't paid the rent in six months, and that piece of news was *after* the landlord took the escrow account."

Seeing her this way hurt, but he dared not interrupt with questions. Somewhere in the universe was an answer to why people did what they did.

She tucked a loose strand of hair behind her ear. "The cops put out a warrant for his arrest, but technically, half of everything belonged to him. Because of the amount stolen, they still consider the crime as grand theft, and he can't return to Harrisburg until the statute of limitations passes."

A child ran across the asphalt path after a soccer ball.

Deems stopped Lauren until the little boy retrieved the ball and returned to his game. "Go on," he encouraged. "Has he ever contacted you to explain?"

He nudged her to continue on the path.

"Not a word. If he wanted out of the engagement, all he had to do was say so. I'm grateful my important papers, diplomas, and art work were stored at the farm. Otherwise, they'd have disappeared with the rest of my stuff."

She leaned against him as they strolled, a gesture that made him believe she'd accepted his trust. Not like he had an inkling of psychology crap, but the feeling was the nicest compliment a woman could give a man.

"His desertion happened two weeks before my scheduled departure for New York. Antonio's class was prepaid and non-refundable, but I had no money to travel here or to live. I almost canceled and swallowed the loss when my parents' church offered me a loan." She adjusted her pack's strap. "Initially, I refused because they had earmarked the money for an expansion project, but they talked me into an arrangement that benefited both parties." She gave him a lopsided grin. "A charge card. What I spend is what I repay. So, I skimp when possible, walk everywhere, and make my own meals to keep my costs low. Bad enough I'll have to live with my parents until I accumulate enough cash for a place of my own." Her arm tightened on his. "I'm a woman with a Master's degree, and my life is a mess."

"I'd say you're handling the situation well enough." For a woman with such a run of bad luck, she kept her head high and mind focused. Add maturity and drive to the list, and she exhibited a set of character traits far beyond any woman he'd ever met.

A breeze caught a few strands of her dark hair. Just that simple act of nature made her look so beautiful.

Lauren shook the hair from her face. "I received a lucky break hooking up with Jan—temporarily anyway. Sharing the rent helped a lot."

With his gaze fixed on her face, he cocked his head. "And where are you now?"

"Just a room." While looking down at the asphalt, she shrugged. "The rent's cheap and will do."

"Then I'll ask you out more to make sure you're eating."

She smiled and turned a pair of misty green eyes his way. "I'll be using you."

"I won't mind as long as you're honest with me." For a chance to gaze into those gorgeous eyes, hell, yeah, he'd buy her dinner every night.

Looking away, she grunted. "Honesty isn't a word in my fiancé's vocabulary." She shook her head. "I'll never understand what happened. He had dreams of opening his own dealership and becoming the king of used cars. All he needed was financing."

Deems stopped, grabbed her shoulders to turn her, and then met her startled gaze. "I'm not him, Lauren. I'd never do anything to hurt you. My promise is mere words, but they're all I have."

She rested a palm against his cheek. "Thank you for being a friend."

Her touch was like a warm feather caressing his skin, gentle yet sensual. She tingled nerve endings that caused a rise in a part of his anatomy where friends shouldn't go. He flicked a finger under her chin. "Then, can I take you home to see where you live?"

She re-hooked her arm through his and urged him to continue on the path. "You probably need to return to work."

"I left for the day."

Tilting her head, she met his gaze. "You just gave me the impression of a man too busy to relax."

"You are correct...until today." He wasn't lying either. Ordinarily, he'd never stop work for any reason, but this woman from apple country inadvertently dragged him away from his desk, forced him to look at the blue sky, and sniff the freshly cut grass. Nature made her happy. His happiness derived from a new business deal.

Maybe she had the right idea to call themselves friends. Their disparities were too wide to compare. Depressing but realistic. He patted Lauren's hand. "Which way?"

She shook her head. "Not yet. Please understand."

"Oddly enough, I do." After hearing about her fiancé and then Eric, small wonder she trusted any man. And then, of course, she had the Hispanic's obsession with her backpack. The woman couldn't catch a break. Somehow, he needed to reverse the trend.

Chapter Eight

"Lauren?"

They had exited Central Park at Seventy-Eighth and Fifth Avenue and joined the always-flowing crowds on the sidewalk. Late afternoon. The beginning of the evening rush hour where an increase in people and cars made for the traditional gridlock.

She said her goodbye without a kiss or a handshake, merely two friends parting to go separate ways. But she remained on the street corner waiting for the green light to cross, her back to him. The light came and went, and still, she stood.

Deems wanted to believe he caused the hesitation, and at any second, she'd whirl and throw herself into his arms.

Wishful thinking. That typical scenario happened whenever a woman discovered his bank account. Any woman, even Lauren, could guess that his job paid well by the look of his tailored suits. He wasn't an off-the-rack man and hadn't been for quite a few years, but Lauren knew him as Jan's brother who worked at High-Rise International. Technically, a mere real estate agent. For the time being, he intended to keep his real identity under wraps. "Is anything wrong, Lauren?"

Brows furrowed, she turned slowly to face him. "I'm contemplating fate." She left the curb and strolled toward him. "If I hadn't been financially strapped, I'd never have met Jan and ultimately you." A slow smile spread onto her lips. "Given different circumstances, this friendship of ours can go in the opposite direction."

The comment certainly boosted his ego. His hopes soared. "You mean lovers?"

With her gaze fixed on his face, she nodded. "I won't, though, and you know why. You're a nice guy, Deems, but we're from two different worlds."

So much for hope. He scowled. "You say that as if you want to convince yourself."

A slight smile touched her mouth. "Maybe."

His gaze scanned her face and searched for a glimmer of want, but he glimpsed only questions. He could provide so much for her—if she'd let him. Ever since his early twenties, he lived by the old adage of patience being a virtue. He once waited three years for a client to come around to his way of thinking. With Lauren, he'd wait longer. No woman intrigued him more than this beauty from apple country. He gave her a slow, lingering look. "I'm a patient man, Lauren, probably the most patient you'll ever meet."

She acknowledged the comment with a lift to her brow before turning to join the crowd crossing the street.

Given *what* different circumstances? If Lauren had come to New York as planned, with money in her pocket, she'd have no need to bunk with Jan. She'd still be engaged, and he'd have no opportunity to meet her. Truthfully, her present situation suited him just fine. He enjoyed helping her, and for a brief moment in the park, he glimpsed happiness on her face. The park or him, he couldn't tell, but he'd like to see her smile more often, especially when the smile glowed from her gaze.

But an ex-fiancé left her financially strapped. No money and no job, along with emotional scars, would make any woman cautious. What possessed the man to disappear and take everything? A loan shark pressing for payment? Another woman? The whole premise smacked of desperation. But why steal her clothes and leave her high and dry without a penny to spare?

On the other hand, Deems should thank him. Lauren was free.

His gaze followed Lauren as she strolled along Fifth Avenue toward Seventy-Seventh Street. She walked with strength in her stride, head high, and her pace leisurely, in no hurry to get anywhere. The woman definitely filled out a pair of blue jeans. Nice ass. Long legs. Not the pampered type so common on his arm.

For some unfathomable reason, he started in her direction with every intention of following for a single block and then calling Lou Zane to swing by with the limo. Fifth Avenue ran parallel to Central Park so heavy foot traffic cluttered both sides of the street. He stayed on the Central Park side close to the parapet separating the park from the sidewalk and kept within the crowd in case she turned, but he needn't worry. Her distance stretched almost a full block ahead, and unless she had damn good eyesight, she'd never pinpoint him among the others.

One block stretched into two then three. Guilt consumed him, but still, he followed. She'd made her need for secrecy perfectly clear, yet something propelled his feet forward. An uneasiness for sure, judging from the tightness in his gut. He should have insisted on walking her home. Hell, he had a good excuse after witnessing the Hispanic's desperation.

Lauren crossed at the Seventy-Second Street stop light, and Deems slowed his pace. Five blocks was enough. Why take a chance to destroy her fragile trust simply because he fought this powerful need to protect her? Stepping closer to the parapet and away from the foot traffic on the sidewalk, he reached into his pocket for his cell phone when a man in a black leather jacket dashed from one of the park entrances and ran across Fifth Avenue, dodging traffic in his quest to reach the other side.

The Hispanic!

His gut wrenched. "Well, I'll be a son-of-a-bitch." What was the man's obsession with Lauren's backpack? Would the friggin' bastard follow her to the end of the earth? He hurried after him.

Deems debated calling 911, but what could he say, that he was following a man who attacked a woman earlier in the day? He hadn't asked for the name of the officer who met them in the park, and since the incident occurred only a few hours ago, the chances of the officer having the time to file the report were slim to none.

A minute later, Lauren turned left onto Seventieth Street and out of his sight.

The Hispanic ran to the corner and peeked before following.

The call forgotten, Deems sprinted across Fifth Avenue, scooted around a crawling black sedan with tinted windows, and barely escaped being run over by a tour bus. At the intersection of Seventieth and Fifth Avenue, he peeked around the side of the building and then rounded the corner.

The street was like so many others in New York—

one way for traffic, parking allowed on both sides, and the through-lane tight since cars grew in size while the streets stayed the same width. This neighborhood, like so many, was a mixture of residences and businesses, from brownstones to brick to gray stones, all connected in one long row. Scaffolding was a common sight as was the sound of jackhammers, but neither concerned him as he scurried to catch up.

Lauren crossed to the opposite side of the street.

The Hispanic followed and strolled about a half block behind.

From his lackadaisical walk, he had no intention of overtaking Lauren, and the revelation raised Deems' blood pressure a few notches. Deems wanted to shout and warn Lauren, but to do so would reveal that he, too, followed. So, he stayed on his side of the street and observed both, keeping to their pace but a discreet distance behind.

A car horn blared. Deems glanced over his shoulder to see the black sedan with tinted windows crawling along, creating road rage for the driver tailgating. When an opening alongside the curb occurred, the sedan rolled in to let traffic pass, and then quickly pulled out to continue its slow crawl. *Looking for a house number, no doubt.*

A little boy, pedaling furiously on a tricycle, zoomed around Deems, imitating the sounds of a race car, nearly colliding into a parcel delivery girl intent on the package in her hand. Down the block, a painter descended a ladder with a bucket of paint in hand while a helper rolled up the canvas covering the sidewalk. Everyday life in the city.

Another car horn blared, breaking into his

thoughts. With a quick glance over his shoulder, Deems jerked to a stop. The same black sedan! The car again rolled into an open space alongside the curb to let the cars pass, but this time, Deems stood against the steps of a brownstone to watch the vehicle drive by. Two men sat in the front seat, both wearing suits and ties. The side windows were too dark to see if anyone occupied the rear seat.

What was wrong with this picture? Was the driver a complete idiot and unable to find his way? No one drove this slow in New York unless...

No, the idea wasn't possible.

He waited for the sedan to drive far enough ahead before continuing. Who were they tailing—Lauren or the Hispanic? *What the hell is going on here*? Was Lauren being honest about her stay? If so, what possible interest could these people have in a woman supposedly taking an art class?

Thinking back, he knew so little about Lauren Howell. Her story about being from Pennsylvania's apple country could be a cover. Perhaps, she had a more covert reason for her visit to New York and *had* to leave Jan's apartment, because Eric discovered the truth and threatened to expose her. Maybe she wasn't attending an art class at all and hid her location to prevent a slip in identity. What proof had he that she was really an artist?

His instincts had served him well over the years, and every fiber told him he was right about Lauren Howell. She displayed more integrity than any woman on his social list. Nothing and no one could convince him otherwise.

With that belief in mind, he quickened his pace but

purposely stayed behind the sedan. Another block later, the Hispanic stopped with a jerk, whirled his head and body in all directions, ran a hundred feet, stopped again and whirled.

Lauren had disappeared!

Panic gripped Deems' chest. Where the hell was she? Had she entered a building without him noticing? But the Hispanic's frantic search eased the knot in his gut. Resisting the urge to run down the street, Deems slipped into the shadow of some scaffolding as the black sedan sped toward the Hispanic and screeched to a halt.

A man in a brown suit jumped from the front seat, grabbed the Hispanic, threw him onto the rear seat, and then slipped in beside him. The door slammed, and the car sped off. The abduction took no more than fifteen seconds.

Stunned frozen, Deems stared while his mind raced. What possible reason could anyone have to grab the Hispanic in the middle of the street and in broad daylight? What kind of trouble was he in, and was Lauren involved? And where the hell was she?

Curiosity colliding with concern, he took two steps away from the scaffolding. At the same moment, Lauren jumped from the open rear doors of a parked box delivery truck and scanned the area.

Seconds later, also from the rear, the uniformed driver of the truck appeared. Turning, Lauren shook his hand, adjusted her backpack, and continued down Seventieth Street.

Biting his tongue, Deems suppressed the laughter about to erupt at how she accomplished her disappearing act without anyone noticing. This woman could definitely handle herself, and he released a long, satisfied breath. She'd be fine for the remainder of her walk home.

But what about the black sedan and the Hispanic? Shouldn't he notify the police? Not like he could tell them much. He failed to look at the license plate on the vehicle. The man who jumped out had a buzz cut and no neck. Big deal—the clues were brown suit and brown hair.

Something made him hesitate to retrieve his cell phone. He wasn't sure what. Only a bad feeling. He glanced in Lauren's direction to see her walking as leisurely as before. Had she witnessed the abduction, or a worse thought, had she anything to do with the two men in the sedan?

Dear Lord, if he read mysteries, he'd love every sordid detail uncovered, but he hadn't picked up a good book in years. So, why was his imagination running wild?

Gut instinct kicked into gear. He learned early in life not to ignore the feeling. Too many questions with no answers. He nudged his feet to move in Lauren's direction. If anything, he had to ascertain her safe return home. He hurried to shorten the distance between them.

Two blocks later, Lauren ascended the steps to a brownstone with a sign over its door, *Rooms To Rent*. Deems stopped alongside a small tree to take in the surroundings, grateful for the rest. He hadn't walked such a distance in years. Sixteen blocks at a guess. All concrete and hard on the legs.

"You lost, mister?"

An old man had exited a shoe shop, carrying a pair of black leather shoes under his arm. They were spit-polished but worn with new leather soles tacked to the bottom. With a jerk of his head, Deems nodded toward the brownstone. "What can you tell me about that rooming house across the street?"

The old guy scanned Deems with one swift glance. "You can afford better than that dive."

He forced a smile. "I'm casing the place for a friend."

"The joint isn't fit for a dog." Shaking his head, he moved on.

Not the most pleasant piece of news. In outward appearance, the brownstone looked all right. No derelicts hung around the door, and no obvious drug dealers lurked in the nearby alleys. A small coffee shop stood a few doors down, and on his side of the street at the corner was Maria's Market with vegetable stands out front.

All right. Now what? Lauren had arrived safe and sound, and the Hispanic had been whisked away to places unknown. A quick call to the police would be the sensible course of action. Hell, he had to do *something*. If he spotted the man's photo on the eleven o'clock news after being fished from the Hudson, he'd feel guilty as sin.

Again, he reached for his cell phone but instantly froze. A familiar head of stringy hair caught his eye. Eric darted between two parked cars and, without a second of hesitation, took the brownstone's steps two at a time. With a quick glance over his shoulder, he disappeared through the door.

Deems' fists clenched. Eric found her. How? Or had she told him? *Why do I have so many doubts?*

Because women had fooled him before. Perhaps

Lauren and Eric connived a scheme to…what? Bilk Jan's brother? *Oh, right, so she moves out to make the plan easier to execute.* He either believed Lauren, or he didn't. And at that moment, he believed her. The more they talked, the more he recognized a woman with her head screwed on tight, with no pretense and no airs—a woman who'd stand her ground and fight, as evidenced by her bruised right hand and Eric's left jaw.

A strong sense of possessiveness took hold. He didn't want Eric within ten feet of Lauren, and damned if he'd let him reach her. After checking for traffic, Deems sprinted across the street and followed Eric's path into the brownstone.

Chapter Nine

The shabbiness of the lobby struck Deems first. Furniture not fit for curbside pickup decorated the main entry room. A man with a potbelly straining his shirt buttons lounged on a filthy sofa, its cushions long past comfortable. He chewed on an unlit cigar while staring at a flat-screen television hanging on the wall—the newest object in the room. Worn linoleum covered the floor, and down a short hall, a gated cubbyhole with an Office sign hanging overhead stood empty. The whole place smelled of stale cigar smoke and burnt bacon.

Deems approached the man. "You the manager?"

The man gave Deems a quick glance before returning his gaze to the TV. "Can I help you?"

Jaw muscles twitching, Deems sucked in a calming breath. "I'm looking for Lauren Howell."

He rolled the stogie to the other side of his mouth and cast a more intense perusal over Deems. "Popular lady tonight. Second floor. Room twelve. Some other guy is ahead of you, although I'd say you're several notches above the likes of him." While pointing a fat index finger, he turned slightly to face Deems. "I don't want no trouble in this place, hear?"

"I'll do my best." He headed for the stairwell.

Every step creaked along the way, making stealth damn near impossible. As he neared the second floor landing, he could see Eric with his forehead pressed against door number twelve.

"Come on, Lauren. Open up!" Eric pounded with an open palm.

"Go away, or I'll call the cops!"

Like a floodgate opening, heat swept through Deems as muscles tensed and pulse quickened. Just from Eric and Lauren's verbal exchange, he had absolutely no doubt about Lauren's side of the story being the truth. Jan was a fool.

"This door can't hold me back, Lauren." Eric readied his shoulder as a battering ram.

Fists clenching, Deems slammed his foot onto the landing. "Do you plan to force your way inside?"

Eric whirled, hair swinging to slap his face. A cold, hard gaze glared. Recognition registered, and his face drained of color. "Yo, man, what are you doing here?"

"Obviously, not for the same reason you are." He fought the urge to wring Eric's skinny neck, but given the least provocation, he'd swing with pleasure at his ugly puss. Sucking in a calming breath, Deems placed his other foot on the landing and stretched to his full height, doing his damnedest to look imposing. "How long have you known where she lived?"

Thrusting out his chest, he stepped away from the door. "Not since yesterday—and you promised to call me."

"I made no such promise." Jaw tight, he approached. "For the record, I found out five minutes ago."

Eric's gaze darted from Lauren's door to the staircase behind Deems.

He looked every bit a caged animal searching for an opening. The man wasn't a total moron. To fight

Deems meant an end to his meal ticket—namely Jan. Little did Eric know Deems Lambert hadn't raised his fists to any man. In his entire life, he talked his way out of every bad situation, and living in Chicago, he'd faced a lot of scary moments. Today, he might finally connect his fist to another man's jaw.

"Jan wants her back, Deems." Avoiding eye contact, he rubbed his palms against his hips. "She's heartbroken so I came to talk some sense into Lauren."

"By ramming down her door? Come on, Eric, how stupid do you think I am?" He took another step forward, purposely splaying his fingers to prevent a swing at Eric's face. "And while we're on the topic, I listened to one story from Jan and another completely different one from Lauren. You want to try for a third version?"

Cringing, Eric shifted from foot to foot. "That night was a gross misunderstanding. I was half asleep when I wandered into the living room and thought I jumped Jan on the sofa." With a weak grin, he rubbed the bruised area on his jaw. "I made an honest mistake, man. Lauren usually stays in her room, but boy, she freaked and slugged me."

"Well, I don't think Lauren has any intention of returning to the apartment." His gaze never deviating from Eric's, he crossed his arms over his chest. "She doesn't trust you and, quite frankly, neither do I."

"Look, man." He raised his hands, palms outward. "I can stay out of her way. She only has a few more months left in New York, right? And her being with us again will make Jan real happy."

What Jan saw in this man was beyond any comprehension. Of course, she was still young and easily influenced, and Eric, being much older, probably took advantage of as many women as possible.

Deems shot a quick glance around the landing. The four doors on this floor were in serious need of new paint. Duct tape sealed tears in the thin carpet, and mildew scented the stale air. No way in hell did Lauren deserve such a dump.

Clearing his throat, Eric dropped his hands. "Talk to Lauren for me, pal, and tell her I'm sorry. Both of us want her back." He nodded toward Lauren's door. "Jan's apartment is a hell of a lot better than this flophouse."

Deems silently agreed. Only one bulb lit the entire landing, creating too many areas of darkness. God forbid what creatures wandered at night. "Take a walk, Eric, and do not come here again, understand?"

"I can't guarantee that, man. I want to make Jan happy."

Eric leaving Jan would make Deems happy. Actually, ecstatic. Forcing himself to maintain eye contact, Deems stepped to the side and pointed to the staircase. "Go!"

Something about Eric's posture put Deems on the alert. The man wasn't the least willing to leave. Eric stood a few inches taller and had a long arm reach but was nowhere near equal to Deems' weight. Deems stiffened his back. "Don't challenge me, Eric. I can make your life miserable."

Eric cocked a brow then nodded. His shoulders slumped, and walking past Deems, he lowered one foot onto the first step then paused, his jaw tight. "Jan doesn't know I found Lauren."

"I'm sure she doesn't. Did you plan on surprising

her by dragging Lauren home with you?"

"Something like that." His forced smile twitched. "Talk to her, Deems, for Jan's sake." He ran down the stairs.

Jan's sake, my ass.

Across the hall, the door to room eleven cracked open to the length of a metal security chain. An old woman peered through the opening. "Is he gone?"

Deems stepped toward the door. "Yes, ma'am. Has he been here before?"

She motioned with her head toward Lauren's door. "He picked the lock yesterday. I called the cops, but they got here too late. They always come too late around here."

Through tight teeth, he sucked in a breath. "Did he break in?"

"Yeah. I heard him moving around, but he rushed out, cursing and empty-handed." She clucked her tongue. "That girl doesn't belong here." She slammed the door in his face.

If Eric's sole purpose was to return Lauren to Jan's, why would he bother searching her room and risk a burglary charge? What the hell was he looking for? Shaking off the frustration of too many questions, he knocked on door number twelve. "Lauren, Eric's gone."

The doorknob rattled, and a scraping sound followed.

When the door flew open, a woman drained of color fell into his arms. Breathing in her familiar vanilla scent, he held her tight. Gone was the proud, confident woman of an hour earlier. She trembled in his embrace, and a longing too emotional to ignore swept through him. Every fiber in him wanted to protect her, and he fought the overwhelming desire to scoop her into his arms and carry her to safety.

After a time, the trembling subsided, but she stayed in his arms, face buried against his chest, and her hands in loose fists. His heart ached to see her so afraid, and he silently cursed Eric, and then Jan. No one should live in fear.

She sniffed. "I won't ask why you're here."

"I'll tell you anyway." He tilted her chin upward to see two glistening emeralds clouded with tears. "I spotted the Hispanic guy following you. When did you see him?"

"About a block off Fifth Avenue. He kept his distance, so I figured he wanted to know where I lived."

"What about the black sedan?"

She jerked back slightly, eyes wide. "What sedan?"

"A man grabbed the Hispanic and threw him into the rear of the car."

"Oh—wow! I wondered what became of him. I guess he pissed off someone else." She replaced her head onto his chest. "Not like I care." She rubbed her nose. "So, you followed me, too?"

"All I wanted was to see you home safe. Even when the sedan whisked away the Hispanic, I still followed only to see Eric run inside." Slipping his fingers under her hair, he rubbed the nape of her neck. "Please don't be mad."

She made no attempt to leave his arms, and her trust created a manly sense of pride to swell within his chest. What if he hadn't followed? Would that lazy piece of shit in the lobby get off his ass to call the cops? He kissed the top of Lauren's head. "Your neighbor claims Eric already broke in."

"Yes, she told me. I can't imagine what he wanted." Patting his chest, she stepped from his arms and used her hands to wipe the tears from her cheeks.

The color had returned to her face, but her eyes stayed an extraordinarily deep green. They were so beautiful they literally took away his breath. Using one finger, he lifted her chin. "You're not mad I followed?"

With a strained smile, she met his gaze. "You're watching out for me in ways no man has ever done. Thank you." She cleared her throat. "I had just grabbed my phone to call the police when I heard your voice. Your timing was perfect." Taking a step toward him, she stroked her fingers along his jacket lapel. "I wet your suit."

"Like I care." He closed the door and took stock of its security, which was none. No dead bolt, chain, or latch. The only lock was a keyhole in the doorknob, and any hairpin would do the job. How the hell did she sleep at night? He jiggled the loose knob. "This door won't keep anyone out, Lauren."

"I know. When I'm home, I jam a chair under the doorknob. I'd buy a chain, but I'll need tools. The landlord offered to put one in for fifty bucks."

"How kind of him." He scanned her room.

The dimensions were no more than eight by ten with a single bed, its mattress indented in the center from age. A hot plate stood on a rickety wooden table along with a two-cubic-foot refrigerator. The table looked ready to collapse from the weight. No TV or rugs, one dirty window with duct tape covering a broken pane, and a yellow-stained roller shade for privacy. On the dresser sat a white plastic bag folded down to reveal a half dozen Granny Smith apples.

Fighting a shudder, he'd seen bigger closets. However, one noticeable absence struck him. "Where's the bathroom?"

She pointed to an opening near the bed.

Walking over, he pushed on an accordion door to see a toilet with a rust-stained sink. No shower. His gut wrenched. "You're not staying here." He faced her. "Come home with me. I've got a spare bedroom."

Eyebrows furrowed, she shook her head. "As tempting as that sounds, no, Deems. I'm indebted to too many people already."

Struggling to keep his voice level, he waved an arm at the door. "But Eric can return at any time. What then?"

Jaw set, she crossed her arms over her chest. "I'll look for a new place tomorrow, but I doubt I'll find a cheaper room."

"Will you at least take some money?" He whirled his hand toward his back pocket.

"Don't you dare take out that wallet!"

Eyeing her closely, he scowled. "You are a stubborn one and too damn proud for your own good." He scanned the room with scorn. "You don't deserve a place like this."

"I don't deserve my life turned upside-down either, but shit happens." She approached and splayed a hand on his upper arm, her gaze tender. "Thank you for coming to my rescue, but time for you to leave. I'm tired." She kissed his cheek. "I'll be all right."

Her words accomplished very little to alleviate the dread growing in his chest. *One last night and no way in hell will she stay in this hellhole.* He vowed to find her a decent place to live.

Chapter Ten

Damn that Eric.

Lauren cussed him repeatedly as she hurried to class the next morning, defying the law by crossing on the red light like so many others. *Lock me away, I dare you!*

Eric would return. The man was determined to get in her pants. *Well, guess what, Mr. Eric Drummer?* She'd defend herself and beat the crap out of him. From the day she watched him saunter into the apartment, she hadn't liked his lecherous looks and secretly questioned his loyalty to Jan. But how the hell could Jan believe that Lauren Howell would hurt their relationship by going after her boyfriend? *Like I'm so friggin' desperate.*

All right, so he found me. How was the question? No way in hell could she miss that tall, lanky body with his mop of stringy hair. Unless he followed in his car. But his jalopy had a hole in the muffler the size of a watermelon. She'd hear the rattle two blocks away. Not to mention his notorious trail of smoke from the bad head gasket. Regardless, come lunchtime, she'd buy a newspaper and scan the ads for another place.

Damn men with their gutter morals. They took what they pleased without considering the implications. Her ex qualified for the top spot on the shit list. Jo-Jo played her for a fool. He asked her to marry him, suggested joint bank accounts, and then took over the bill-paying, because keeping the books was his job at the car dealership. As early as high school, he had always been good with numbers. She hadn't realized how good until he cleaned house. Then, to discover he withheld the apartment rent from as far back as her layoff. What a shocker. With the security deposit depleted, she sold her engagement ring and borrowed the remainder from her parents to pay the overdue rent. Otherwise, a collection agency would hound her to the brink of insanity.

She glanced both ways before crossing at Seventy-Third Street. Thinking back, her sudden unemployment triggered a change in her ex. He converted from a cheerful, gregarious man to a sullen and argumentative one, and they fought for the most asinine reasons. All too often, he stormed out, threatening never to return, and then crawled in like a puppy who wet the floor, begging for forgiveness. Hell, she hardly understood what to forgive. As the best car salesman at the dealership, he made enough money to pay the rent and utilities *without* her paycheck. So, what happened?

He'd left no clue as to why he disappeared. His family denied knowing his whereabouts. Her happily-ever-after dream had shattered into a thousand pieces. Now, she was flat-broke, owed money to the church and her parents, and had no place to live except over her parents' garage.

The last fact irked her the most. From the first day of college, she'd managed her life and survived on her three-D murals plus food server jobs at several Gettysburg restaurants. She alone paid for her college education straight to a Master's degree with only minimal help from scholarships. But now, with the educational system in shambles, she might be forced to forget teaching as a career and concentrate fully on her art. Three-D murals and stained glass were two of the biggest options in interior design.

At the next crossing, she hurried as the light turned yellow. The morning was beautiful, a perfect day to walk with the air crisp and the overhead sky a clear blue. She missed the sights and scents of spring back home, mostly the sweetness of apple blossoms floating through the air and their soft, white petals blanketing the grass. The predominant odors in New York were car exhaust and the occasional whiff of garbage from a nearby alley. *Damn city-slickers don't know what they're missing.*

Her cell phone rang midway up the next block. With her heart rate kicking into high gear, she smiled at the sight of Deems' name. If she ever decided to give a man another try, she'd definitely choose Deems. He showed when she needed him most, like the proverbial light at the end of a dark tunnel. If she wasn't careful, she'd break her own rule of staying clear of men and fall in love with him. She lifted the phone to her ear. "Hi. I'm on my way to class."

"What time is lunch?"

"One o'clock. Antonio gives us an hour. Why?"

"I've a new place for you and within walking distance from the studio."

She stopped and stared at her phone before returning the unit to her ear. "How do you know where the studio is?"

"Simple deduction, my dear, and the use of the Internet. You mentioned the name Antonio a couple of times, and maybe that's how Eric found you and followed. Want to see the place?"

She winced. The area around the studio was too swanky. "How much?"

"I'll meet you outside the studio, and we'll discuss the details. And no, I'm not taking you to my place. See you at one." He disconnected.

A car horn blared and scared her half out of her skin. She had stopped in the middle of a crosswalk, shocked by his news. Pulse racing, she mouthed an apology and hurried to the curb.

Why was this man always coming to her rescue? He was the most thoughtful man she'd ever met and wasn't sure whether to be flattered or leery. She had absolutely no excuse to turn him away, except for her do-not-get-involved vow. But, in truth, she was drawn to him in a way she hadn't expected.

Instincts told her he had more than a casual interest. Yesterday at the park, she had seen the smile tugging on his lips and the shine in his brown eyes, and unable to resist, she kissed him. Not deeply, but she pretty much killed their friendship agreement. After Jo-Jo, she hadn't wanted any part of a relationship until she arranged her life into some semblance of order. Friend or otherwise, Deems complicated her entire situation. And so what? A woman couldn't ask for a nicer complication.

As the time passed, she counted the minutes for the clock to strike the one o'clock hour and barely listened to a word out of Antonio's mouth. Deems was the reason for her pounding heart and scatterbrain, not the prospect of a new apartment.

"Hey—yo! You're soldering the wrong side!"

Lauren jumped at the sound of Barbara's voice, her partner for the day. She stared at the glass pieces on the table in front of her. "Where?"

Barbara flipped a glass piece and pointed. "Shiny side down."

"Oh." She almost ruined the entire design. "Sorry."

With her sleeved arm, Barbara brushed her straight black hair from her face. "You're in la-la land today. Maybe you should give me the solder gun." She took the gun from Lauren's hand and soldered the two pieces together. "Want to talk about what's bothering you? I know the look, honey. A man's involved."

Lauren couldn't deny the accusation. All morning, her gaze darted to the front windows. Deems would be waiting outside, and that handsome man affected her in ways she hadn't expected. Smiling, she turned to her classmate. "I'm heading out the door at the stroke of one whether Antonio approves or not."

No exaggeration either. When the clock chimed one, she grabbed her backpack and flew toward the exit. Deems stood on the sidewalk alongside a big, black man, both impeccably dressed in business suits. A silver limo stretched behind them, polished to perfection and glowing in the afternoon sun—although, the black man's bald head created the brighter glow.

After marveling at the beauty of the limo, she locked gazes with Deems. He smiled, and her breath hitched. The man had become her knight in shining armor. She desperately fought to control the desire to throw herself into his arms. Clearing her throat, she raised a brow and pointed at the silver limo. "Yours?"

Deems waved a nonchalant hand. "Company limo and our driver, Lou."

With a polite tip of his head, Lou nodded. "Nice to meet you, Ms. Howell."

The chauffeur had at least fifteen years on Deems, but his size and broad shoulders plus a six-foot-five frame left no doubt that he doubled as a bodyguard. With bright dark eyes but a serious expression, he opened the rear door.

Deems took her elbow and waved toward the opening. "I said we were within walking distance, but I don't want you to waste your lunch hour. We'll eat on the way."

Eat? With her heart fluttering and butterflies threatening to pop out of her mouth? *He must be joking.*

Her steps faltered by the door while her gaze shifted to Lou then Deems until resting on the inside of the limo. She'd seen this type of scenario in the movies, where strangers lured the unsuspecting victim into an expensive car only to meet The Enforcer and die a horrible death. *I really should stop watching late-night movies.* She trusted Deems. He wouldn't come to her rescue then toss her to the wolves, right? So, taking a deep breath, she removed her pack and stepped inside.

He slipped alongside her.

The smell of new leather hit her nose. Combined with pristine carpeting and sparkling chrome, hell, this vehicle had rolled right off a showroom floor. Giggles threatened to erupt. She'd never been in a limo, not even for a funeral, but she couldn't ignore the sudden lift in her spirits. She'd been down-in-the-dumps for months and always questioned her decision to come to New York. Now, sitting next to Deems and in this plush limo, she let hope seep into her psyche...at least for today. She would enjoy Deems' company and the luxury of the brushed leather seats beneath her butt. She ran her fingers along the carpet-covered door to feel the softness. "Wow! If you're trying to impress me, you've succeeded."

"Seatbelt, please." He pointed.

She snapped the belt before the limo glided into traffic.

The buildings zipped by as Lou skillfully maneuvered around buses and illegally parked cars. They left the studio's location on Seventy-Fifth and Madison, and Lou stayed on Madison, traveling through the upper east side of Manhattan, an area she hadn't seen since everything was way out of her price range—food included.

Deems stretched forward and opened a small, glass-covered cooler full of wine, beer, soda, and water. A white deli bag had been crammed in the middle.

After grabbing the bag, he opened the fold and took out a large, paper-wrapped sandwich. "We'll share a ham and cheese." He handed her several napkins, opened the wrapping, broke apart the sandwich, and handed her half. "Water or soda? I won't feed you the wine or beer. I don't know if you drink alcohol, but mainly, I don't want you drunk for your afternoon class."

She smiled at his thoughtfulness. "Water, please." She spread a napkin across her lap and then pointed to the fridge. "What, no champagne and caviar?" She bit into the sandwich and rolled her eyes as the flavors of honey-roasted ham and melted Swiss cheese hit her taste buds. "Oh, my God, this is so good!" She hurriedly ate another bite.

"Champagne and caviar are for dates, Lauren.

We're on a mission." He grabbed two water bottles from the cooler, unscrewed both, and placed them in the fold-down cup holders between their seats. He spread napkins across his suit before taking a large bite.

She pointed to the driver. "What about Lou?"

"He'll eat while we look at the apartment." He took another bite, chewed, and then shifted the rest to the side of his mouth, bulging his cheek. "I've no need to impress you, Lauren. Lou belongs to the company owner and drives whoever and wherever he's told. I'm privileged because I'm the North American agent, and a lot of my properties are here in Manhattan." He chewed then swallowed. "This city has some of the most expensive real estate in the world. We're currently heading to one."

Nearly choking on her food, she lifted her napkin to her mouth and stared. "You know I can't afford much."

"That's why you'll have a job."

The hand with the napkin fell to her lap. "What are you talking about? I don't have time for a job."

"For this one, you will." With a napkin, he wiped his mouth while gesturing with his hand toward her backpack. "I see you don't carry a purse. Do you keep everything in your shoulder bag?"

"No. I keep my cell phone and room key in my jeans and my wallet in my jacket pocket. Otherwise, I carry nothing else of value." She sipped her water. "I started the habit the day I arrived and spotted all the derelicts at the train station." She shook her head. "I can't wait to leave this city."

There. She reminded him not to waste his time. Obviously, Deems Lambert was a great catch, but she wasn't fishing. Even though the man had returned hope to her heart, she'd never allow herself to fall in love. In her mind, a city-boy versus country-girl pairing would never work, and if she kept her distance, she should emerge from their friendship unscathed.

Yeah, right.

His musk cologne swirled around the inside of the limo and distracted her to no end. She barely took notice of where they were or where they were going.

The limo slowed.

Deems stuffed the remainder of his meal into his mouth, removed the napkins, and swept the crumbs off his suit. After swallowing, he glanced out the window. "We're here, Lauren. You can finish on the way back."

Quickly, Lauren rewrapped her sandwich and shoved the bundle into the small cooler. After unbuckling her seatbelt, she kicked her backpack to the side and followed Deems onto the sidewalk. Mouth agape, she froze.

Chapter Eleven

Eyes nearly popping from their sockets, Lauren gawked at the most beautiful marble-faced high-rise with glass double doors for an entrance. The building stretched upward to God only knew how many floors. No doorman or overhead canopy were visible, but nevertheless, the place was way out of her league. To make matters worse, Central Park sat across the street with all its green splendor.

A sense of disorientation hit. The tall building before her, the beautiful park behind, and a limo at the curb. Definitely not her world of tractors and apples, and a fluttery feeling filled her belly. What was he thinking? She knew enough about the expensive properties surrounding the perimeter of the park. They provided homes for some of the richest people in the world. Swallowing hard, she met Deems' twinkling gaze. "We're on Fifth Avenue, right?" She gripped his jacket sleeve. "Are you out of your mind?"

As a gentle smile curled his lips, he patted the hand on his sleeve. "Trust me, you'll love everything about this arrangement. Unfortunately, the Stewarts' condo doesn't face the park, but you can't have everything."

Have everything? What the hell is he talking about?

With his warm palm on the small of her back, he ushered her through the two glass doors and into a marble-tiled lobby where a crystal chandelier hung from the ceiling. White marble paneled the walls, held together by strips of gold metal. Every inch sparkled, and one dared not track in any dirt.

From behind a desk full of computer screens, a security guard shot to his feet. "Afternoon, Mr. Lambert."

"Hi, Robert. We're heading for the Stewarts'."

"Right. Hold on." He lifted a desk phone to his ear, spoke briefly, and then ended the call. "They're waiting, sir." Slipping from behind the desk, he headed toward an open elevator while pulling a ring of keys from his belt.

Still with his hand on her back, Deems nudged her forward. She forced her legs to move, and together, they stepped into the elevator.

Robert inserted a key into the slot near the fourth floor button but backed out with a smile and a quick salute before the doors closed.

Polished to perfection, the marble paneling continued in the elevator, and she glided her fingers along the cold surface. The elevator control panel sparkled with glossy brass, boasting of fifteen mother-of-pearl floor buttons.

"Close your mouth, Lauren."

Heat seeping into her cheeks, she slapped her lips together and met his amused gaze. "You don't really expect me to live here, do you?" He'd taken her to an exorbitant neighborhood, fully aware of her problems with money. Was he deaf? Hadn't he heard anything at all?

"You will live and work here. They need a condo sitter."

Heart racing, she whirled to face him. "A *what*?"

A smile tugged the corner of his mouth. "Someone to watch their place while they travel. Here we are."

The elevator doors opened onto a long carpeted hall with two heavily-carved wooden doors opposite each other. Three small, lit chandeliers brightened the way. At the far end alongside a fire hose encased in glass, a fire exit door stood with its lit sign overhead. No marble on the walls, just ordinary gray paneling trimmed with wood. Still elegant but without the opulence.

"Come on, Lauren."

Her feet refused to move. "Deems—" Her mouth resembled the Sahara, and she swallowed hard.

He gave her a warm smile. "They'll love you."

Slipping his hand over hers, he urged her from the elevator.

The warmth of his hand distracted her from the growing panic but not enough to shake her from a stupefied state. Was she dreaming? Hell, she must be. Any second, she'd awaken and find herself still soldering in class.

He advanced toward the door on the left where he tapped a mother-of-pearl doorbell.

Church bells chimed from deep within to announce their arrival. She wasn't sure why, but she glanced upward as if expecting to see the bell tower.

A woman in her late fifties swung open the door with a flair. She had fly-away, bleach-blonde hair firmly lacquered in place, a diamond the size of a boulder on her left hand, and a string of pearls around her neck. She flashed a brilliant smile. "You brought her. Oh, Deems, I'm so glad. Come in, come in."

Stepping aside, she waved toward the living room.

Lauren entered a spacious room fit for a king. White furniture, white rugs, and sparkling gold-trimmed lamps with dangling tassels dominated the interior. Crystal figurines decorated tables and shelves, and potted plants covered every nook and cranny, layered on stands, tables, and the floor. The whole room looked like a forest surrounded by snow.

A man trudged from the right hallway carrying two heavy suitcases, which he plunked alongside four others already resting by the door. Bald, round, and not much taller than his wife, he gasped and sputtered from the exertion.

Deems used an elbow to nudge her forward. "Carol and Bill Stewart, meet Lauren Howell."

Both appraised her with a satisfied nod.

Like meat on a skewer. She glanced at Deems for some affirmation as to what the hell all the scrutiny was about but received only a grin in return.

Carol touched Lauren's arm. "Can you start tonight?"

"Deems hasn't filled me in, Mrs. Stewart." She glowered at Deems.

Carol dismissed him with a wave of her hand. "Just like a man. As if women are mind-readers." She scrunched her face at Deems then looped her arm through Lauren's and guided her toward the center of the living room. "Well, dear, last night, I ran into Deems and told him of our woes about finding a reliable person to take care of all my babies." She fingered a leaf on one of the plants. "Our housekeeper will stay if I ask, but she's made plans to visit her family out in Arizona. Our dilemma boiled down to our neighbor across the hall lending us her housekeeper, but I never liked the woman—our neighbor, not the housekeeper. Way too snobby for my liking." She nudged her farther into the room. "Anyway, Deems mentioned you needed a place to live until you finished school. The timing was perfect. We'll pay you a thousand a week, and we'll need you for at least a month. Are my terms suitable?"

Mouth agape, Lauren staggered then shook herself. "A thousand dollars a week?"

Loosening her hold on Lauren's arm, Carol Stewart raised her brows. "What, not enough? Fifteen hundred then."

Lauren's head spun. She reached with a hand to her forehead, as if to hold her head in place. "Mrs. Stewart, please—no, a thousand is good enough."

"You'll help us then?" Carol patted Lauren's arm before releasing. "Oh, I'm so pleased. You're house-sitting along with caring for the plants and keeping the place clean." Whirling, she grasped Lauren by the shoulders. "Can you start immediately? We leave tonight." She dropped her hands.

Stunned at the sudden turn of events, Lauren simply nodded. This job was her best break in months. And all because of Deems. Eyes wide, she shot him a glance.

He responded with a wink.

Heart pumping wildly, Lauren barely contained her joy. "After class tonight, I'll run and pack my things. What time do you leave?"

"Our transportation is arranged for seven. If you arrive before then, good. I'll leave a list of the feeding schedules for the plants on the kitchen counter. If by chance you're late, you can obtain the key from Robert at the security desk." She wagged a finger at Deems. "Make sure Robert knows her."

"I'll do that." He headed for the door. "Come on, Lauren. Let's return you to class."

Class? Why? Shaking herself, she thanked the Stewarts and followed.

Bill Stewart led them to the elevator. "You made my wife very happy." Reaching around Lauren, he jabbed the Down button for the elevator. "You don't know what you're in for, but I can honestly admit you should have taken the fifteen hundred. My wife sings to her plants. She'll probably expect you to do the same."

Hell, if required, she'd sing soprano. What a friggin', lucky break.

The elevator doors opened. He inserted a key into the lobby slot and turned, removed it, and held out his hand to Deems. "We'll see you when we return."

As the elevator descended, Lauren stared at the closed doors while placing a palm onto her forehead. "I can't believe what just happened."

Gazing upward, Deems followed the changing overhead floor lights. "I'd say you're perfect for the job." Lowering his gaze, he leaned toward her. "You'll be safer here."

Safer and with a salary. How had she become blessed all of a sudden? Dropping her hand, she met his gaze. "Why are you doing this?"

His brow cocked. "I'm helping friends. I've known Carol and Bill for years, and then, of course, there's *you* until we say goodbye."

Say goodbye? She shook herself. *Yes, naturally, until we say goodbye.* She again stared at the doors. "A thousand bucks a week. What I don't spend, I can put toward my loans."

Like the floodgates opening, the reality hit. She shrieked with glee, whirled, and threw herself into his arms. She regretted not meeting Deems earlier. He had become her good luck charm, and because of him, she would spend the remainder of her New York stay in comfort.

Deems responded by wrapping his arms tight around her. "Don't thank me yet, woman. You've a forest to attend, and I hope you know something about plants, being from the country and all."

Tilting her head, she gazed into his twinkling eyes. "I know quite a bit about plants, Mr. Lambert. My mother grows all kinds of flowers." As the elevator slowed, she pecked his lips. "Thank you, Deems." The doors opened.

He released his arms but clamped onto her hand. "Hold on. Some instructions are in order." He pointed to the control panel. "I'm sure you noticed how a special key inserted activates the elevator. The key works only for that particular floor. Also, you'll notice two elevators, but you can only use this one. The other is reserved for the penthouse."

Leading her through the open doors, he paused in the middle of the hallway and pointed to the fire escape at the end. "All the staircase doors have alarms to alert security so no one can sneak up to bother you. No one can visit unless they go through Robert or the night guard, Johnny. I'm sure you noticed how Robert called the Stewarts before allowing us into the elevator. He follows standard procedure for all of our high-rises."

After glancing at the sparkling marble and then his

exquisite suit, she cast him a one-eyed squint. "Your company owns this building?"

"Yes, and I'm responsible for the management. The structure is fifteen stories high plus a penthouse, two condos per floor—except for the penthouse which occupies the entire floor. The penthouse is also the only unit with access to the roof." He turned toward the lobby, still holding her hand. "For tonight, I'll lend you Lou. He'll wait by the studio, drive you to your room, and then here. He'll save you a lot of time and be your bodyguard should Eric come calling."

They approached the security desk. Robert already stood, watching them.

Deems squeezed her hand. "Robert, Lauren Howell will be staying in the Stewarts' condo until they return."

Robert gave her a warm smile. "Glad to have you, miss. If you need anything, call me."

Need? She'd have money, a nice place to live, and security a phone call away. What could she possibly need? She felt so damn happy she might break down and cry.

Chapter Twelve

"You're certainly cheery."

Deems glanced up from his laptop to realize he had been whistling. Betty, his executive assistant, had walked into the office with more paperwork—and he didn't care! "You're making exceptional coffee these days, Mrs. McGann."

She peered over a pair of eyeglasses. "I make the coffee the same every day so I'm sure your attitude influenced your taste." She placed the paperwork into his Inbox. "Did you have a nice lunch?"

"I had a wonderful lunch." Having Lauren by his side in the limo, watching her finish her half sandwich, and knowing she'd be safe in the Stewarts' condo, hell—yeah, he was a happy man. His mood hadn't been so light in years and all because of one woman. In the elevator, when Lauren had thrown herself into his arms, she bubbled with an enthusiasm that caused her face and eyes to glow. The shadow clouding her had disappeared, and she changed into the most beautiful woman in the world. Once reseated in the limo, he almost told Lou to take a round-about route to the studio.

"You're whistling again."

So he was. He cleared his throat and slipped the top paper from the pile. "What's this?"

"The fax from Dan Williams in Argentina. You

know, the report you requested about Mark Jordan." She adjusted her glasses.

Deems read the list of attributes. Aggressive, confident, dependable. "My gut said Mark was good, and Dan's had several months to evaluate my new hire." He leaned back in his plush leather chair and smiled. "Mark reminds me of me, a real go-getter and not afraid to stick out his neck." He glanced at Betty. "Has he landed in New York yet?"

"Yes, he cleared Customs. I sent Lou to the airport."

"Good. I'm sure Dan told him he's in the running for a promotion." Finished with the fax, he placed the paper to the side. "Let me know when he arrives."

"Right."

Betty stood with a big smirk on her face. Since he recognized that crafty little glint in her eyes, he narrowed his gaze. "Something on your mind?"

"You've been rearranging your busy schedule a lot these days. I'm hoping this woman forces you to work less." Gaze twinkling behind the glasses, she left, closing the door after her.

He hadn't become a successful man by sitting idle. Yes, he always had his schedule book full but rarely for social activities. Until Lauren, he hadn't made any exceptions. No getting around the fact. Life was wonderful. The business was doing well, and his new hires were working out better than anticipated. He'd met a fascinating woman who excited him in ways he hadn't experienced in years, and he actually whistled in tune. Lauren had changed his perspective on everything. Closing his laptop, he grabbed a few papers from the Inbox and skimmed through the contents.

The only detail souring his euphoria was their friendship agreement. He'd like to move their relationship in a different direction, but she hated New York and used the excuse to keep him at arm's length. Well, guess what, Lauren Howell? He would love to make her happy, shower her with gifts, and never have her worry about money again. Yet, caution prevailed. In the past, he'd made the mistake of trusting a woman only to discover her loyalty centered on his money. Would Lauren be the same or remain the level-headed, down-to-earth woman who captured his heart? Time would give him an answer, so he mustn't blow his identity too soon. He picked up his pen and scribbled a response on the first letter.

A knock sounded on the door.

Without waiting for his reply, Jan popped her frizzy mop through the opening. "Hi. Got a minute?"

"Jan, come in!" He threw his pen on the desk. "What brings you here?"

"Oh, you know, I was in the neighborhood."

His office building was a far cry from her apartment and school, but he let the comment pass. Whenever Jan visited—which wasn't often—she usually bounced into the office full of youthful vigor, but not today. She entered with a hesitant step while clutching a large canvas purse to her chest. Since a frown wrinkled her forehead, he glanced at her gladiator sandals just to see if the laces were too tight. "Have a seat."

She flopped into one of the two big leather chairs in front of his desk, dropped her purse to the floor with a thud, and curled onto the seat, legs tucked close to her chest.

At a guess, she wanted to blend in with the leather. Impossible with her flowery clothes. He'd swear on a stack of bibles she wore pajamas as her everyday garments. He leaned back and studied his sister. "What's bothering you, Jan?"

While toying with her pant leg, she sighed. "I wondered if you've seen Lauren."

She'd said the words so softly he actually wondered if Eric was right all along about Jan missing Lauren. His eyebrow ticked. "I have. Why?"

Shooting him a quick glance, she hugged her knees. "Lauren and I talked about a lot of things, Deems. You know, sister stuff. I miss her." Smirking, she shrugged. "I guess I want to know if she's okay."

"She's fine." *After I secured her safety from Eric, found her a decent place to live, and assured money for her to eat.* Oh, how he wanted to tell Jan what a douche bag Eric was and the trouble he caused, but he'd waste his breath. She wouldn't hear a word. While gazing carefully at his sister, Deems rocked in his chair. "Do I detect a hint of regret?"

Waving aside his question, she met his steady gaze. "Are you dating her?"

"I can't call us dating." Picking up his pen, he tapped the tip on his desk pad. "I've seen her a few times, more to check on her than anything else."

Jan fussed with a string of beads dangling around her neck. "I'll never forgive her, Deems."

So ended the question of whether Jan wanted Lauren back. He again dropped the pen and studied her. "Lauren's story is substantially different from Eric's, and quite frankly, I believe hers." He leaned forward to point a finger. "Lauren hit him with a solid right hook for a reason, and she has the bruised knuckles as proof."

She shook her head. "Eric said the bruise came from the car."

A classic case of blind love. How could he possibly convince his young and naïve sister about a man like Eric? She had picked the worst kind of opportunist—a man who took whatever he pleased without guilt or remorse. And right now, the man had everything. He screwed Jan while feeding her lies about false love, and then secretly pursued Lauren while Jan attended class. Without a doubt, Jan needed some sense slapped into her small brain.

Again, Deems sat back. "Lauren is very beautiful, Jan. She has no need to chase men, especially one dating her friend. You know yourself she doesn't want any involvement with a man, and she's already told me that very thing more than once." He cocked his head. "Deep down, you believe her, don't you?"

She stretched out her legs and slumped into the chair. "I don't know what to believe."

If Jan wasn't careful, she'd slide right off the leather cushion and look like a bouquet of flowers hitting the floor. But this visit was more than her feigned concern for Lauren. He let a gentle smile slip onto his lips. "Why don't you tell me what's really bothering you."

Jan shuffled her sandals on the rug. "Eric's done some things that have me wondering."

Well, this revelation was a welcomed opening. Not like he had any expertise on the inner processes of a woman's mind, but he understood men like Eric. And to have his sister associating with his type was enough to make a brother's blood boil. Deems reclined his chair and lifted his feet onto the corner of the desk. "What's Eric doing?" *Besides stalking Lauren.*

She shot him a sideways glance. "I never told anyone—not even Lauren, but while we were in the Bahamas, he disappeared for an entire day. I almost contacted the police, but then, he strolled through the door and never even apologized. The time was close to midnight, and he refused to talk about where he'd been."

A man who disappeared while on vacation with a girlfriend almost always created one scenario. Deems cringed. "Another woman?"

"I can't be certain." Lips pursed, she drummed her fingers on the armrests. "He talked me into a trip to the Bahamas, because he said I studied too much. Then, he turned around and said we're leaving, because I'm missing too many classes." She sighed heavily and straightened in the chair. "We paid for six days but left in three with no chance for refund." She met his gaze. "I thought he'd gone bonkers, you know, like too many hours in the sun. He knows we're not rolling in dough."

His gut tightened. "You paid for the trip?"

She grimaced. "Actually, *you* did since you pay all my bills."

With his blood about to boil out his veins, Deems toyed with the crease in his trousers while mentally counting to ten. Jan's spending options necessitated serious reconsideration with Eric in the picture. He'd already warned her about the rent. Maybe his next action was to cancel the credit card he gave her, but such an action left him with a tricky situation. He wanted Jan to have anything she desired, and to cut her off would break his heart. Yet, in the same breath, he refused to allow her to support her slug of a fiancé.

"And another point." Jan swung her legs over the chair's armrest, brows creased together. "When we arrived at the Bahamas airport, Eric turned into a bundle of nerves. He couldn't sit still. Once home, he relaxed completely but then got real bad after Lauren left. He's snapping at me for the oddest reasons, disappears for hours, and paces like he's some caged animal." She frowned at the floor.

Should he tell Jan how Eric found Lauren, all under the pretense of returning her to the apartment? Somehow, Jan's naïve mind would twist the story and make Eric the hero. He pursed his lips. "What do you expect me to do?"

Shrugging, she forced a smile. "Be my sounding board. I've no one else to talk to—except Mom, but she'll tell me to abide by your decision." She scratched her head then shot him a quick glance. "Lauren won't let you beyond the friendship part?"

He often marveled at how his sister's mind worked. She inquired about Lauren's well-being then switched to Eric's odd behavior before circling back to Lauren. He shook his head. "She hates New York, and yes, she told me about her fiancé. I can't blame her for being leery." His desk intercom buzzed.

Dropping his feet to the floor, he leaned forward and flipped the switch. "Yes, Betty?"

"Excuse the interruption, Mr. Lambert, but Bill Stewart is on the line and wants to know if the check arrangement for Lauren Howell is okay."

"Tell him it's perfect." He'd have a great reason to see Lauren at least once a week, whether she wanted to see him or not. Inwardly, he smiled at the thought.

Jan's eyebrows rose halfway into her hairline. "Is Lauren working for Carol and Bill?"

Shit. He should have forewarned Betty about a call from Bill. Propping his elbows on the desk and shooting Jan a sharp glare, he wagged a finger. "Lauren's condo sitting, and don't you dare mention anything to Eric."

"Oh. Well…good for her. Look—" She slid to the edge of the seat, straightened her shoulders, and placed her feet flat to the floor. "I'm thinking of getting a summer job at the end of the semester. Any objections?"

They were words he never expected to hear. She'd probably acquire a job faster than Eric. "Great idea, Jan. You'll feel a sense of control with your life and maybe meet new friends." *And hopefully, a better boyfriend.* "Just don't pull an irrational stunt like run off and marry Eric when he's filled you with so much doubt."

She waved aside the comment. "He suggested that already, but I want a big wedding, and planning one takes time."

Thank God for small favors. "Then don't let him talk you out of your dreams."

The intercom buzzed again. Betty's voice crackled through the speaker. "Mark Jordan is here."

He flipped the switch. "One second." Meeting Jan's gaze, he raised a questioning brow.

Jan jumped to her feet. "No problem. I've grocery shopping to do." She grabbed her canvas purse.

"Send him in, Betty."

A man in his early thirties strolled through the door, showing a healthy set of white teeth inside a broad smile. With blond hair, brown eyes, and his skin an impressive tan, he displayed every ounce a confident man. He wore a business suit and tie, impeccably tailored to fit a small frame. Hand outstretched, he walked toward the desk.

Deems stood to take the hand. "Glad you arrived okay. My sister, Jan."

Turning to Jan, Mark flashed a smile more brilliant than ever. His gaze scanned her from head to toe and gave no indication of displeasure at her flowery appearance. He took Jan's offered hand. "Mark Jordan. Nice to meet you."

Jan acknowledged Mark with a tilt of her head, her gaze equally taking him in. Her mouth opened to speak, but she slapped her lips shut.

Dare I play matchmaker? Mark had a future with High-Rise International and was by far a better catch than Eric. But convincing Jan to break her engagement and try another man would be a lesson in futility.

Jan cleared her throat. "I was just leaving." She headed for the door but not without a quick glance over her shoulder at the newcomer.

Hope surged within Deems' chest. She was definitely interested. If he could somehow arrange a date without seeming too obvious...

Once the door closed, Deems waved Mark to a chair before sinking into his own. "Dan Williams sent an impressive evaluation of your work. He tells me you speak Spanish so fluently he can't follow." Leaning back, he rested his elbows on the armrests and steepled his fingers. "Dan also mentioned you have a knack for dialects, and he wants to put you in charge of the western side of South America. How do you feel about the responsibility?"

Sitting, Mark beamed. "I can't complain about a promotion, Mr. Lambert. Chile and Peru have some nice properties available, and I'd like to approach the owners."

Deems extended a finger. "As long as you ascertain that the structures meet our building codes. I don't want a collapse five years down the road." He gestured toward the world map hanging on the wall above the leather sofa. "Also, be aware of the fault line traveling along the coast. I'd like to see some sort of earthquake prevention built into the foundations."

"Yes, sir. I'll follow all the company codes."

"Good. You'll receive a substantial pay raise, of course." He sat forward. "I want you to spend some time with our accounting manager. He'll help you organize the office in Peru. Your next stop will be to meet with our legal department. They've already done a ton of research on South America." He paused to smile. "While you're here, you might like to see your family."

Nodding, Mark returned the smile. "Already arranged, sir. My mom and sister are driving here to meet me. We'll spend a few days together before they head home."

"Excellent. Accounting will give you your own credit card. Treat your family to New York at the company's expense." He stood and extended a hand. "We'll have dinner together before you leave." He shook Mark's hand. "Head to accounting. They have an advance in salary waiting."

"Thanks, Mr. Lambert." He turned toward the door then quickly turned back, an eyebrow cocked. "Is your sister…single?"

Well, well, he's interested. Studying Mark, Deems

chewed on his inner lip. "She's engaged to a jackass." His own words twisted his gut into a knot.

Mark grimaced. "Sorry, she wasn't wearing a ring."

"He can't afford a ring or anything else." He mustn't say too much. Otherwise, he'd make his sister look like an idiot. Sighing, he rubbed his forehead. "I don't approve of the match, Mark. Even if I urged her to join us for dinner, she'd probably drag along the jerk."

Mark's blond brows creased into a frown. "That's a shame. She's cute."

And just your size. He shook his head. "Mark, I'd like nothing more than to see you two hook up, but I don't think she'll leave the slug. You have my blessing to try."

He flashed a grin. "Wow, thank you, Mr. Lambert, but my time in New York is limited. I won't have the opportunity to pursue a relationship."

A noble man. Don't that beat all. Mark Jordan was the best recruit he'd seen in a long time. According to Dan's report, the man could sell a motorcycle to a blind man.

Over the next two hours, the pile of paperwork on his desk slowly diminished. As the clock struck five, a soft tap sounded on his door. He glanced up to see Lou Zane step in.

"I'm about to leave to collect Ms. Howell. Do you want me to swing back to drive you home?"

"No, thanks, Lou. I'll take a cab." He threw his pen on the desk then leaned back and clamped his hands behind his head. "Did you do a little covert activity?"

Lou approached the desk. "Yes, sir. After I

dropped Mr. Jordan at his hotel, I swung by the studio. Eric Drummer slumped in his car a half-block away, watching the place. He looked like he'd been in a barroom brawl with cuts and bruises all over his face. Pretty obvious, even with my quick drive-by." He tugged on his ear, his face thoughtful. "Someone worked him over real good."

Jan hadn't mentioned Eric being in a fight. In all probability, Eric told her he fell onto his face, and naïve Jan believed him. He gritted his teeth. "I'd like to know what the hell my sister sees in that man."

Stroking a hand across his bald head, he sighed. "If she's anything like my oldest daughter, she'll wise up too late."

"Yeah, precisely what I'm afraid of." Chest tight, he swiveled in his chair and stood to face the large picture window behind his desk. Here on the eighteenth floor, he had a bird's eye view of Manhattan and the Hudson River, but the floors above had the best views and, of course, the higher rent. Stuffing his hands into his trouser pockets, he turned back to Lou. "All right. Follow my original order and don't let Lauren out of your sight until you safely deliver her to the condo building. She'll protest, so don't let her win."

Smiling, Lou nodded. "I'll do my best." He headed for the door.

"And Lou—"

Lou glanced over his shoulder.

"Be careful, will you? I smell a bad fish."

Chapter Thirteen

At five thirty, Lauren exited the studio to see Lou waiting alongside the limo.

With a big smile, he opened the rear door and waved her in.

Dear Lord. She'd be the talk of the class tomorrow. A limo twice in one day. And she with hardly a dime to her name. She eyed Lou warily. "I don't need such fanfare, you know. Can I sit in the front with you?"

"Sorry, miss. I must follow proper procedure. If you like, I can keep the window open between us." He cocked his head. "Shall we go?"

She removed her backpack and slipped onto the seat. Once again, the giddiness threatened to overtake her. The rich smell of leather combined with the plushness of the upholstery was a luxury far beyond her wildest dreams. After spending several months in New York, she understood the need for a limo and driver. People parked their cars and left them, only daring to move the vehicle when public transportation just wouldn't do. Like when they ventured out of the city. Or had a special function to attend. And in Deems' case, when he visited his many properties.

Lou slipped behind the steering wheel, opened the connecting window, and glanced over his shoulder. "Seatbelt, miss. And so you know, Mr. Lambert gave me specific instructions to stay glued to your side until we reach the condo building."

She inwardly smiled. Deems would win her heart yet, and if truth be told, she was damn close. "Thank you, Lou. I won't mind." Not with Eric hanging around. After buckling her belt, she rested her head on the seat cushion and closed her eyes.

For the first time since leaving Jan's apartment, she breathed a sigh of relief. Everything would be all right and mainly because of one caring man. He had lifted her from a living hell and returned peace to her soul. How could she ever thank him? *Maybe he'd like a fresh apple pie.* She lifted her head. "Deems won't get in trouble, right?"

Lou glanced in the rearview mirror, his dark eyes twinkling. "He'll be fine, miss."

True to his word, Lou stayed by her side, even as she packed her belongings and turned in the key. By six forty-five, he escorted her into the lobby of her new home as Robert emerged from the elevator with a cart full of suitcases.

Facing her, Lou gave a brief salute. "I will leave you, miss, unless you want me to accompany you upstairs."

She took her suitcase from his hand. "I can manage. Thank you so much, Lou, for everything."

"Anytime, miss." He bowed slightly, waved to Robert, and left.

Robert eased the loaded cart toward the door. "I think the Stewarts packed enough for a year." Smiling, he turned to Lauren. "Nice to see you again, miss." He pointed to the lone suitcase in her hand. "You want me to carry your luggage?"

Panic gripped her. *Dear Lord, he'll expect a tip!*

Smiling, she shrugged. "I'm good, Robert, but will you—"

Before waiting for the rest of her sentence, he whirled toward the elevators while stretching a key ring from a retractable device on his belt. "Happy to oblige, miss." He inserted the key into the fourth floor slot then stepped out with a quick salute. "Welcome to the building, Miss Howell."

The whole scene had a surreal effect on her psyche. First, Lou with the limo and his personal escort, and then, Robert in his perfectly pressed uniform of blue shirt and black pants. Both treated her as if she possessed a wad of dough. *If they only knew.*

Reaching the fourth floor, the elevator doors opened. Throat tight, Lauren squared her shoulders, took a deep breath, and stepped onto the hall carpet. Her stomach jumped around inside her gut, causing a queasiness to increase with every tread. She couldn't shake the feeling of walking within a dream, and at any moment, she'd awaken and find herself back at the boardinghouse.

Ever since the budget crisis hit Pennsylvania, nothing but bad luck had come her way. Consolidated schools meant limited need for teachers, crowded classrooms, and decreased time for one-on-one tutoring. Her fiancé left her flat broke and disappeared without explanation. Jan kicked her out of her apartment and wouldn't listen to reason, and now, Eric wanted to climb into her pants despite her lack of interest.

All these incidents paled because of Deems. He'd become the good luck charm she desperately needed. He'd broken the pattern of bleakness surrounding her life, and thinking of him forced her to step toward the door, head high, and press the doorbell.

The door flew open before the chimes faded.

Carol Stewart looked a trifle flustered with a few golden strands dangling from her perfectly sculpted hair.

"Lauren, dear, you're here. Put your luggage anywhere and come into the kitchen. We don't have much time." She waved as she hurried toward the kitchen counter.

Stepping in, Lauren placed her suitcase and backpack by the sofa and followed where Carol, like a whirlwind, picked up a coaster, put it down, grabbed a flowerpot, and then put that down until zeroing in on a sheet of paper. The kitchen, enormous in size, sparkled from stainless steel appliances and polished marble countertops. A curved counter with six stools separated the food prep area from the living room.

Carol thrust the sheet of paper into Lauren's hand. "Here is the watering schedule for my babies. I've written out everything and labeled all the containers. The plant food is in the sunroom." She waved in the direction of an open archway.

"This other list—" She thrust a second piece of paper in Lauren's hand. "These are emergency numbers—the main desk in the lobby, and our cell numbers. We've already stopped mail delivery so Bill arranged for your check to go to Deems." She touched Lauren's arm. "I hope that's okay, dear. We didn't know what else to do on such short notice, but I'm sure Deems will drop off the check." She tapped the paper in Lauren's hand. "The phone number on the bottom is our accountant. If you want, you can make other arrangements."

"Deems is fine."

Bill Stewart approached while throwing on a blue sport jacket. He reached into his pants pocket and extracted his wallet. "We're not leaving much food in the refrigerator. Here's a couple hundred for shopping." He fished out the bills.

At the flow of green, Lauren's eyes widened. He withdrew more money than her monthly unemployment check. "I don't need that much!"

"Take it anyway." He shoved the bills in her hand then extracted two keys from his shirt pocket. "Here's the key to the elevator and the key to the front door. Don't give them to anyone."

"Yes, sir." She took the keys.

He wagged a finger in her face. "No wild parties. No drugs. I'm going on Deems' word about your reliability. If you entertain the opposite sex, make sure he's as trustworthy as Deems."

Carol patted her husband's arm. "She may prefer her own sex, dear."

With one eye closed, he scrutinized Lauren. "All right, make sure *she* is as trustworthy as Deems. The spare bedroom—that's the third door toward the end of the hall—is yours. Make yourself comfortable." His cell phone rang. He hurriedly answered. "Good. We're coming." He disconnected. "Car's here, honey. Let's hit the road." He turned to Lauren with fingers poised over his phone. "Give me your cell number, young lady, just in case I need to call."

Lauren relayed the number.

He punched quickly on his keypad.

"I'll take good care of the place, Mr. Stewart."

Carol grabbed her purse, jacket, and straw sunhat.

"I know you will, dear. We have Deems' assurances, and because of him, I'm leaving with a light heart. Try not to call unless you've a real emergency, you know, like the building's on fire."

Lauren laughed. "Have a good time."

While throwing open the front door, Bill gestured for Carol to hurry.

Lauren stood outside in the hall and waved as the elevator doors closed on their happy faces. *Wow.* A lightning bolt introduction to the world of the wealthy. *I'm spending a month in luxury and getting paid for the privilege. Who woulda believed?* Lauren chuckled, closed the door, and collapsed against the wood frame to catch her breath. After a few minutes to allow the quiet to settle her nerves, she let her gaze wander over the interior.

Her original assessment of a condo with a forest hit dead-on. Miniature palm trees, rubber plants, cactus, several African violets, and ferns. The list was endless. And in the kitchen along the counter stood an array of herb pots. She pushed away from the door and meandered toward the kitchen.

The herbs she recognized since her mother grew a variety of her own. A large aloe plant stood on a corner stand near the end of the counter. The plant underneath on the small shelf…no clue. And the plant alongside? Stretching across the counter, Lauren grabbed the list to compare names and labels. *Okay, this system will work.* First item of importance, find the plant food.

The sunroom was situated off the dining room in a large alcove with tables and chairs surrounded by foliage. An array of windows showed a city view— large buildings intermingling with small. A church steeple, covered with copper sheeting, sparkled in the early sunset, its distance perhaps five or six blocks away. Between the steeple and the condo was a rooftop with a raised-bed garden with two people, a man and a woman, working hoes through the dirt.

Shelving, along the front and both sides of the sitting area, contained more than two dozen flowering plants, crowding the sunroom and creating a closed-in feeling. Several flowers were in bloom—daisies, tulips, gardenias, and one over-sized miniature tea rose bush in the far corner. She sniffed the tiny red rose and, surprisingly, no scent.

Against the wall in the other corner, two tall, wooden cabinets stood. She opened one door then the next to see an array of plant food and marveled at how so many plants had their own special blend. Her mother simply fed them water and only occasionally threw on some horse manure.

Using the time to reflect on her good luck, she leaned against the window frame and stared at the sunset on the church steeple. Her parents' house of worship floated into her mind and how the committee had willingly given her a loan. The parishioners worked so hard to raise the money for the expansion project, and yet, they agreed on a delay so Lauren Howell could go to New York. Without their generosity, she wouldn't be here.

Oh, how I miss Arendtsville—the greens instead of concrete gray with the air crisp and clear instead of full of car exhaust. In another month and a half, she'd be living over her parents' garage, scanning the want ads, mailing out résumés, and putting her life together again. Summer would be in full tourist swing, and many of the

Gettysburg restaurants needed extra food servers. To accumulate cash, she'd try for two jobs, and if her luck held, she'd have a teaching position by fall. Whether college, high school, or grade school, art had no age limit. Even if her job search took her halfway across the state, she'd always return home on weekends to help with the fall harvest.

This peaceful, contented feeling filled her eyes with moisture, and Deems floated into her thoughts. He'd made life bearable again, and for the first time, doubts surfaced about their friendship agreement. Every time her gaze drifted to his lips, she imagined the softness brushing feather kisses along her skin. When he'd held her at the rooming house, he squeezed her to his chest, and her fingers itched to slip inside his shirt. She'd grown accustomed to his smile and his relaxed state of mind. Nothing fazed him. He was a man secure with his place in society.

Could she learn to tolerate New York? She'd be so far away from home, and the sights, smells, and sounds of the country were in her blood. How long before she yearned to walk among the hills and valleys? Deems, being city-bred, would never understand the driving force of working with nature. Short term in New York? Possibly. But full time? *Unlikely.*

So, she reverted to her original conclusion. A relationship with Deems would never work and shame on her to think otherwise. Case closed.

Meaningless words when her heart ached to see him again. *This indecision will never do.* She whirled from the window and headed for the living room, turning on whatever light she passed. The brightness of all the white furniture forced her to squint, but the green foliage helped lessen the glow.

Three separate sections divided the main living area. The center, near a large picture window with the same view of the church steeple, contained the long, white sofa with two matching chairs. On the right, two tan recliners sat beneath a large-screen television positioned on the wall. To the left were the kitchen and formal dining area with a rich mahogany dining table and eight chairs along with matching china cabinet. In the kitchen, a white phone hung on the wall above a two-seater table, which Carol had quickly explained connected directly to the security desk.

Off the kitchen, a long hallway led to the bedrooms. Lauren grabbed her suitcase and backpack and headed for her room, passing a huge master bedroom, an enormous bathroom, a smaller bedroom, an office with computer, and finally, the end bedroom where she threw her luggage on the mattress. While running her fingers across the soft comforter, she looked around.

Compared to her last residence, the room was a palace. Neutral colors of gray and white, a walnut dresser with mirror, and small-screen TV on the wall gave the appearance of a first class hotel. She fought back tears at the Stewarts' generosity. Her thousand dollars a week plus working her butt off would help repay her loans in no time, hopefully by the end of December. Then, she'd start the new year with a clean slate. After Jo-Jo and Eric, she had doubts about trusting men, but Deems proved good men still existed. He'd done so much for her in such a short time and all without asking anything in return. Because he cared. Or felt sorry for her. She wasn't sure which. Either way, he made her feel safe. After a quick trip to the bathroom, she returned to the kitchen.

An inventory of food staples was next, starting with the refrigerator. As expected, no perishables, not even ice cubes in the freezer. No coffee in the cabinets, only tea bags, a few cans of soup, flour and sugar in bins, salt and pepper. The basics. A bit of shopping was necessary. Since she had her ID, money, phone, and condo keys on her and hadn't removed her jacket, she headed for the lobby.

Robert stood behind the security counter, talking to another man wearing the same blue-and-black uniform. Robert was an older man, perhaps in his fifties, in great shape with strong arms and wide chest. The other man was in his thirties, tall and trim, but without the muscles to fill his shirt. Both wore guns on their hip. They turned and smiled.

"This is Johnny, your night-shift guard." Robert slapped the younger man on the back. "Johnny, meet Lauren Howell. She's staying in the Stewarts' place while they're away."

"Nice to meet you, ma'am. If you'll excuse me, I need to do a security round so Robert can leave." He disappeared into the elevator.

Lauren turned to Robert, a brow raised. "Security round?"

Smiling, he nodded toward the computer screens. "Security cameras can only do so much, so we do a visual inspection of every floor from the penthouse down via the stairwell. Fire regulations prevent us from locking the doors to the stairs, but each door has a motion-activated sensor that lights up our board. Here, take a look." He gestured for her to come around the desk. "Johnny's already on the fifteenth floor and will climb the single flight to the penthouse then walk his way down."

The videos were crystal clear and in color. When Johnny arrived at the stairwell door marked with a big P, he jerked on the handle.

Robert nodded at the screen. "The fire escape access to the penthouse is always locked because opening the door puts someone directly into the resident's living room. There's no hallway like the other floors." He pointed to a video square. "Johnny will use the stairs and stop on every floor for inspection. We follow this procedure on each shift change."

"Who lives in the penthouse?"

Wagging a finger, Robert gave her a polite smile. "Sorry, ma'am. We can't disclose who lives in our building. Company rules." His gaze twinkled as he crossed his arms over his chest. "How's it feel to live like the wealthy?"

Sighing, she placed a hand over her heart. "Ask me another time. I'm still in shock." She cocked her head toward the entrance doors. "I suppose we're standing in one of those costly high-rises I've read about?"

Smiling, Robert tugged on his ear. "Oh, yeah. We're not the most expensive building in the city, but to give you an idea, the fourth floor condos sell for ten mil apiece. The higher you go, the more expensive. The penthouse goes for twenty-one mil."

The numbers were mind-boggling. Her mouth lifted to one side. "The Stewarts trusted me that quick?"

"Well—" He tugged on his ear. "Mr. Lambert had something to do with their decision." He glanced at the monitors. "Johnny's almost done. He'll check the hall behind me and then the alley. Everything must follow company code. Any questions?"

"Just one. Where can I do some quick grocery shopping?"

He checked his watch. "At this time of the evening, your best bet is a mom-and-pop store on Eighty-Second Street, two blocks off Fifth Avenue. Some of the bigger stores deliver since most of the residents in this building won't know the inside of a supermarket if they fell through the roof. Shall I call you a cab?" He reached for the desk phone.

New York cabs cost a heap of money, and she'd rather spend her stash on food. Besides, with just a three to four block walk, she'd be back before Eric or the Hispanic found her. She smiled at Robert. "No, I'll walk. I won't buy much tonight."

He held up a finger. "Before you leave, miss, you should know the main doors lock promptly at nine every night and stay locked until seven in the morning. A buzzer by the door alerts the guard on duty."

Security plus. Impressive. She might have the best night's sleep since leaving Jan's.

After thanking Robert, she passed through the double doors, stepped onto the sidewalk, and promptly collided into Deems.

Chapter Fourteen

Lauren's breath hitched as two strong hands gripped her arms, causing all thoughts to disappear. On the surface, Deems hadn't the appearance of a muscular man, but she stared with a new appraisal, sucking in the scent of his musk aftershave while locking her knees to prevent an inadvertent slide to the sidewalk. In a flash, she conjured images of the physique beneath the business suit with his slim build transforming into a muscle-bound champion of justice. That vision accelerated her heart rate. Deems Lambert *was* her hero, because he always appeared when she least expected. The vision burst into a puff of smoke as a car horn blared her into reality.

His light brown eyes glowed. "Sorry about that."

In the twilight, his iris had the color of honey. Funny how she hadn't noticed until now. And he had cute ears, too. What more would she uncover as she leaned toward dissolving their 'only friends' arrangement?

He dropped his hands but not without a gentle caress along her arms. His touch caused an erotic shiver straight to her core. Since she wore a short-sleeve T-shirt under her jacket, she almost wished she'd left the jacket upstairs. "I'm equally at fault."

Oh, God, help me. Her mouth had gone bone dry, and her heart thumped so hard, she swore he'd hear.

Resisting the urge to throw her arms around his neck and kiss him senseless, she fussed with her jacket sleeves. Deems unknowingly excited all the right buttons. Dare she tell him? Or worse, show him how his touch affected her?

She really should be sensible about her feelings. Deems might as well be from another planet. They had disparities wider than the Grand Canyon and definitely too numerous to list. If he would only stop gazing with eyes as beautiful as a honeycomb. Smiling, Lauren stretched to kiss his cheek. "Hi."

His gaze brightened. "Hi, yourself. What's the kiss for?"

"A friendly kiss. For looking out for me. I appreciate all you've done."

"That's what friends are for." He stepped back. "Bill called and told me you looked a little overwhelmed."

Since they stood in the middle of the sidewalk with people walking around them, she urged him to move toward the building. "Stunned is the word, Deems. I'm a farmer's daughter, and a woman used to barns and tractors and not all this opulence." Was she crazy to fight the desire building inside? She'd believed Jo-Jo was the perfect man and look what an idiot he'd made her. What if Deems agreed to a short-term affair? No commitments. No strings. *Hmm.*

He looked around. "Where are you heading?"

Thankfully, his voice broke her train of thought. "I need food. Robert told me of a place on Eighty-Second Street. Want to come?"

"I'd like that."

She slipped her right arm through his left and

allowed herself the luxury of a companion. No one could possibly mistake them for being on a date. She wore blue jeans, T-shirt, and sneakers, and Deems, as usual, had on his impeccably-tailored suit with silk shirt and tie. He wore a diamond-studded gold watch on his left wrist, which glistened under the street lights, and a ruby-adorned pinkie ring on his left hand. And here she wore a common variety watch and her gold ring from graduate school. As different as night and day. "Where are the Stewarts going?"

"A month-long cruise. Caribbean. Panama Canal. Mexico. California. They're flying home from Oregon."

She smirked. "Must be nice to have money. My parents barely scraped by with the fluctuation in apple prices from year to year. That's why they encouraged me to go to college."

He glanced her way. "But your brother will suffer the same fate."

"Oh, he knows, but he's also a good machinist and one of the best tractor mechanics in the county. He's in high demand." She met his gaze. "Even if he sells the orchards, he'll still make a decent living."

At an intersection, they stopped for a red street light. When the light changed to green, and they crossed with the crowd, he nudged her arm. "Bill's computer is password protected, and he asked if I had a laptop to loan you. If you're interested, you can connect to his Wi-Fi."

There he goes again, giving so much in his kind and generous way. How in the world had she gotten so lucky? "I'd appreciate that." Damn, her voice cracked. She swallowed hard. "I used Jan's computer on occasion, mainly to research some of the information Antonio feeds us." *And save on my cell phone bill.* She glanced his way to see a soft smile curling one side of his mouth. With every look, the man melted some part of her. How could she possibly survive any more chance encounters if her body struggled to remain in solid form? She cleared her throat and cast her gaze forward. "On lunch break the other day, I accessed the High-Rise International website."

"Oh?" He squeezed her arm. "Curious about me?"

She playfully nudged him. "Your website didn't tell me much. Every link goes to your public relations woman."

"We're a privately-held firm, Lauren. The company doesn't follow SEC rules about posting salaries or a board of directors. Worldwide, our staff is roughly twelve hundred employees of which a third are overseas."

"Then, I can honestly say I'm glad you're the North American agent. Otherwise, we'd never have met." She smiled because she meant every word.

He patted the hand on his arm and smiled in return.

Ordinarily, she'd avoid any after-dark walks on the streets of New York, but strolling on Fifth Avenue with a handsome man by her side on such a beautiful spring evening flipped her viewpoint from leery to cheery. Lit street lamps created a romantic air. A cool breeze blew from the direction of Central Park, which helped disperse some of the car exhaust from the passing traffic. A perfect night for a walk. Her light jacket sufficed, but some people were bundled like the wind blustered straight out of the arctic.

An odd feeling swept over her. She strolled with a

man who obviously made good money, yet he accompanied a woman with hardly a dime to her name, just to do a little grocery shopping. His job surrounded him with clients like Carol and Bill Stewart, the muck-a-muck of New York society while her friends included the offspring of other farmers. She was so far out of his league, her heart took a nosedive.

As they turned onto Eighty-Second Street, he lifted her hand to his lips and kissed her fingers. "What are you thinking?"

Too many thoughts, unfortunately. Like how your kiss makes me feel warm all over. She'd never say the words out loud. "Oh, you know." She stared into the distance. "How different we are, and yet how comfortable I feel around you." She shot him a glance. "You don't strike me as the domesticated kind."

His mouth twitched. "Then you perceive me as the big-city bachelor who parties all night and sleeps all day?"

She hid a smile and lowered her gaze. "Something like that. We're heading to a food market of all places."

"Like an ordinary couple?" He intertwined his fingers with hers. "When I arrived in New York and for quite a few years after, I shopped on my way home. These last two years, my schedule prevents any leisurely trips to the market, so I delegated the task to my housekeeper. In a lot of ways, I miss such a simple part of life." He patted her arm and pointed to a store. "I think this is the place."

She followed his finger to see the last of a vegetable cart bounce over the threshold as a young boy tugged it into the store. A woman in a stained white apron swept a broom across the pavement and toward the curb. She gave them a quick scan and nodded.

Stepping toward the woman, Lauren pointed at the door. "Are you still open?"

"Twenty minutes," she said with a thick, German accent. "My husband's inside. He'll take care of you."

Lauren hurried to the fruits and vegetables first. A couple of green peppers, some tomatoes, onions, and, of course, Granny Smith apples. Then over to the bread aisle.

Deems followed with a small shopping cart of which he snuck in some chocolate chip cookies, fudge brownies, and peanut butter.

She glanced at the latter and raised a brow. "No jelly?"

Grinning like a kid in a candy shop, he grabbed a jar of peach jam. The whole scene filled her with a warmth she hadn't experienced in a long time. He was great company, and yes, they were turning into good friends.

"Store closes in ten minutes!"

Dragging her thoughts away from Deems, she hurried to the refrigerated section. Eggs were next. Then milk, cream, butter, and topping her mental list, coffee. "Mr. Stewart gave me money before he left. Even at exorbitant New York prices, I think I can pack the fridge. Since you're with me, you can help carry the stuff."

"I'm paying. Save your money."

She opened her mouth to protest, but he held up a finger to stop her and grabbed a bag of cheese curls before heading to the register.

Dangling plastic bags from their arms, they talked all the way to the condo, laughing at stupid jokes, and exchanging stories about their youth. He sold comic books from a red wagon at the age of seven. She made her first apple pie at the age of nine and won first prize at the county fair.

Once inside the Stewarts' condo, they plunked their packages onto the counter. She unpacked while he rummaged through the bags.

With a soft cry, he took out the chocolate chip cookies, ripped open the bag, and shoved a whole cookie into his mouth. She prayed he didn't choke to death, since her Heimlich maneuver might be a bit rusty. "You'll spoil your dinner."

He stopped chewing and stared. "You're inviting me?"

"If you give me a cookie." Holding the egg carton in one hand and the butter in the other, she opened her mouth, and he obliged, brushing his fingers ever so softly across her cheek. His simple touch caused a shiver to travel the length of her spine. Damn, he made her feel good.

He popped three more cookies into his mouth before she finished her first.

The poor man's starving. She emptied another bag. "Where do you live?"

"Not far. I'm in a company-paid condo."

Wow. Not to worry about paying the rent, she'd be in heaven. Finished with the groceries, she opened the carton of eggs. "Since the time's late, we'll eat light. How about an omelet?"

"Sure, if you allow me to open a bottle of wine. Bill has a wine cooler in the corner here." He opened a glass-covered door and bent over to study the contents.

Whoa! She whirled. "Wait a minute, Deems. I can't

replenish what we drink."

"But I can. I know Bill's taste. Ah, this wine will do nicely." He straightened while holding a long-necked brown bottle. "A German *Spatlese* to go with the food purchased from the German couple." He grabbed a towel and wiped the moisture from the bottle.

Lauren searched the lower cabinets for an omelet pan, found one, and then broke the eggs into a bowl. "I don't know the first thing about wine, except apple and peach. Some of the orchard farmers make a batch every year." From one of the drawers, she extracted a cutting board and prepared to chop a green pepper and onion. "One farmer makes this fantastic grape juice. Gad, is that good!"

Deems opened one drawer after another until a soft exclamation escaped from his throat. "Success!" He held a corkscrew and promptly popped the wine cork.

A strong wave of comfort swept through her. She hadn't experienced such contentment since she finished her first three-D mural for a swanky Harrisburg hotel. She and Deems acted like any domesticated couple, preparing a meal as if they'd done it a thousand times.

She shot him a sideways glance. A curl of a smile moved his lips. Sexy as hell, and such a simple expression melted her knees. But the tug he created was so damn puzzling, yet exciting, and downright dangerous. She'd love to drag him to the bedroom and unveil the man under the suit.

Oh, shit.

She had whipped the eggs into a dense froth. Dumping in the vegetables to cut down the foam, she stirred and then poured enough of the mixture into the preheated pan for the first omelet. "You realize I know very little about you." A statement more than a question since he hardly talked about himself. She wasn't sure if that trait was good or bad. Jo-Jo bragged with every opportunity.

Deems lifted two wine glasses from an overhead rack and poured. "Know that I am not married, never have been, but plan to marry someday as soon as I find the right woman to tolerate me."

She smiled down at the pan. "You shouldn't have trouble finding the right woman, Deems."

"So you say, but I find dating incredibly hard." Reaching across the counter, he grabbed napkins from a holder. "Do you mind if we eat at this small table?" He pointed.

He had indicated the two-seater table against the wall, a more intimate setting than sitting on one of the bar stools. "No, I don't mind." She flipped the omelet. Cheese would have been nice to add, but she totally forgot to buy some. Maybe tomorrow. "Why do you say dating is hard? You seem like a great catch." She probably shouldn't have been so blatantly truthful, but the words poured out before she had a chance to stop them.

After placing napkins and silverware on the table, he turned to face her. "I can't find a woman with substance. They want the easy life, you know, shop all day, party all night, like money grows on trees. They hook onto me as if I'm Fort Knox." He retrieved the wine glasses, placed hers on the table, and took a sip of his own. "Do you want to know how I analyze women these days? I observe their cell phone use. If they constantly talk and text or interrupt a conversation to answer a call, then they have no meaningful purpose in my life." He frowned into his wine glass. "Cell phones have made people rude and self-centered and are a killer for any serious relationship." He lowered his glass to the table. "Being with you is refreshing. Your phone never rings."

"I don't have the gift of gab, Deems." She slid the omelet onto a plate and handed him the dish. "Besides, I'm usually working and don't have time to talk. My family and friends know my routine so they'll call at night." She poured the remaining omelet mixture into the pan.

"What do you expect in a relationship?" He placed the plate on the table.

His simple question caused her breath to hitch. Why, she wasn't sure. She stared at the bubbling eggs. "I thought I knew. Jo-Jo proved me wrong on all counts. He made good money as a car salesman and was well on his way toward his own dealership, so I don't understand why he disappeared." With the spatula, she fussed with the edges on the eggs.

"Maybe he started his dealership in another state."

"The cops investigated but came up empty." She flipped the omelet. "Jo-Jo took the bank money in cash." She glanced his way. "I discovered he put in a withdrawal request three days prior to his disappearance." Just saying the words gave her a headache. For the first time in her life, she nearly fainted on the spot when the bank teller told her the news. After the initial shock, she turned into a raving maniac.

"I'd call him a foolish man."

She slid the second omelet onto a plate and turned. "The warrants for his arrest will remain active for seven years. When they expire, who knows what will happen? He certainly can't return to Arendtsville." She put the plate on the table then paused, her gaze intent on the steaming eggs. "If I had one word to describe what I want in a relationship, I'd say honesty." She shot Deems a sideways glance.

A guarded expression passed onto his face, and her gut sank. Was he already hiding something? *Yeah—well, so what?* They were in a new friendship. What he did when they weren't together was his own business. "Come on, let's eat." As she lowered onto the chair, she drifted her gaze toward the wall clock. Nearly nine. "My mother would have a fit if she discovered how late I eat in this city." After tasting her omelet, she shook on some salt. "Dad always wanted dinner on the table at five and even earlier during the harvest so we could eat and continue picking until dark." She pointed to his plate. "You might need a little more salt and pepper."

Acknowledging with a nod, he pulled out his chair and settled onto the cushion before digging into his omelet. "Perfect."

She hated to always point out their disparities, but someone had to remind him. His world of concrete and asphalt contrasted to hers of fresh air and open spaces. Plus, he was a businessman used to the hustle of a big city. She was an unemployed teacher slash artist who recognized the origin and taste of every apple on the planet. What could they possibly have in common?

Except a mutual attraction.

She sipped her wine. *Not bad.* A gentle sweetness to complement the omelet. "How'd you know I was trustworthy? You recommended me for this job, and we barely know each other."

Wiping his mouth, he leaned back and smiled. "There's something about you, Lauren. You have two feet on the ground. I like that trait." Gaze twinkling, he sipped his wine.

So odd. She hardly knew him, yet one look flipped her heart within her chest. How could he affect her to the point where she hardly knew her name? Hell, she almost married a guy she thought was her everything, and all he ever gave her was heartburn. Looking away, she toyed with her omelet. "I'm from a hard-working family. I may have my own career, but I still help at harvest time." She met his gaze. "And I won't ignore the town's annual apple harvest festival. Everyone participates because people come from around the country." She leaned forward and waved her fork to emphasize her point. "You should visit some time. The first two weekends in October, rain or shine. Lots of stuff to eat, countless crafts and demonstrations, and my favorite, folk dancing. Two solid weekends of fun." She sipped more wine.

A smile tugged the corner of his mouth. "See what I mean? Two feet on the ground. You'll make any man fall in love."

Including him? She sure as hell teetered on the edge, and that tidbit of truth scared her half to death.

Chapter Fifteen

After dinner, Lauren expected Deems to leave, but he helped with cleanup, found a cork for the wine, and even wiped the table. She wanted so much to loosen his tie and relieve him of his suit jacket, but one touch would turn into two, and she'd never stop herself. Her heart felt the tug of a man falling in love—like the way his gaze maintained eye contact over dinner. She couldn't allow him to love her and purposely avoided physical contact.

Earlier, she had considered the possibility of an affair. But without the slightest nudge, she'd fall head-over-heels for him, and then what? Say goodbye and thanks for the memories? He deserved a woman from his own world, someone who lived and thrived in a big city. She wasn't that woman.

"You have a dishwasher, Lauren."

She looked at her sudsy sponge. "I can't waste water for such a small number of dishes." She glanced over her shoulder. "Water is precious to a farmer, Deems. We learn early not to waste such a valuable resource." *The ever-practical farmer's daughter, that's me.* Her heart sank.

If she was a different type of woman, she'd go after Deems and never again worry about money. Hell, he lived in a company-paid condo. What if the place was just as swanky, high in the sky, and away from the noise and traffic on the streets? Would she reconsider?

Her gaze scanned the sparkling kitchen, the modern appliances, and the spaciousness leading into the brightness of a living room all in white. He couldn't possibly have a condo so luxurious. Otherwise, women would be breaking down his door.

All her life, she had lived within the confines of a small space. At the first opportunity, she moved out on her own. Now, of course, she'd be moving back in with the family. A definite setback. The farmhouse was a four-bedroom, two-story structure that housed her parents, her brother and his wife, and their two kids. The only available spot to park another bed was a tiny office over the garage. Even her apartment with Jo-Jo wasn't big—merely adequate for a young couple saving for marriage.

Living a life in cramped quarters probably influenced her love for the outdoors. The open space gave her room to breathe. And, of course, picking apples from the time she could walk certainly helped. For four years, she taught in Harrisburg, and when she could, she'd run to the farm to work in the orchard as an excuse to leave the city. Jo-Jo never had an itch to leave, and she hadn't quite understood why he disappeared. They both grew up in Arendtsville, attended the same high school, and knew each others' families. Even at an early age, Jo-Jo had an inner drive to become a big shot and to make tons of money so he could thumb his nose at the world. Ironically, he'd been on his way.

Deems cleared his throat. "I should go. It's getting late."

Agreeing with a nod, she tossed the kitchen towel

on the counter. What else could she say? No, don't go? She'd love for him to stay, but the suggestion wouldn't be wise. Her fingers still itched to undo his tie. She followed him to the front door.

With his hand on the knob, he paused and gave her a faint smile. "Thanks for dinner."

"You're welcome. Thanks for helping to carry the stuff."

My, my, so formal. Just two friends maintaining a safe distance. She should slap herself silly.

He kissed her lightly on the cheek but hesitated as he stepped into the hall. He said nothing and merely searched her face with unasked questions in his gaze. Was he waiting for an invitation to stay? *Oh, God, should I? Do I even dare?* She wanted so much to be in his arms and hadn't had the pleasure of a man in her bed since her ex took a long walk. But Deems deserved more than a brief affair. Someday, he'd find the right woman and live the happily-ever-after dream.

Their gazes locked. The man was so friggin' handsome. Not a touch of arrogance showed. Just a man looking at her with an unreadable expression. She started. No, not unreadable at all. Something shone within the honey gaze, and her breath hitched. "You don't have to leave." *There. I blurted the words.* A heart-before-brain impulse. What man had the ability to resist an outright invitation from a woman?

His gaze tender, he brushed her cheek with two fingers. "Yes, I do." He lightly tapped her nose. "I'll see you again, Lauren, sooner than you think." Turning, he headed for the stairwell at the end of the hall.

Whoa. Nothing like crushing a woman's ego then stomping on the pieces. Maybe she misinterpreted his signals and suddenly flunked Body Language 101.

Since he chose the stairwell instead of the elevator, then he was obviously in a big hurry to leave. The thought totally devastated her psyche and created a jumble of mixed feelings, none good. Embarrassment. Regret. Confusion. Surprisingly, no anger surfaced. He was the smarter one by keeping their friendship status quo, and she felt like a fool for blurting the offer. With a whole month to fight his strange pull, maybe she should think twice about any future dinner or lunch invitations. Truthfully, all she had to do was remind herself about his fast exit down the fire escape. With a heavy sigh, she closed and bolted the door.

His musk cologne collided with the scent of the forest. She sucked in a large breath and smiled. Deems might have rejected her, but for the first time in months, a man had awakened the woman within, despite her fiancé leaving her devoid of emotions. Her heart had come alive and was ready to love again. Maybe not with Deems, but he opened the door to her heart. She would let in love, and she had Deems Lambert to thank.

The doorbell rang. Since she stood halfway to the sunroom, she snapped her gaze toward the door. Carol Stewart had left specific instructions, and one was how security called first to allow a visitor to the floor.

Peeking through the peephole, she immediately jerked backward.

Deems stood on the other side.

Elation and puzzlement conflicted, and, heart thundering, she threw open the door, fighting desperately to remain neutral. She cocked her head. "Forget something?" His tie was off with his silk shirt partially unbuttoned. Even his hair was slightly mussed.

Brows high, she stepped back. "Have you been running?"

"Good guess." A brief smile touched his lips, and he crossed the threshold. "I rushed out for something, but before I tell you what, I need to modify our friendship agreement." He closed the door.

Backing away, she put distance between them. Why, she wasn't sure. Perhaps because he might touch her, and she'd melt into a puddle. The look in his eyes had her mesmerized. His gaze glowed with something so intense, he caused her heart to somersault.

He stopped, a brow cocked. "Are you afraid of me?"

"No—yes!" Afraid of him being the perfect man, and she'd have to say goodbye. "Deems, I—"

His long arm reached to press a finger against her lips. She still moved away, even though she wanted to throw herself into his arms. Maybe the wine deteriorated her brain cells, because she sure as hell couldn't understand her own actions. Her thighs hit the sofa arm, and she caught herself before falling over.

Stepping close, he gave her a one-eyed glare. "You want to know something, Lauren? After all our time together tonight, you never once told me to take off my tie. How come?"

Staring, she gaped.

"I'll tell you why." He pointed a finger in her face. "You considered the removal of my tie as an act of undress. You couldn't have that, could you?"

Heart thundering, she slapped her mouth shut. "I don't know what you're talking about."

"Oh?" He backed off, a smile curling his lips. "You hung onto me in the park and even on the way to the market, yet here, you avoided touching me like I had the plague. Why?"

Do I dare admit the reason? My God, the air crackled with sensuality. She wanted him so badly, yet fought like mad not to reach out and touch him. She swallowed hard. "What do you mean modify our friendship agreement?"

His smile disappeared, and he slid his gaze up and down her body. "You know damn well what I mean."

Yes, she did, and her heart rate skyrocketed. She sucked in a large breath. "I can't touch you, Deems. I…won't stop."

He smirked. "Precisely what I thought."

Locking onto her gaze, he removed his suit jacket and tossed the garment onto a side chair. Then, he removed his watch and slipped the timepiece onto the end table. Slowly, with his gaze still locked onto hers, he unfastened the cuff links on his shirt sleeves and placed those on the end table, as well.

His casual little strip-tease activated a flood of moisture between her legs, and she couldn't recall the last time a man aroused her so quickly. Hell, she wanted this man and everything he had to offer. Yet, the yearning both frightened and thrilled her. Her brain said to run, but her heart said grab him and never let go.

He smiled. "You asked me to stay, Lauren. Did I misinterpret?"

Eyes wide, she shook her head, unable to form words.

With an outstretched finger, he poked her shoulder. His easy push knocked her over the sofa arm. She landed on the cushions and stared upward, totally tongue-tied.

Placing his hands on his knees, he bent over. "You can tell me to leave, and I will, but I understand your dilemma. You don't want to get involved, because you won't stay in New York. I, of course, won't leave since my life centers around this big city. So, we have a relationship going nowhere. Yet—" He settled alongside, nudging her closer to the sofa back. "We are attracted to each other in the worst way. You can't deny this pull we have, and if you do, then your ex has destroyed your ability to trust your own feelings." With one finger, he stroked her cheek, his smile gentle. "Trust them now, Lauren."

The man was a psychic, reading her heart and soul as if they displayed like a neon sign. She wanted Deems more than she cared to admit, but she wasn't sure if her feelings were the result of loneliness or Jo-Jo's crushing abandonment. Chest heaving, she licked her lips. "You deserve better than me, Deems."

His brow arched. "I can think of no one better than you, Lauren Howell." He lifted the hair away from her face and smiled. "I ran out for condoms."

With one hand on the sofa back and the other on the cushion above her head, he leaned close to her face. "I want you, Lauren, and I want you until we say goodbye."

Oh, my God, how can I refuse? His dark gaze exploded with heat, and the intensity seared straight to her core. He had her so turned on, even a cold shower in a freezer wouldn't suffice.

He brushed his lips across hers then lifted his head, his gaze searching her face.

Does he expect me to respond? How can I when I can't even breathe?

Again, he brushed his lips across hers and repeated the search of her face. "Do you want me, Lauren?"

What a question! "You know I do." She placed both palms on his chest. "But I don't know if I can withstand another broken heart."

Resisting her hands, he leaned over with his hot breath close to her lips. "Maybe I can convince you to stay."

"And maybe I can convince you to come home with me." She slipped both arms around his neck. "But are we wise to start something we might not finish?"

"We're not wise at all." He kissed her right ear. "But I want to be more than your friend." He kissed her left ear. "Not a day goes by without me thinking of you, and I'm willing to endure the pain of separation if you allow me to love you while you're here." His lips slid to her neck.

She shuddered from the moist heat of his mouth. The man stood in a league of his own and beyond any man she'd ever met, including her ex. From the moment she'd walked into Jan's kitchen and shook his hand, she experienced something so foreign, so unbelievably fierce, the sensation startled her. Over time, his presence threw her mind and heart into turmoil, and nights of mental analysis proved nothing. She questioned her sanity and blamed all her confusion on a hormonal imbalance.

Now, with her body anticipating the intimacy denied for so long, she again questioned her wisdom. Her heart hammered against her rib cage as she relished the feel of his lips against her throat. Even though his hands hadn't moved from the sofa cushions, her skin tingled with a hyper-awareness of the man hovering.

Any other man, she'd hesitate to give her heart, but she trusted Deems, and *that* bit of insight surprised her more than anything. Taking his cheeks into her hands, she lowered his mouth to hers.

Without wasting a second, he slipped his arms beneath her and lifted her close to his chest. His lips, hot and moist, suckled with a gentleness until his arms tightened, and he deepened the kiss. Tiny atoms exploded throughout her body, awakening a part of her she swore died with her fiancé. She melted into his strong arms, and her thoughts shattered as she relished the sensations of a core coming alive. Hell, the man felt so damn right.

He stood with her cradled in his arms. "Which bedroom?"

His voice had a husky need. A turn-on, for sure. She kissed his ear. "Last one at the end of the hall. My luggage is still on the bed." Not like luggage would squelch their mood. Hell, the place was immaculate, and they could easily have sex on the rug.

Once in the bedroom, he kicked her suitcase and backpack to the floor, lowered her to the bed, and then zeroed in for another long kiss. He wasn't a man in a hurry. He suckled and tasted down the length of her neck to the V in her T-shirt, brushing feather kisses across her chest while biting the material covering her skin.

He stopped to gaze into her eyes. "I don't think you realize how beautiful you are, Lauren. I'm sorry I hadn't visited Jan earlier."

Muffling her reply, he crushed his lips to hers, forcing her mouth apart to thrust his tongue deep. Heat surrounded them, like a furnace on high, and if she sensed a brief loosening of his arms, she'd strip herself naked to allow some cool air to hit her skin.

Her fingers ached to touch more than the outline of muscles through his silk shirt. Unable to contain herself any longer, she pushed on his chest. His head popped up with a cocked brow, his gaze clouded with passion. She hurriedly unbuttoned his shirt and yanked apart the edges to expose his chest. A little chest hair greeted her, several rippled abs, and two muscular breasts. *As easy on the eyes as the fingers.*

While pinching her T-shirt, he grinned. "My turn."

Before her next breath, her shirt was off, bra unsnapped, and his mouth traveled straight to her breasts, biting the protruding nipples to release a waterfall in her pants. "Oh—damn!" She sucked in a long, shuddering breath and became lost in the skill of his tongue. If she wasn't careful, she'd come before her jeans were off. Gripping his shirt collar, she groaned.

He lifted his head. "Time?"

The man wasn't an idiot. He had her so incredibly turned-on she could hardly breath.

He unsnapped her jeans and lowered the zipper then stopped to tickle her belly button.

"Oh—shit!" She nearly jumped halfway off the bed.

"My, my, you certainly are sensitive." He slid her jeans and panties down her legs then tossed them to the floor. Standing, he reached into his pants pocket and, with a big smile, dangled a long string of condom packets.

Cocking a brow, she shot him a wry grin. "You plan on staying a while?"

"Until you throw me out."

"Ha! Not until the harvest moon, big guy." She might even tie him to the bed. From the puzzled expression on his face, she laughed. "The harvest moon is in September."

Grinning, he removed his clothes and stood naked before her, his erection waiting.

Oh, my God. The man was beautiful. Broad shoulders tapered to slim hips with subtle muscles on chest, arms, and legs. He obviously worked out but not to the extent where his body rippled like Adonis. Mouth bone dry, she swallowed hard. "I'm serving apple pancakes in the morning."

Chapter Sixteen

If ever a man had doubts about his ability in bed, he needed a woman like Lauren to stoke his ego to unimaginable heights. After his last fiasco affair, Deems swore off women, fully believing he'd never find a suitable mate. Most of his women were city-bred, the majority from New York, and accustomed to the high-life of fine wine and dining. Obviously, he looked in all the wrong directions. Who'd believe he'd fall for a country girl as gorgeous as Lauren Howell?

Heart full, he looked at the beauty cuddled under his arm and tucked a strand of loose hair behind her ear. They'd gone three rounds so far and each more powerful than the last. She gave without inhibition and made sex fun again. Every kiss from her luscious lips drove him crazy, and he performed for this woman like no other. Never in his life had he such a wonderful night, and the 'L' word tittered on the tip of his tongue. Of course, caution squelched any verbal expression. He knew damn well she felt the same. Every kiss and touch told him so, but she had been through too much. Her life was in turmoil, and if he could ease her mind for a little while, then he'd pat himself on the shoulder.

With his fingertips, he stroked her bare back, and she stirred, her long hair tickling the skin on his chest. She had a beautiful body, proportioned at chest and hips with flawless skin, and a build with strength. A woman used to hard work. Yet, she was soft as fleece.

From the moment Lauren opened the door to Jan's apartment, she had floored him with her unbridled allure. Her voice—hell, even the air she breathed—captivated him. Because of Jan's comment about Lauren's fiancé, he put on the brakes and followed Lauren's lead. But how could he possibly endure their simple friendship when her stunning beauty was impossible to ignore? Without debate, she had become the one to marry...except she hated New York.

His universe. The city with the most expensive real estate in the world. He couldn't possibly leave, and why would he? The hub of his business centered in Manhattan. Once Lauren caught a glimpse of how comfortable her lifestyle would be, she'd never need to work again.

Lauren walked her fingers across his chest. "What are you so reflective about? Having second thoughts about us?" She stifled a yawn.

Rotating his head, he met her sleepy gaze. Her cheek rested on his shoulder, and she had the glow of a sated woman. Looking at her turned his heart to mush. He smiled. "No second thoughts, Lauren, but I am thinking about you, me, this bed, and our wonderful night. Need I go on?" He should have her in *his* bed and in *his* condo, but not yet.

She kissed his nipple. "Thank you."

One brow arched. "For what?"

"For allowing my confidence to return. My ex shattered me to pieces, you know."

"The man's a fool, Lauren. Whatever prompted him to disappear must have been a humdinger."

She lowered the sheet to toy with his belly button.

In doing so, she also exposed more of her strong back.

He slipped his hand under the sheet to rub her pretty butt.

"I think I may have the answer for Jo-Jo's disappearance." She kissed his ribs. "The other day, my mother called. Two FBI agents stopped by the farm to question me. Apparently, Jo-Jo embezzled a hundred grand from the car dealership." She rotated her head to meet his gaze. "He was also the bookkeeper and had easy access to the money. The auditors found a series of withdrawals, all cash." She returned her attention to his navel. "One of the agents called me, but I couldn't tell her anything. I haven't the foggiest idea where he went." Her hand slipped under the sheet and caressed his penis.

Her touch was hot enough to scorch, and he hardened within her palm.

"My ex fell off the face of the earth, Deems. No one has a clue as to his whereabouts."

Was she aware of what her hand did to his body? Dear Lord, her fingers were magic. And of all things, they conversed as if they lounged at the kitchen table with coffee.

She looked up with a smile curling one corner of her mouth. "Did you really run out for condoms?"

Somehow, he found his voice. "I wasn't carrying, Lauren." He shot her a one-eyed glare. "Please don't tell me you had a purse full."

With a faint smile, she returned her head to his shoulder. "Not a one. I hadn't planned on any sexual activity while in New York." Her fingers glided over the tip of his penis.

Holy damn! This woman completely stole his

breath. He shuddered.

"You've made my New York visit very memorable, Mr. Lambert."

If she asked him to be her slave, he'd bow and readily agree, especially if she continued her fondling during every conversation. He kissed her hair. "I'd like to convince you to stay."

Green eyes wide, she propped herself onto an elbow. "You mentioned that earlier. Are you serious?"

"Never more so than now." He nudged her shoulder. "New York is a mecca for art. You can profit from the location." Her fingers traced along the muscles on his chest with her touch so erotic, the sensation intensified his erection. His heart nearly beat out of his chest. She *had* to hear the thumps against his rib cage. But when her gaze met his, she gave no indication of noticing *anything*. She was a man's sinful fantasy.

She shifted on her elbow. "I have no aspirations to become a well-known artist, Deems. I do art because I enjoy every aspect, and the work helps put food on the table. Otherwise, my career is teaching."

"You mentioned you wanted your own studio."

"More for a hobby if and when I marry and have children. I'd love to have a studio big enough for a class. Like Antonio, who teaches only six students a year. That kind of schedule would be a lot of fun. A summer recess class, for example. Now—" She gripped his shaft and grinned. "I realize what effect I've had, so do you want to fool around one more time before we turn in for the night? I don't know about your work schedule, but I have a class in the morning."

Swallowing hard, he desperately fought the urge to enter her without any intention of foreplay. "How about

I walk you so you won't lose yourself along the way? Newcomers have a tendency to become disorientated in a big city."

She kissed his cheek, lingering long enough to brush her breast against his chest. "I'd like that."

He rolled her onto her back while glancing at the clock on the nightstand. "The time is only one in the morning, and I still have some condoms left."

Her gaze twinkled. "You want me to fall asleep in Antonio's class?"

He kissed the mound of her breast. "I'll make coffee strong enough to curl your hair."

****

As promised, Lauren prepared the apple pancakes for breakfast and even concocted her own syrup using butter, vanilla, and sugar. He never tasted anything so delicious. And as promised, he made the coffee and waited for her reaction. She looked so cute all puckered up.

He couldn't remember the last time he'd experienced such a strong surge of happiness. Never had he strolled along Fifth Avenue with the early-morning crowd while a beautiful woman held onto his arm. Most of his dates demanded the limo, and they walked no farther than the distance from the curb into a restaurant. Not so with Lauren. She insisted they leave early and take their time to enjoy every moment together. Damn, she was special.

At the next street corner, Deems glanced at Lauren's glowing face, and she returned a smile brilliant enough to melt his bones. Their night of lovemaking had transformed her from a gorgeous woman to an absolutely breathtaking one, and she walked by his side, her arm draped in his, looking as happy as he felt.

Despite the threat posed by dark clouds overhead, the morning was pleasant with cool air and temperatures hovering in the low sixties. With summer a few weeks away, sweltering city heat would follow. Definitely not his favorite time of year, but for a born-and-bred city boy, he rarely concerned himself with the change of seasons.

Lauren would. She struck him as a woman always outdoors, regardless of the weather. For a city dweller, so what if the air changed from one day to the next? No one noticed. No one stepped outside to suck in a large breath since all they'd receive was a snoot-full of car exhaust.

He shouldn't think about how different she was, but deep down, he couldn't ignore their disparities. Maybe she would grow to love New York. Maybe her love for him would be enough to change her mind. He hoped so. His options were few.

They turned off Fifth Avenue and headed along Seventy-Fifth Street.

Antonio's studio was a few blocks from the Metropolitan Museum of Art, which made sense since he was a well-renowned artist. Scanning the line of parked vehicles alongside the curb, Deems caught movement within a gray sedan several slots away from the studio. An older man scrutinized them from behind the steering wheel, his gaze unwavering. The car had the familiar chrome spotlight within reach of the driver's window and an official license plate—two tell-tale signs of a cop car. Seconds later, the door swung open, and the rotund driver stepped onto the pavement.

He wore a black suit, black shirt, and white tie, as if he played a hitman in a gangster movie. Gray hair covered a round head, and a pair of gray eyes shifted from Lauren to him.

Approaching with a clipboard in hand, he blocked their path to Antonio's door. "Lauren Howell?"

"Yes?"

Lauren showed no recognition, but her hand tensed on his arm. Instinctively, he stepped a few inches in front.

"I'm Detective Rick Baylor from NYPD." He produced a gold badge. "I went to the address on your mugger's report, but the landlord told me you packed up and left. I called your cell, but your phone was off."

Shrugging, she shot Deems a quick look. "I only turned on my phone this morning. Sorry."

A pink flush rose onto her cheeks. Deems inwardly smiled, because he hadn't a clue when she had the time to turn off her phone.

"Miss Howell, you reported three attempts by a man to steal your backpack. Is this the man?" He extended his clipboard to show a mugshot of a Hispanic male, containing front and side views.

Nodding, she gasped. "You caught him!"

The detective ignored the comment and pointed to her shoulder. "Are you carrying the same backpack?"

"Yes."

The older man tugged on an already long earlobe. "He's dead, ma'am. Knifed from behind. We identified him as Rafael Torres, a two-bit smuggler with a rap sheet a mile long." His brows furrowed into a deep crease. "I'm curious why he wanted your pack when he had a nicer one in his apartment. May I take a look inside?"

"Sure." She slipped the strap off her shoulder and handed him the pack.

Detective Baylor carried the bag over to his car, placed his clipboard on the hood, and unzipping the main compartment, extracted the items one at a time. He inspected each and then placed the item on the engine hood. Her stuff was ordinary—safety glasses, leather gloves, a notebook, T-shirt, a set of keys, and a small bottle of perfume.

Deems smiled at the last one because Lauren's vanilla scent lingered on his skin.

The detective dangled the keys in front of Lauren.

"They're the keys I use for home," she explained. "They serve no purpose for my visit to New York, so I keep them clipped to the inside of the pack."

He nodded, lifted out a large sketchpad, and flipped through the pages. "These are good." He held up a likeness of Deems.

Brows high, Deems took the book. "Wow, Lauren, you never showed me."

She shrugged. "That's because I'm still practicing."

Deems placed the pad on the car to flip through the pages. Several faces he failed to recognize. One was Jan and another Mr. O'Reilly, the landlord. Her details were phenomenal. "They're great!"

With a shy smile, she closed the sketchbook. "I'm hoping to do portraits one day, maybe when I grow too old to do large murals."

Baylor turned the backpack upside down and gave the bag a vigorous shake. Then, he ran a hand along the lining.

Lauren cocked a brow. "What are you looking for?"

"Something to pique the interest of a two-bit smuggler, but I don't see or feel a thing." He replaced the contents into the pack and drew the zipper. "Torres offered to buy it, right?"

"Yes." She slipped the strap over one shoulder. "Contents included. I wasn't interested."

Deems' posture stiffened. "You don't think his murder had anything to do with her pack, do you?"

Again, Baylor tugged on his ear, his gaze distant. "Hard to say. Crooks like Torres hang with the wrong crowd." He released his ear and grabbed his clipboard. "He probably looked cross-eyed at someone and got repaid with a knife. Happens all the time."

One down, one to go. Now, if someone would take care of Eric... Nasty thoughts. He shook them away. "Detective, I witnessed this Torres guy being shoved into a black sedan." He relayed the events of following Lauren home. "I completely forgot to report the incident." He had been too distracted by Lauren's shabby room. All his concentration centered on improving her situation.

Baylor flipped to a clean page on his clipboard and, with a pen from his breast pocket, scribbled several notations. "A black sedan with tinted windows is common in New York, and without a license plate number, we're up a creek without a paddle." He dotted a few i's and then looked at Deems. "Hard to say if the abductors killed him, but I'll keep an eye out for the one man you described. Torres had fresh bruises on his face. So, someone worked him over pretty good."

The detective's cell phone rang. He excused

himself to answer while, again, scribbling on the clipboard. An occasional "uh-huh" escaped from his throat until he thanked the caller and disconnected. His gaze shifted from Lauren to Deems. "Do either of you know an Eric Drummer?"

Lauren's eyes widened to show white surrounding the green. While biting her lower lip, she flashed a glance at Deems.

Suppressing a sigh, he had hoped to have one day pass without hearing the man's name. *Obviously not.* Chest tight, he spoke through gritted teeth. "We both know him. He's my sister's fiancé. Why?"

With his pen, the detective motioned over his shoulder. "He semi-hid in a sedan at the corner curb. As you two approached, he took off. Out of curiosity, I called in the plate."

Deems yanked on his belt as if his pants were falling. In truth, Baylor's news rolled his stomach. That friggin' Eric just defied logic. Taking a calming breath, he explained Eric's obsession over Lauren. Just verbalizing the words turned his blood into lava.

"Infatuated, eh? And engaged to your sister?" Clucking his tongue, Baylor replaced the pen to his pocket.

Lauren tucked a loose strand of hair behind her ear. "The word isn't infatuated, Detective. He has a determination to conquer."

Her last word twisted Deems' gut. Without question, his sister required a serious talk, but at present, Lauren's safety was paramount. He had to arrange security, but dammit, she'd argue every step of the way.

Baylor leaned toward Lauren. "I recommend a

restraining order, miss. Legal action gives the police a reason to arrest him." He handed her and Deems his card. "If you think of anything else about Torres, give me a call. As for Drummer, stop into the court clerk's office and file a petition to restrain. The process isn't easy these days, but you'll start the ball rolling. Thanks for your help." He stepped into his car, turned the ignition, and joined the flow of traffic.

Brow wrinkling, Lauren stared after him. "Jan will dispute anything I claim when I go to the court clerk."

"Doesn't matter. I don't want him near you, and truthfully, I don't want him around Jan either." He hadn't liked any part of the detective's information. All right, so this Rafael guy was dead, but to know Eric sat outside the studio irked him to no end. Eric spotted Deems with her and took off. He'd return later to follow her to the condo—if he hadn't already. Scanning the area for Eric's clunker, Deems made a mental note to give the condo security Eric's description. Under no circumstances must Eric approach Lauren Howell.

Chapter Seventeen

The next day, Lauren informed Antonio she'd be late, and she used some of Mr. Stewart's money for a cab to the court clerk's office. The male clerk had a lackadaisical air and only begrudgingly handed Lauren the paperwork for the restraining order, while advising of the severe backlog in the court system. The man explained the process took weeks and, more often, months. Lauren would be home in Arendtsville by then so her effort to keep away Eric was fruitless, not to mention expensive. Jaw clenching, she tore up the application and headed to the studio.

If her father and brother were here, they'd handle Eric in ten seconds flat. One punch a piece. They always watched out for her, as did some of the men in the apple-processing warehouse. Here in New York, she had only Deems.

Already, she missed him. Deems' smile and liquid-honey gaze warmed her like no other man, but after yesterday's meeting with Detective Baylor, he received a phone call from his assistant. He promptly called Lou for a drive to the airport. Something to do with a problem in Dallas.

So much she didn't know about him—except how he captivated her in ways she never experienced. As if by magic, she'd become a puppet dangling by strings. He was attractive and kind, generous and protective, and above all, a fantastic lover. He restored her self-esteem and filled her heart with happiness. Because of Deems, nothing would prevent her from rebuilding her life.

That night, after a stop for more groceries, Lauren entered the building lobby to see Johnny, the night watchman, jump to his feet.

He gave her a big smile. "Evening, Miss Howell. A package came for you."

"Oh?" She approached the desk and rested her bag of food stuffs on the counter. "I'm not expecting anything."

Johnny handed her a rectangular box. "A laptop, miss. A special courier delivered the package about an hour ago."

A thrill coursed through her. She'd forgotten Deems promised her a computer. But she hadn't anticipated a new one. The box was still sealed. Thanking Johnny, she tucked the package under her arm, lifted the grocery bag in the other, and headed for the elevator.

In record time, she connected to the Stewarts' Wi-Fi and gleefully accessed the Internet. Since her phone budget lacked unlimited web surfing, the laptop gave her the freedom to roam for however long she wished. She was dying to find out more about Deems Lambert and High-Rise International.

With the computer on her lap and her legs stretched across the sofa, she began her search and easily accessed a slew of information on the company. High-Rise International was a multi-billion dollar conglomerate of five-star buildings located throughout the world. She found no list of employees, but an itemization of the properties filled a page. New York, of course. Dubai. Paris. Virtually a building in every major city around the globe. The only contact information was through a public relations executive named Cynthia Patterson.

Her next search was on the man himself. After typing his name in the box, a list of his addresses popped onto the screen—all in Chicago, but nothing for New York. No social media sites, no professional listing, and only one mention of his attending the University of Chicago. If Deems had done a similar search on her, he'd have discovered her website for three-D murals, her affiliation to the Philadelphia Museum of Art, and her artist work with the underprivileged children in Harrisburg. So basically, she uncovered nothing more about this wonderful man. Releasing a heavy sigh, she closed the laptop.

After a quick shower, she crawled into bed and lay awake, staring at the ceiling. Without Deems, the bed felt cold, but his musk scent lingered on the pillow. Smiling, she hugged the pillow and sniffed only to have her reverie interrupted by the shrill of her cell phone. Her heart skipped a few beats to see *Deems* pop onto the screen. The mere sound of his voice lifted her spirits. She was falling hard for the man and way too fast. *Until we say goodbye.* They both understood the limitations to their relationship, but every time she repeated the mantra, the words stuck in her throat.

At the end of class the next day, Lauren exited the studio with the rest of the students and felt a tug on her jacket.

"Lauren, wait a minute."

Marylou, one of her classmates, stopped her.

The poor woman had bright orange hair and skin loaded with freckles, but she displayed an extraordinary sense of color with design ideas good enough to impress Antonio. With a raised brow, Lauren nodded toward the street. "You usually walk in the opposite direction."

"That's the reason we need to talk. Face me."

An odd request. Marylou put her back to the street, forcing Lauren to pivot a hundred and eighty degrees.

"Do you see the white SUV down the block?"

Lauren glanced over Marylou's shoulder and spotted Eric sitting behind the wheel of his old jalopy. Heat immediately flushed up her neck. Looking farther, she caught sight of a pearl-white luxury SUV sparkling in the late afternoon sun. She met Marylou's gaze. "So?"

"I think he's following you." Biting her lip, she shifted on her feet. "I don't know for sure, but yesterday after class, the vehicle drove slowly behind you. I noticed because I'm walking toward him."

Great. Obsessive Eric and now a white SUV. What next, a red car to make a caboose? She glared at the sparkling vehicle. More tinted windows. "Did you get a look at the driver?"

"No, the windows are too dark." Marylou touched Lauren's arm. "Be careful, will you? We have a lot of weirdos in this city."

Lauren took Marylou's hand and squeezed. "Thank you. I'll be careful. See you tomorrow." She stole one last look at the luxury model, glared at Eric, and then turned to head home.

After several peeks over her shoulder, Lauren confirmed Marylou's suspicion. Eric's bucket of bolts blocked the traffic behind him by driving too slowly. The white SUV followed several cars behind. But was the SUV tailing her or Eric?

Under normal circumstances, she'd be terrified someone followed, but annoyance surfaced, along with the strong need to pound Eric's face into the concrete. Her usual route was to leave Antonio's studio on Seventy-Fifth Street and walk straight up to Fifth Avenue, always traveling in the direction of traffic. But since two cars followed, and they were in the throes of rush hour, Lauren turned right onto Madison Avenue then left onto Seventy-Six Street where she walked opposite the traffic flow. Unable to follow, her two pursuers continued on Madison, and she sprinted toward Fifth Avenue. Not bothering to wait for the green traffic light, she continued across the street and entered Central Park, dodging behind several trees to wait.

Eric's smoke-spewing jalopy passed moments later. Cussing up a storm, Eric slammed his fist into his steering wheel and hit the gas, screeching around the corner and out of sight.

A black sedan with tinted windows followed.

Lauren's gut jolted. Was this the same car involved in Rafael's abduction? And where was the white SUV? *What the hell is going on*?

Knowing Eric would break every law to circle the block, Lauren walked along Fifth Avenue at a brisk pace. When his smoke trail fogged up the next street light, she, again, darted into the park. Eric and the black sedan passed and still no white SUV. *All right, the sedan is following Eric. Why*? Several blocks later, she hurried into her condo building to see Robert wiping his computer screens.

He looked up with a broad smile. "Evening, miss. How's the glass artist doing?"

"Hopefully, getting good enough to make some money." With a quick glance over her shoulder at the front door, she strolled toward the desk. Should she tell Robert about being followed? She opened her mouth to speak when Eric's smoke-spewing sedan inched by the glass doors.

Eric's gaze searched into the lobby. Too late to hide. Nothing stood between her and the front door.

A minute later, the black sedan drove by, the windows too dark to see within. With hands balled into fists, she fought the urge to run out and strangle Eric. With her luck, they were *his* friends in the black sedan.

Finished with the last computer screen, Robert threw the wipe into the trash bin. His gaze studied her. "You looked ready to confront that Drummer fellow."

Her brows rose. "How'd you know about him?"

A small smile curled his mouth. "Mr. Lambert left his description."

Deems again, taking care of her, and always making sure she remained safe. A warm glow settled in her chest.

Robert motioned with a nod toward the door. "Drummer's already been by several times, miss." He pointed to the computer screens. "We monitor the exterior of the building, too."

She peeked around the corner of the desk at the screens. Crystal-clear pictures. The sight of so many camera angles loosened the tightness in her gut. "How about a white SUV?"

His eyes widened. "Excuse me, ma'am?"

"Pearl-white, a luxury model. Whoever he is has been hanging around the studio."

Frowning, he ran a hand through his crew cut. "Mr. Lambert mentioned a black sedan with tinted windows, which I've seen twice already, but no white SUV." Grabbing a pen, he wrote a quick note on a pad. "I'll tell him what you said. Oh, and, miss, rest assured. Drummer won't step foot past this lobby."

Those words were wonderful to hear. She released a long breath and smiled. "Thank you, Robert. Too bad the cops can't lock him away for being ugly." With a wave, she headed for the elevator.

After arriving at her floor, she let herself into the condo. At least here with all the cameras and security, she felt safe, away from the weirdos, but hell, the list grew every day. Rafael wanted the backpack, even offered her money, and then ultimately, attempted to steal it. His purpose was clear and no longer a threat. Eric wanted *her*, and his intention was also clear. The guys in the black sedan abducted Rafael, and the poor guy wound up dead. Now, the sedan tailed Eric. Where did the white SUV fit in? *What the hell is everyone's obsession with me?*

Releasing a heavy sigh, Lauren tossed her backpack and jacket onto a kitchen counter chair before heading to the bathroom to freshen her face. The water wasn't cold enough, not like country water—clear, fresh, and invigorating. After returning to the kitchen, she grabbed a water bottle from the refrigerator and took a long swig.

Her gaze drifted to the backpack. Jan had carried the bag everywhere before they switched, but Jan made sure she'd emptied the contents. Even Detective Baylor inspected her supplies and then shook the bag. So, what interested Rafael? And since the black sedan returned to the picture, was Eric interested in the pack, too? But that would mean Eric and Rafael knew each other.

Nothing made sense.

The condo phone rang, jarring her thoughts. She lifted the receiver. "Hello?"

"Mr. Lambert is here, Miss Howell. Shall I send him up?"

Her heart flipped. *He's home!* "By all means." Did Robert have to ask?

She didn't know what to do first. Fix her hair? Brush her teeth? Start dinner?

Restraint, that's what I need. But as soon as she opened the door, she flew into Deems' arms with a happy shriek. Not willing to draw attention from the neighbor across the hall, she grabbed his arm and hurried him inside, shut the door, and then pushed him into the living room.

With a wide smile, Deems dangled his tie between two fingers. "I feel undressed."

Knocking the tie from his hand, she pushed him onto the sofa and held him down with her body while showering kisses all over his face. Her heart was ready to burst at the sight of him. *So much for restraint.*

"Wow." Gaze sparkling, he wrapped her in a tight embrace. "This welcome-home is the best I've ever received." With a whirlwind of a maneuver, he reversed their positions and pinned her to the sofa cushions.

His lips captured hers with full force, deep and probing, causing a groan to escape from her throat. He tasted so good.

His mouth slid to her forehead. "I've missed you,

Lauren, and you know what?" He lifted his head to meet her gaze. "I never imagined I'd say those words to a woman." He kissed her nose. "Have you eaten?"

Eat? What, food? She gazed into a pair of tender, brown eyes. "I haven't decided what to cook."

"Then, let's go out. We're wasting a beautiful evening. We'll do a little window shopping and maybe try this new Italian restaurant on Park Avenue."

She'd rather stay wrapped in his arms and to hell with food. As hard as she tried, she couldn't push him out of her mind. He'd become more than a friend in so short a time, and because of him, she'd treasure her memories of New York forever. Her fingers slipped into his hair. "We could stay in."

"Sure, but you're the one who made me appreciate the beautiful outdoors."

Manhattan's outdoors was no comparison to the country, but she let the comment pass. "I still don't have anything other than blue jeans to wear. You're not taking me to a fancy place, right?"

"I don't think so, but we'll find out." He kissed her nose again and slipped off the sofa while extending a hand to help her to her feet.

She threw on her jacket, double-checked her pockets for condo keys, wallet, and cell phone, and followed him out the door.

As the elevator descended, she leaned against him and brushed her lips over his because she wanted to, and nothing in the world stopped her. The man destroyed all her inhibitions. She no longer doubted her ability to trust another man or fall in love. If he again asked her to stay, he might hear a yes.

They reached the lobby, arm-in-arm.

Standing, Robert waved Deems to the desk. "Sorry to tell you, sir, but Drummer is outside. Just pulled alongside the curb five minutes ago. You'll see his sedan parked near the corner."

Deems' arm tensed in hers. "Show me."

Robert pointed to a square on his computer screen. The camera angle caught a good view of Eric with his arm dangling out the car window with the evening breeze rustling his stringy hair.

Whoa! Deems' gaze changed from alert to full fire within seconds.

He turned to Lauren, jaw tight. "Go upstairs. We'll have dinner another time. I'm stopping him right now."

Chest tight, Lauren gripped his arm. "What will you do?"

"For starters, drag him to my sister's."

She stroked his cheek. "Please don't let him hurt you."

With his gaze boring into hers, he stroked a finger along her chin. "Thank you for worrying, but if I need help, I'll yell for Robert. Now, go upstairs."

Gut clenching, she cringed. "Will you call me?"

He nudged her toward the elevators. "I won't be long."

Oh, God. He might kill Eric and ruin his successful career. How would she ever forgive herself if this wonderful man got hurt?

Chapter Eighteen

Fists tight, Deems closed his eyes and counted to ten. If he stepped outside with his temper boiling out of control, he'd kill Eric. What the hell was the man's problem? Was he so friggin' dense he couldn't see Lauren's lack of interest?

Throughout his entire Dallas trip, Deems thought of nothing but her and barely had the concentration for business. Her smile, always so beautiful, brightened the world around her. Her expressive green eyes and alluring touch revealed her feelings better than words. Every part of her felt right, and no woman ever had him more mesmerized. Whoever this Jo-Jo was had to be a complete moron for letting her go. *And I'll be damned if I let Eric lay another hand on her.*

Moving around the security desk toward the rear hall, Deems pointed to Robert's phone. "If you see Drummer swinging, call the cops. I'll use the Exit door and sneak around from behind."

"I can come with you, sir."

A worthwhile suggestion. Robert was built like a brick shit-house with muscles bulging from every seam of his clothes, but no, Eric was a personal problem. The privilege to break every bone in his face belonged to Deems. "I'll handle him, Robert. I don't think he's man enough to fight me, but just in case, my order stands with the phone call."

Deems hurried along the hall to a door marked Emergency Exit, which opened to an alley between this building and the next. Using the side wall as cover, he peeked around the building's corner. Eric still had his arm dangling out the window, like he had all the time in the world to wait for Lauren to appear. With every muscle tense and ready to fight, Deems approached and yanked the driver's side door with enough force to rattle its handle.

Eyes and mouth wide, Eric snapped his head, flying his stringy hair every which way. "Yo, man, you startled me!"

The waning evening light revealed bruises on Eric's face. He had a whale of a lump on his right cheekbone, a cut over his right eye and lip, multiple contusions, and probably a few loose teeth. The injuries made his ugly face uglier. Dismissing the temptation to add some bruises of his own, Deems urged Eric to slide across the bench seat. "I'm driving you home. I've had enough of this stalking."

Eric stiffened. "Look, man, I want to apologize."

Gut boiling, Deems jabbed a finger on Eric's shoulder. "Like hell. You're after her for a reason, and I don't like it. Move over!"

"All right, all right." He slid to the passenger side. "I can drive myself, you know."

Deems slipped behind the steering wheel. "I'm kicking some sense into my sister's thick head. I've had it with you." He turned the ignition key to hear a grind and a squeal before the engine sputtered to life, sending a cloud of black smoke into the air. He threw the gear shift into Drive and rolled into traffic.

The stench of motor oil filled the car's cabin, along

with exhaust fumes and dirty laundry—all causing his nose to itch. Deems couldn't tell if the smell came from Eric or the upholstery. Maybe both. Grimacing, he waved a hand in front of his face. "What the hell is the smell?"

Eric forced a laugh. "Hey, man, this car's a classic! You don't see many of these on the road."

No surprise there. Cars spewing pollution like a smoke stack should be condemned. He turned onto Seventieth Street. *Small wonder I still remember how to handle a car.* He rarely drove anymore and hadn't bothered to buy a vehicle since moving from Chicago. With Lou chauffeuring him everywhere and cabs available at all hours, he had no need to drive himself.

After a few blocks, Eric hung his arm out the side window while his other arm draped across the bench seat. A sneer twisted his lips. "Jan won't believe you."

Deems shot him a glare. "I'll *make* her believe me."

Twenty minutes later, he found a parking spot a half block from Jan's brownstone apartment, which, these days, was a sheer miracle. His chest tight and with the unmistakable urge to hit something—like Eric—he cut the engine and tossed Eric his keys. "Let's go." He'd approached a now-or-never time. His sister might hate him for what he was about to do, but for Lauren's sake, he'd do anything to keep away this asshole. Deems stepped from the car and slammed the door behind him, half expecting the hinges to snap from rust.

Moving in a nonchalant fashion and still with that sneer on his lips, Eric patted the car hood on his way around to the curb. "You're wasting your time, man."

Since he'd rather be with Lauren, he couldn't agree

more. Using his right hand, Deems splayed his fingers on Eric's chest to stop him, matching him sneer for sneer. "Who worked you over, or are you planning to tell me you tripped on your roller skates?"

Eric's lips twitched. "Me and a friend got into a disagreement."

Must have been an argument fit for a boxing ring. Deems shook his head. "You hang with the wrong crowd, Eric." He leaned close enough to smell Eric's onion breath. "Jan better not be in any danger."

Eric backed away. "Aw, man, I won't hurt her."

"I'm not worried about you hurting her. I'm worried about your *friends.* Come on. I've better things to do than hang with you." He grabbed his arm and shoved him toward the brownstone.

At that moment, from the opposite direction, Jan turned the street corner, carrying two canvas shopping bags, one in each hand. Her eyes widened to the point of popping as she met them at the apartment building's steps.

Her gaze shifted from Eric to Deems. "What's going on?"

Deems shoved Eric toward her. "Your so-called fiancé is stalking Lauren."

Palms outstretched, Eric faced Jan. "I only went to apologize. For your sake, Jan, so you and Lauren can be friends again. This way, she can move back and help us with the rent."

Jan thrust a canvas bag into Eric's arms. "You have no reason to apologize for anything. Besides, I don't want anyone with us. We're a couple now. A third person will be in the way."

The woman wore ear plugs and blinders. What

189

could Deems possibly say to persuade Jan to listen? Hell, he would willingly introduce her to a half-dozen potential mates. Mark Jordan for one. The man had a good head on his shoulders and a far-better future. Somehow, some way, Deems wanted to arrange a date between the two. He stared directly at Jan. "From here on, I no longer pay your rent. If you want to be a couple, then act like one and keep this joker away from Lauren." He narrowed his gaze. "He's frightening her, Jan. Don't you even care?"

Jan's complexion changed to ash, and she gripped his arm. "You agreed to a couple more months, Deems. You know we can't afford the rent."

Fighting to control a rising explosion, Deems shook off his sister's hand. She hadn't heard a word about Eric frightening Lauren. All she cared about was the rent. He hated to punish Jan because of her choice of mate, but he had his limits. Deems shook a thumb in Eric's direction. "If this wise-ass looked for a job instead of spending his days stalking Lauren, maybe he can solve your money problems."

Since he fought the urge to grab his sister's shoulders and shake some sense into her, he stepped back, out of reach. "I'm sorry, Jan. I'll continue to pay your tuition, but the rent and credit card stop today."

"I'll tell Mom and Dad." She jutted her chin.

Oh, cripes. She pulled this shit when she was five years old. He snorted. "Please do. I can inform them what a loser you found."

Eric spread his arms wide. "Hey, hey, I'm standing right here, you know."

"And what about my allowance, Deems? You stopping that, too?"

Deems' gaze shifted from his sister to Eric. "I won't stop your allowance, because I don't want to deprive you of basic necessities...like soap." He scanned Eric's smudged clothes.

Eric glanced down at himself and, with the use of two hands, flicked his hair off his shoulders. "I've got prospects brewing. I need a little more time for everything to work out."

Stepping close, Deems glared into Eric's face. "Then I suggest you wait here and not wherever Lauren is."

Jan nudged her way between the two men, placing her back to Eric, her gaze fixed on her brother. "You're asking me to choose between my fiancé and money. I'll choose Eric, you know."

Under better circumstances, he'd be proud of Jan's choice, but not with Eric. She had the potential to do so much better. Maybe he *should* call his parents and let Mom give Jan an earful.

The brownstone's door flew open. Mr. O'Reilly stepped out, waving his arms. "Where've you been? Your apartment's been ransacked!"

Jan gasped. Eric cussed, and both ran into the brownstone.

Deems silently groaned. What else could keep him from Lauren? Shaking his head, he followed. Once reaching the third floor, he approached the apartment's open door to see Jan with a hand over her mouth.

Everything was askew. Books from the shelving lay tossed to the floor. Every conceivable drawer was opened and dumped. Even the sofa had been turned on its front with the underside lining ripped.

Pacing, Eric grumbled some obscenity.

Deems waved a finger about the room. "I'm no detective, but obviously, someone was looking for something. Your television and stereo are still here, DVD collection, and laptop, too." He turned to the landlord. "Did you see or hear anyone moving around the apartment?"

O'Reilly shook his head. "The tenant on the second floor called to complain about the noise." He pointed to the door. "They busted the lock. When I got up here, I found the door open and no one about. Whoever broke in probably used the back fire escape." He surveyed the mess. "We should all the police."

Shoulders stiff, Eric stepped forward. "No cops, Mr. O'Reilly. One of my buddies is playing a practical joke."

Jan cocked a brow and stared. "Who?"

"Never mind who. I'll even the score."

Her mouth fell open. "None of my business? I live here!"

With two hands, Deems gripped Eric's jacket and glowered close to his face. "I don't know what you're involved in, but rest assured, if anything happens to Jan or Lauren, I'll make sure the court ships you straight to Sing-Sing." He dropped his hold.

Eric raised his hands, palms outward. "I know who's responsible. Just two old friends, okay?" He adjusted his jacket.

Deems bristled. Probably the same *friend* who used Eric's face for a punching bag. For some reason, a black sedan with tinted windows came to mind.

Chapter Nineteen

With her stomach in a knot, Lauren paced in front of the sofa. The minutes passed and dragged into hours. If she wasn't careful, she'd wear a spot on the rug straight down to the padding. How could she possibly relax with Deems out with Eric? What if Deems walked in all bruised? She'd burst into tears and bawl. And Jan, would she believe her brother? In all probability, Jan would convolute some sob story to counter her brother's arguments. The girl was too damn young and inexperienced, and no amount of words or evidence would convince her otherwise.

The condo phone rang. With a quick glance at the wall clock—nine-fifteen—she flew toward the kitchen to grab the receiver. "Yes, Johnny?"

"Mr. Lambert's here, ma'am."

"Good. Send him up."

Calm down. He's alive. Staring through the peephole, she hurriedly opened the door before Deems reached for the bell and yanked him into the condo. Ignoring his amused gleam, she thoroughly inspected his face and then his hands. His suit was still impeccable. No smudges of dirt or blood. Everything appeared perfectly natural, and relief flushed to her toes.

Chuckling, he flicked under her chin. "No, I did not hit him." A half grin quirked on his lips as he closed the door. "Sorry I took so long. Jan's apartment was ransacked."

Wincing, Lauren gripped his arm. "Is Jan okay?"

"She wasn't home at the time. Now, where were we?" He wrapped his arms around her.

"Wait a minute." She nudged on his chest, not hard enough to break his embrace but enough to look up into his face. "You're not giving me any details. What was taken?"

"Nothing was missing, just everything turned on end. Eric claims his buddies were playing a joke and refused to call the police."

Somehow, the comment about Eric and the police came as no surprise. The man probably had a rap sheet well hidden from Jan. The poor girl was so dense. "What was Jan's response about Eric?"

His arms slipped down her sides, and he sighed. "Jan took his side, of course. Since I've known her to be a stubborn little mule, I had no other option but to stop paying her rent. If she wants to live with a man, then she needs to take responsibility for her actions. I'll continue paying her tuition and allowance, but—"

Lauren's eyelid twitched. Perhaps she'd misheard. "Hold on a minute. What do you mean you paid her rent? Since when?"

"Oops." He grimaced and looked away. "Sorry. Cat's out of the bag. I've been supporting my sister since she arrived in Manhattan."

"But I paid half the rent—eleven hundred dollars a month." She gripped his suit jacket lapels and narrowed her gaze. "Did I pay the full rent?" Truthfully, she shouldn't complain. The amount was still cheaper than a room at the YWCA.

A smile tugged at the corner of his mouth. "You paid less than half, Lauren." He yanked her into his arms until she stood flush against his chest. "I don't want to talk about Eric and Jan. I've spent two days in Dallas, and all I thought about was you." He lifted her chin and captured her mouth.

All her worries disappeared as the warmth of his kiss shattered her thoughts like leaves blowing in the wind. His musk cologne swirled around her head, and she sucked in his scent with relish. She missed him so much. In such a short time, he'd become the most extraordinary man to enter her life.

Wrapping her arms around his neck, she deepened the kiss. *How can I possibly let this man go?* Deems made her body come alive. He weakened her bones and forced her to question her own sanity. Most of all, the fullness he caused in her chest was enough to explode her heart. Plain and simple, she loved Deems and would never get enough of him. Whenever they were together, she felt safe and whole. *To think I almost married a man who was nothing more than a roommate.*

But upon her return home, she still had to contend with her limited finances and basically restart her life from the day she'd left for college. She couldn't take the easy route and sponge off Deems.

Deems slid his lips from hers and bit her earlobe. "I'm contemplating a position change at the company." He took her hand and guided her to the sofa. Sitting, he urged her onto his lap. "I'll allow someone else to have a shot at the North American territory."

She traced a finger along his lower lip, enjoying the feel of the softness. "What will you do?"

"I have other options." He kissed her finger.

Every touch had her reeling, even the soft, gentle ones. With her gaze on his lips, she tilted her head to the side. "Not because of me, right?" She met his gaze. "You obviously have a good-paying job. And you have Jan to support."

Pulling back slightly, he pursed his lips. "Is the money important?"

"I'm saying don't quit a job you like for a woman who is temporarily in your life." Damn, those words were hard to say. The fullness in her chest turned to an ache. As hard as she tried, she couldn't shake away the sadness surrounding her heart. Avoiding his gaze, she toyed with the buttons on his shirt. "I'm not sure I can take this city full-time, Deems, and I will never ask you to leave."

With a gentle nudge to push her off his lap, he stood and extended a hand.

She slipped her fingers into his and followed him to the picture window where a nighttime view of city lights greeted them. Even at this height, she wasn't impressed.

He waved an arm. "This world is mine, Lauren. I can't leave."

His voice sounded like a prisoner locked in a cell. She cocked her head. "You *can't* leave, or you *won't*?"

Facing her, he gave her a tired smile. "I won't."

Could her heart sink any lower? *Well, what did you expect?* Gaze cast downward, she nodded. "I understand, Deems, but you have to consider my point of view, too. I love to lie in an open pasture and stare at the stars." She pointed out the window. "All I see now is the church steeple reflecting light off its copper sheeting. The city's light pollution hides everything in the sky except for the moon." Turning, she patted his chest and gave him a light peck on the cheek before breaking away. "If you're hungry, I've some leftover chicken. Then, maybe we can relax in front of the TV."

Lowering his head, he gazed with a one-eyed glare. "You've been on my mind for two days straight. TV is not uppermost on my agenda."

"The suggestion was in case you were exhausted." She flashed a wry grin. "TV is not uppermost on my mind either." She hooked her arm through his and led him to the bedroom.

****

Deems jostled through the crowded cocktail lounge toward the curve in the bar where available standing room eased the sardine effect. Ordinarily, he'd avoid a Friday night date at Billy's Bar and Grill, but he promised Lauren a dinner. Come hell or high water, he'd give her one—provided Antonio stopped being so hard-nosed.

The bartender, who looked no older than the legal age limit, gave him a nod. "What will you have?"

"Scotch on the rocks." He wanted to swing by the studio to save her time, but the art students were coming down to the wire, and Antonio spent every minute cramming his knowledge into their brains for fear of missing a crucial point. Lauren's classes stretched into the evening hours and delayed her arrival home, effectively curtailing any together-time because of exhaustion.

The bartender placed a napkin then his drink onto the bar.

Slipping onto the only empty stool, Deems tossed him a twenty dollar bill and sipped, his gaze scanning the crowd. He should level with Lauren and explain about his business and career. So what if he made good money and supported his sister? Why not tell Lauren the whole story? She displayed a sensibility far beyond any woman in his past. Like now. He suspected her late-class excuses were a rational need to place a wedge into their relationship, which made sense. Neither wanted to say goodbye, yet the outcome of a successful union slapped their faces every time they slept together. Nowhere was their inevitable separation more apparent than the countdown of her time left in New York.

Tonight, he would, once again, raise the subject of her staying. Maybe persistence would wear her down. Somehow, the idea caused a chuckle to reverberate in his throat. Lauren was, if anything, a strong-willed woman. If she agreed to stay, she'd stay on her terms, not his.

"Are you alone?" said a sultry voice.

He rotated his head to see a woman with too much cleavage leaning toward him. Since they were packed against the bar with no place for a quick escape, he smiled politely. "I'm waiting for someone."

"I can keep you company while you wait."

Her breath smelled like gin as she looped her arm through his. Feeling as if ants crawled beneath his shirt, he used a two-finger hold to lift her arm from his jacket. The last thing he wanted was for Lauren to see another woman hanging on his arm. He scowled. "I'm meeting someone. Move on."

She huffed then turned to the man behind her.

Thank the Lord for small favors.

No matter where in Manhattan, on a Friday night, crowds packed every bar, restaurant, and nightclub as people sought relief from a hectic work week. This particular bar and grill offered a casual atmosphere with no particular dress code, and Lauren should feel perfectly comfortable. He, of course, donned his usual suit and tie since he felt undressed in anything less.

As he surveyed the entrance for the woman of his dreams, he spotted a familiar face holding the door for two women—one elderly, the other in her twenties—both hurried toward the ladies' room.

Mark Jordan caught his wave and made his way to the bar, hand outstretched. "You're the last person I expected to see, Mr. Lambert."

Taking Mark's hand, Deems nodded in the direction of the ladies' room. "Were the two women your mom and sister?"

"Yeah, two deer caught in the headlights." He chuckled. "I've been showing them the sights. They come from a small town, so I don't think they're impressed. More in awe of so many people."

A typical reaction for anyone's first visit to New York City. Deems recalled Lauren's look of confusion when she stepped into the deli restaurant on their first date. *Wait 'til she gets a load of this place.* He sipped his drink to hide his spreading grin. "Big city life isn't for everyone. I'm seeing a woman who's from a small town. She can't wait to leave."

Mark's mouth quirked to the side. "Sorry, boss, I can't believe any woman would leave you. You're a great catch." His gaze wandered over the crowd before drifting back. "By the way, I'd like to meet your sister again. She's cute."

The best news he'd heard all day. "Nothing I'd like more, Mark, but her fiancé is a foot taller than you, and he won't think too highly of your interference."

Squaring his shoulders, Mark smirked. "I can defend myself. How about we meet in your office?" He waved away the bartender. "You come up with some excuse for her to visit, and then, I'll pop in like before." He grinned. "I'll throw on the charm."

Deems almost laughed. With Mark's good looks and easy smile, he might be the man to draw Jan from her loser fiancé or, at least, put some doubt into his sister's brain. His gaze scanned Mark. A nice dresser. Suit but no tie. Open-collar white shirt. He wore his clothes well. "My sister is thickheaded and probably more trouble than she's worth, but you know what, Mark? Let's give the plan a try." He slapped the man on the back. "I can extend your time in New York with the pretense of learning new accounting procedures, invite Jan to lunch, and then have you unexpectedly arrive."

Chuckling, Mark nodded. "That should work."

The entrance door opened. Deems locked his gaze onto the familiar head of dark hair as Lauren walked through followed by two men. All three were smiling, and a surge of jealousy collided with pride. The woman had a way of exciting his nerve endings, and an erection erupted as proof.

Like a miracle from the heavens above—or just his wild imagination, the crowd separated, and his breath hitched. She looked stunning in a sleek black dress perfectly contoured to show her beautiful curves. Her hair fell loosely onto her shoulders with several strands drawing a man's gaze toward the soft mounds of her breasts. With high heels and plenty of legs, she exemplified a man's fantasy of a healthy woman capable of a night of vigorous sex. Every male in the establishment turned to gawk, but she hardly noticed. Face glowing, she met his gaze and smiled.

As her gaze shifted to Mark Jordan, the smile faded, and her pace slowed. Green eyes wide, she lost all color in her complexion.

Mark's color turned to ash. His posture stiffened, and he gave every indication of preparing to bolt. *What the hell is going on here*? Deems stood and stepped away from the bar.

Lauren approached, and her gaze drifted to Deems. Frowning, she pointed to Mark. "A friend of yours?"

The chill in her voice sent a shiver along his spine. He eyed her warily. "Colleague."

Without a second's hesitation, she slapped Mark hard, snapping the man's head like a volleyball.

"Lauren, Lauren!"

Mark's sister and mother worked their way through the crowd, waving to grab her attention. But Lauren, with chin high and nostrils flaring, locked her gaze onto Deems. That quickly, her head lowered, and she bit a trembling lip before turning on her heel and running for the exit.

The two women struggled to cut off Lauren at the door, but Lauren hurried through the entrance and onto the street.

Shock froze Deems from reacting. He had no idea what happened, and only when the two women turned toward the bar did his brain finally click into gear. Gut wrenching, he gripped Mark's arm. "You're Lauren's ex-fiancé!"

Beads of sweat accumulated on Mark's forehead. "I never expected to see her again." He avoided eye contact.

Deems tightened his grip and struggled with every ounce of self-control not to wring the man's neck. "You stole her money and left her high and dry. What kind of a man are you?"

Hell, Deems answered his own question. Mark Jordan wasn't worth his weight in salt. No wonder the damn man wanted to meet his sister. Easy money for the taking. Deems dropped his hand as the two women approached.

Holding a quivering palm outright, Mark stopped them by gesturing toward the restaurant area. "See if our table is ready. I'll be over in a minute."

The younger woman glanced toward the entrance. "But, Jo-Jo, that was Lauren!"

"Yes, please, go sit. This man is my boss, Mr. Lambert, and I need to explain a few things."

With raised brows, the women started off, glancing over their shoulders at Mark.

Palms outward, Mark turned to Deems. "Look, Mr. Lambert, I made some bad choices, and I panicked. I knew Lauren would be all right."

His blood boiled. "Well, she wasn't all right, Jordan. She's flat broke and had to borrow money to survive."

"But she met you, and I know how generous you are with your money." He shot Deems a weak smile.

Clenching his fists, Deems deliberately kept them at his side. Otherwise, he'd be too tempted to swing. "Lauren won't take money from me, you idiot. She's too proud." He scowled. "For a man engaged to such a strong-willed woman, you should know that simple fact." Another friggin', self-centered opportunist. While studying Mark, he released a long breath through tight teeth. "How did we hire you? The company has strict background checks, and Lauren tells me the police hold warrants for your arrest."

Mark ran a shaky hand through his blond hair. "You hired me before those warrants were issued, sir." Wincing, he shot Deems a pained look. "Lauren had no idea I traveled to New York for a job interview. After I got hired, I figured a clean break was my best move."

"But you took everything she owned."

Mark held up a finger. "Technically, the movers did. I told them they had two hours to clean out the apartment."

"Then, what about the hundred grand from the car dealership?"

Fidgeting, he pulled his shirt collar away from his neck, his gaze focused on the bar stool behind Deems. "I had creditors to pay off." Swallowing hard, he faced Deems. "I truly intended to refund the money, but my boss questioned some of the entries in the books. When I heard he engaged an auditor, I had to leave, and being hired by High-Rise International was my lucky break."

Deems sneered. "Except at present, we have an embezzler and a thief with active arrest warrants on payroll. Not only that, you made your family accessories. All this time, they hid your location."

Casting a quick glance around, he grimaced. "Yeah, they promised to keep my secret, even from Lauren." He forced a smile. "You must admit, sir, I've done a great job for the company. Dan Williams and I work well together, and we've succeeded with the acquisition of three expensive properties, substantially adding to your bankroll."

Like I give a shit. Money was not uppermost on his

mind. He witnessed the pain on Lauren's face, along with a fleeting glimpse of anger and disappointment. At him. Because Mark stood nearby. *What she must think.* He eyed Mark through narrowed slits. "Aren't you on an airport watch list?"

"Probably." After crossing his arms over his chest, he widened his stance and smirked. "I flew into Canada then took a train to Grand Central Station. A quick cab ride to the airport was all I needed to meet Lou. Look, Mr. Lambert—" Dropping his arms, Mark gripped Deems' jacket sleeve in his fist, his gaze pained. "I need this job. I've no other way to repay Lauren and the car dealership."

The man was a friggin' genius at deception, and he pretty much screwed his probation period. Lips tight, Deems shook free of Mark's grip and jabbed a finger onto the man's chest. "You do what's right by Lauren and the authorities first, and we'll discuss your future with the company. As of this moment, you're suspended."

Sucking in a quick breath, Mark nodded. "I'll do everything you say, Mr. Lambert. I'll repay Lauren with interest and return to Pennsylvania to face the warrants. All I'm asking is a chance to prove myself."

Deems only half-listened to Mark's last words. He worked his way through the thick crowd with one thought on his mind...Lauren.

Chapter Twenty

With tears threatening to gush, Lauren staggered more than walked. She ignored the wide-eyed stares from passing people and the loud wolf whistles from men out on the prowl in their fancy cars. Lack of clear vision contributed to poor balance, and she looked every part the intoxicated woman about to fall off her heels. Since darkness descended on New York and Friday being a prime dating night, people and cars crowded every street. So what if she was dressed to the nines and staggering? Heaven help any man who approached. She might seriously kill him.

For the second time in six months, her world crashed. Jo-Jo re-entered her life in the worst way—as a friend of Deems. She felt so betrayed. Deems *knew* what her ex had done. Jo-Jo was a wanted man, maybe not on the FBI Ten Most Wanted list, but certainly Arendtsville's and definitely Harrisburg's. The cops searched everywhere, followed every lead, and even accused her of being in cahoots. All this time, Jo-Jo hid in New York and probably under the protection of Deems Lambert. She choked on a sob.

Her cell phone rang. Deems, of course. She assigned him a special ringtone but debated answering. The painful tightness in her throat convinced her to let the message go to voicemail.

Jo-Jo's mother and sister denied knowing his

whereabouts, but being here with him became proof positive they lied to the authorities and her. Neither one gave a damn about her bleak financial situation.

Again, Deems called. This time, the ringtone jarred her senses. A strange feeling of time standing still enveloped her, as if she created the only movement while the rest of the world remained stationary. Since her arrival in Manhattan, she'd never been out alone after dark, and the phone snapped her to a reality that instantly put her on the alert. Staggering, teary-eyed, and surrounded by strangers...hell, her vulnerability smacked her in the face. She stopped to inspect the area.

Ordinary buildings surrounded her, mainly brownstones intermingling with small shops. Since she stopped in the middle of the block, she had no idea what street, but at least, she hadn't wandered into a slum—if Manhattan had a slum.

I desperately need a tissue. She had forgotten to pack a few in her new clutch purse so she sniffed and gave a discreet wipe of her nose. Somewhere in her brain, the image of a newsstand formed. She had passed one but couldn't remember where. Looking behind her and down the street, she spotted the green-painted wooden structure positioned at the last corner and retraced her steps.

The vendor had a full display of pocket-sized necessities. Tissues were among them.

Grabbing a pack, she sniffed while reaching into her purse for money.

"Keep them, lady."

Lifting her gaze, she met the kind eyes of an elderly man. "Excuse me?"

He nodded toward her hand. "I said keep them. You look like you just got jilted."

Blinking away more tears, she nodded, thanked him, and retraced her steps up the street before stopping to rip open the packet. Several tissues later and vision somewhat cleared, she scanned the area for a cab, and her breath froze. A pearl-white SUV sat at the corner, illegally parked alongside a hydrant. Eric's jalopy wasn't around nor was any sign of the black sedan.

So, the SUV is following me, after all. She was in the mood for a good fight, even at the cost of ruining her new dress and heels. Of course, the driver could easily force her into the vehicle and abduct her to God knows where. But her parents hadn't raised her to be a coward. She wanted to punch someone's face, and the SUV driver made for a good start.

With a quick glance for oncoming traffic, she jaywalked to the opposite side of the street and marched in the vehicle's direction only to watch the SUV squeal away from the curb and around the corner. Tinted windows prevented any visual of the interior. Whatever happened to the laws restricting the use of tinted windows in the driver's area?

If she wasn't wearing high heels, she'd chase the vehicle to kingdom come. Chest heaving, more in anger than exertion, she neared the street corner as the SUV turned left onto the next street. *Probably going around the block to sneak up again.* But the vehicle was so incredibly beautiful, how could he hide?

For the third time, Deems called. Frustrated at an evening shot to hell, she was ready to give him a piece of her mind. Removing the phone from her purse, she answered. "What?"

"Lauren, please, honey, I didn't know! You only called him Jo-Jo!"

Oh. How stupid of me. Jo-Jo was a family name, given as a toddler. Sighing, she pinched the bridge of her nose.

"Lauren?"

The sound of Deems' pleading voice weakened her knees. With a lump choking her airway, she staggered toward the brick-face on the corner building.

"Please let me talk to you, sweetheart. Don't deprive me of how fabulous you look in your dress."

Sweetheart? Her insides melted from the word, and tears streamed down her cheeks. Self-doubt flooded her. How much of Deems' words were true? *Can I even trust him?* She fell back against the bricks on the building and immediately felt the dress snag on the mortar.

"Lauren?"

Oh, God, how I want to believe. The experience with Jo-Jo had filled her with so many questions. Had she done something to cause him to leave? Why had he embezzled money when he performed so well as a car salesman? Was their engagement a total sham from the beginning?

"Lauren—please!"

But Deems was so different. Without trying, he'd swept her off her feet and made her feel loved. He accomplished more in such a short time than Jo-Jo had ever done in their years together. How could she even compare the two? She sucked in a shuddering breath. "Deems—" Her voice cracked. She couldn't utter another word if she tried.

"Let me come to you, honey, okay? Stay where

you are."

Where the hell am I? She blinked to clear her vision and searched for a street sign. Ninety-Eighth and Park. "I definitely walked too far."

"Just stand where you are. I'll swing by in a cab."

She had no desire to move, even though she looked like a hooker waiting for a client to pony-up her fee. The wolf-whistles were unreal. Men hung out of passing car windows, drooling, and arms begging her to come-hither. One car, full of women, stopped and invited her to join their party. *I don't hear this shit on the streets of Arendtsville.*

Jerking her brain into gear, she pushed away from the building and stared at her phone. Not once had she mentioned where she was. How would Deems direct a cab? What if he—

Chest constricting, she glared at the white SUV inching toward her. Undeterred, she squared her shoulders and stood her ground, one fist gripping her purse and the other ready to swing. Her heart pounded wildly, but really, lots of people were around. One scream would cause a scene.

The vehicle glided alongside the curb and stopped. A second later, the passenger window lowered with a whirl.

Knees shaking, she peeked at the driver then shot back with a gasp. "Lou!"

He grinned, showing a set of bright, white teeth. "Evening, miss. Mr. Lambert will be along any minute."

No wonder Deems hadn't asked where she was. He already knew! Every single one of her muscles released all tension, and she clutched the car for support. "Why,

Lou?"

"Why am I following you?" He leaned across the console. "The big man wants to keep you from harm, especially from Drummer."

Deems again, protecting her. *How can I not love that man*!

A yellow taxi stopped alongside Lou's door. Deems jumped from the rear seat, threw a few bills at the driver, and rushed around the SUV to wrap her in his arms.

She almost resisted, but his tender embrace offered her the comfort she craved and warmed her from the evening chill. She hadn't remembered to buy a shawl to cover her bare shoulders. Her anger and walking raised her heat levels. Only as she waited for Deems had the chilly night air penetrated her bones.

Releasing her, he placed both palms on her cheeks. "You scared me by running off . If Lou hadn't gotten stuck in traffic, he'd have been halfway home. Lucky for him, he watched you walk right past the SUV and followed." A worried gaze scanned her face. "Are you all right?"

"No." She felt like a wreck, had sore feet from walking too far in new high heels, and probably looked like a prize fighter with red eyes and nose.

He opened the rear door to the SUV. "Come on. Get in."

They buckled seatbelts under Lou's watchful eye. Deems immediately wrapped an arm around her and eased her head onto his shoulder.

The feel of his strong arm combined with the musk scent of his cologne compelled her body to melt with one big shudder. She stared at nothing in particular—

the white leather interior of the luxury SUV and Deems' polished shoes. Despite a struggle to keep her mind empty, silent drops of moisture tickled her cheeks. As soon as she'd spotted Mark Jordan standing next to Deems, she recalled the moment of entering an empty apartment, searching from room to room and finding only dust balls. Everything she owned, gone, even her late grandmother's treasured costume jewelry. For days, shock consumed her, followed by outrage, and not knowing what steps to take next. When she uncovered the depletion of their bank account, she lost every ounce of self-control. She wanted to kill him, but Jo-Jo had virtually disappeared from the surface of the earth.

Deems handed her a handkerchief. She sniffed the musk before dabbing her eyes. "I'm sorry I ran out on you."

He kissed her forehead. "I wasn't sure what shocked me more—your leaving so suddenly or the slap you gave Mark. You almost snapped his neck."

"I wanted to use a fist but too many witnesses." She sniffed.

Deems nodded to Lou. "You know where we're going."

Lou shifted the car into Drive and eased into traffic.

She ran a hand along the plush seat. *As smooth as a baby's bottom.* "This SUV is beautiful, Lou. Is it yours?"

"No, ma'am. Another company car." His dark eyes twinkled in the rearview mirror.

She rotated her head to look at Deems. "Why'd you keep Lou's surveillance a secret?"

His lips curled into a gentle smile. "I didn't want

any arguments. Keeping you safe and happy is my number one priority." He dropped his gaze to the floor and sighed. "Lou discovered the black sedan following Drummer, the very same one that followed the Hispanic." He shot her a quick glance. "I hired a private detective to keep an eye on Jan while Lou watches you." With his gaze meeting hers, he traced a finger along her bare shoulder. "You've become very important to me, Lauren Howell."

Pulling away, she frowned. "I'm not sure how I feel about all this secrecy."

"Doesn't matter. You can argue all you want, but I won't change my mind. Eric's into something bad, and the break-in at Jan's apartment proves my point." He eased her head back onto his shoulder. "Stay put. I've no intention of letting you go twice in one night."

No man had ever treated her with such possession, as if she was beyond special. The thought filled her soul with a warm, fuzzy feeling. From as long as she could remember, she'd taken care of her own problems, and for the first time, Deems wanted to assume the role. Her brain argued to resist. Her heart convinced her otherwise. Giving in to the warmth of his body, she relaxed against him and slipped her hand under his jacket lapel. "You can explain how Jo-Jo became a colleague."

His arm tensed around her shoulders. "I hadn't any particular insight into Mark's personal life, but I knew of his excellent track record at the car dealership." He passed a palm along the length of his tie. "Our human resources department completed a thorough background check but, unfortunately, before the warrants were issued. Mark, of course, checked out clean as a whistle, and I hired him. Two weeks later, he reported for training." After a brief pause, he sighed. "Human resources never found any financial problems, but Mark said his creditors—"

Huh? Brows high, she jerked her head from his shoulder. "What creditors? Jo-Jo was the most meticulous bookkeeper I've ever met. He had no debts."

"How about illicit ones?"

Gaze focused out the side window, she chewed on her inner lip. "I suppose the possibility exists." Penny-pinching Jo-Jo? The man was adverse to any loan, big or small. She shook her head. "No, he lied."

"He cleaned you out for a reason, Lauren, and don't forget the stolen money from the dealership."

She couldn't argue the point, but creditors? The man counted every dime between them and saved to the point of obsessiveness, but his habit accumulated a sizable saving account. No way had he kept so much money in the bank with creditors on his ass.

With her head again nestled against his shoulder, she toyed with his diamond-studded tie clip. "I've known Jo-Jo since high school, Deems. I don't believe creditors prompted him to steal."

"What then?"

"I don't know. All I can tell you is his sudden change after I lost my job. I still don't understand what happened. I'm disappointed and angry at a man I thought I knew."

He kissed her hair. "As of tonight, I suspended him and canceled his return to South America."

Her breath left in one big whoosh. Pushing on his chest, she jerked from his arm and met his gaze. "South

America? That's where he's been?"

"Afraid so. On Mark's initial interview, he jumped at the Argentina position, and now, I understand why. He had to escape from the country before his plans were destroyed." His finger traced along her shoulder. "Mark returned for his six-month evaluation. In order to keep his job with High-Rise, he needs to repay your half of the money and do his time with the authorities." He eased her back under his arm.

Wow. No wonder the cops couldn't find him. South America. Of all places.

Lou glided the SUV alongside a curb and stopped.

Straightening in the seat, she looked around. "Where are we?"

Deems turned her head and kissed her nose. "On the way to meet you and Lou, I made reservations at one of New York's many five-star restaurants. You dressed for me tonight and deserve the best dinner money can buy. I won't let Mark rob me of a date with the most beautiful woman I've ever seen."

Heat flushed her cheeks, for she had indeed dressed for him. She used part of her paycheck to buy dress clothes, even though she stopped in several shops to find something affordable. She returned the kiss but this time, on his lips. "Thank you. I need a trip to the ladies room to refresh my face."

"I'll save you some time." He opened a flap on the back of Lou's seat. "You look wonderful, but here's a mirror. Are you still hungry?"

"I can eat an entire slab of beef."

"Good, because I called in a favor."

She checked her reflection. No makeup smudges. Not much she could do about her red eyes, except smile a lot. She finger-combed her hair and closed the flap.

Lou opened the rear door, and they stepped out. Deems shook Lou's hand. "Thanks for watching her. We'll take a cab home."

"Have a good time, Mr. Lambert."

Hand on the metal frame, she stopped Lou from closing the door. "You're done following me, right?"

Both men glanced at each other, then her, and simultaneously said, "No!"

Chapter Twenty-One

After saying goodbye to Lou, Lauren took a moment to study her surroundings. She had absolutely no idea where they were, but the black double doors to the restaurant looked ominous, like an entrance to a forbidden castle. Brass lion-headed knockers hung on both doors while scrolled across the top, fancy gold lettering announced the name of the restaurant. "Les Amoureux," she murmured and turned to Deems. "The words translate to Lovers. An odd name for a restaurant."

Chuckling, he placed a hand on the small of her back and guided her toward the door. "The owner fell in love with the woman who showed him the property. They have three kids now." He opened the door and waved her forward. "Shall we?"

Several couples waited in the wide foyer where a maitre d' fussed with the computer on his pedestal. She and Deems approached.

The tuxedoed man glanced up and smiled. "Mr. Lambert, how nice to see you!" After jabbing a finger onto the computer screen, the maitre d' stepped from the reception stand and crooked a finger. "Your table is ready, sir. Frederic was pleased as punch to hear you were coming." He led the way through a dining room of dark brown and maroon in the direction of small oval booths positioned against the far wall. Pivoting the entire table, he waved them toward the center of the round, padded bench seat, waited for them to settle in, and then replaced the table.

Since they sat in such an intimate setting away from the kitchen and front entrance, she experienced an unusual sense of awe. For the first time, she looked at the man beside her and questioned whether she understood him at all. Obviously, Deems had connections, but to obtain a table at a five-star restaurant on a Friday night told more about the man than she imagined. How powerful was he in this huge city? She leaned close. "Do you come here often?"

"Not really." He unbuttoned his suit jacket and draped an arm behind her. "I brought my mom and dad here when they visited."

That piece of information hardly constituted the maitre d' knowing him by name, but she let the comment pass. With a curious gaze, she scanned the dining room. All through college, she'd worked in some nice restaurants but never a five-star one. Nor had she ever dined in anything swankier than the local mom-and-pop establishment. But this place was fabulous. The tables were equally spaced, so settings remained intimate without fear of the next table overhearing the conversation. Every plate was individually carried—no trays or covered dishes—and then promptly whisked away when empty.

Soft music played from speakers overhead, mainly orchestration arrangements with violins and muted horns. Scarce lighting prevented one from gawking at someone's food. Male and female servers, dressed in tuxedos, wore crepe-soled shoes with movements like a whisper of wind.

Deems nudged her shoulder. "What are you thinking?"

Tearing her attention from her restaurant analysis, she met his gaze and smiled. "That maybe I should apply for a job at a place above two to three stars. These guys can make some serious bucks compared to the tips I make."

The wine steward approached, holding a bottle of Bordeaux on his arm. "From Frederic, sir. His finest." With a corkscrew, he extracted the cork and poured a small amount into Deems' glass.

Deems sniffed then tasted. "Nice. Tell Frederic thank you."

With the wine poured, another waiter handed them menus.

She nearly choked on the exorbitant prices.

Lowering his arm to hold the menu with two hands, Deems wagged a finger in her face. "You order anything you want, hear?"

She'd like to order him to put his arm back where it belonged, but the poor man couldn't possibly eat with one hand all night. Her gaze traveled down the list of entrées. "I can get used to this kind of lifestyle, you know."

"I hope you do…within reason, of course."

He flashed a smile that warmed every inch of her skin.

After their orders were taken, Deems entertained her with stories about the trials and tribulations of city life, all geared toward making her smile and laugh. In one tale, he detailed his trip to Phoenix where the owners of a prospective high-rise refused to negotiate until he mounted a horse.

"A horse of all creatures." Grimacing, he gave a short, stifled laugh. "Can you imagine a city boy like me on a horse?" He shot her a quick glance. "The animal scared me half to death. I thought he was huge."

She, of course, handled a horse as well as a car since Central Pennsylvania was a mecca for equine stables. With mountains, pastures, and valleys to ride plus the abundance of Amish with traditional horse and buggy on the road, one couldn't drive two miles without seeing a stud service or hay for sale. But she laughed at Deems' story, because visions of a handsome man on a white stallion stayed in her mind, a man sitting tall in the saddle, like Prince Charming coming to rescue the fair maiden—albeit with muffled screams. Stretching, she kissed his cheek.

He jerked back, eyes wide. "What was that for?"

"For not hurting the horse."

"Humph." A smiled tugged at his mouth.

Arriving with their appetizer, the food server placed a plate of bacon-wrapped figs before them.

Lauren served Deems two then helped herself to the remaining two. She cut one in half, sampled the fruit, and then swooned. "These are good. He drizzled balsamic over them."

In no time, they polished off the appetizer.

Dabbing a napkin to her mouth, she smiled. "This place is nice, Deems. Thank you."

He grabbed her hand and gave her fingers a squeeze. "If you told me about the dress, I'd have made arrangements before the evening started."

Shrugging, she sipped her wine. "I went on a spur-of-the-moment shopping trip. Since Antonio tortured us all week, he cut our day shorter than we anticipated.

The women in our class gave me the names of some shops within my price range." She met his gaze and smiled. "You deserved to see me in something other than blue jeans."

"You're beautiful, Lauren." Without breaking eye contact, he lifted her hand to his lips.

His gaze darkened. The honey gaze connected to hers was so warm and tender, she couldn't look away. Her heart melted, and tears threatened behind her eyes. She was falling for this man, and every argument to counter the feeling sounded so lame. *Oh, God, what should I do*? Suppressing the lump in her throat, she stared at her wine glass. "We shouldn't have let ourselves become so involved."

With a soft touch of his hand on her cheek, he returned her gaze to his. "I don't regret a second of our time together. Yes, we will have difficulty saying goodbye, but I intend to relish every minute together. Who knows? Maybe you'll love me enough to stay."

She already loved him and wanted the man for the duration of time but struggled with the conflict of telling him so. Unable to form words, she kissed his soft lips. He deepened the kiss, and every muscle in her body released its tension. She swore she'd slip right off the bench seat and onto the floor so, as an anchor, she grabbed hold of his suit lapel. Somewhere during those few moments, she became vaguely aware of the food server who removed their empty appetizer dish, topped off their wine glasses, and disappeared as quietly as he came.

Deems touched the very edges of her soul and gripped her heart in ways never experienced. She was powerless to stop the yearnings he created—ones of love, security, and an overwhelming sense of peace. He had proven life wasn't so bad after all.

Someone cleared his throat. They broke their lip-lock to see the server pointing to their entrees.

"Please forgive the interruption," he whispered. With a smile tugging his mouth, the man backed away and disappeared.

The aromas of herbs and onions were enough to break them apart. Deems ordered stuffed pork chops with a delectable blend of rosemary and garlic, tiny potatoes, and asparagus. Hers was a petit filet mignon, medium rare, smothered with mushrooms and wine sauce.

They dug in.

Between the mouth-watering food, splendid wine, and Deems' company, she erased Jo-Jo from the inner recesses of her mind. What's done was done, and she wanted nothing more to do with her ex. He was no comparison to Deems, and she silently thanked Jo-Jo for ending their engagement. She sipped her wine. "How long has Lou followed me?"

Before answering, he shoved a potato slice into his mouth, chewed, and then swallowed. "Since the day he transported you to the condo." His gaze searched her face. "Please don't be mad. Eric's close proximity bothered me."

How could she possibly be mad at a man for watching her back? *God, how I love him*! Her heart felt so damn full. She fed him a piece of her meat. He returned the gesture and fed her a bite of his pork. Her eyes rolled at the succulent blend of rosemary and butter. "Boy, that's good." She buttered a petite roll. "What about Lou's chauffeur job? What does the boss say about him following me around all day?"

He dabbed his napkin on his mouth. "Lou's entitled to days off, and the company has several drivers as backup. Remind me to give you Lou's cell number. If you're in for the day, tell him. He also won't follow if I'm with you."

Swirling a slice of mushroom into the wine sauce, she suppressed a smile. "I'm glad. I want you all to myself."

Deems finished the last morsel on his plate and leaned back with a hand on his belly. He glanced her way, gaze sparkling. "Until morning?"

"You know damn well that's what I mean." Her mouth lifted at the corners. "We still have half a string of condoms to use."

Chuckling, he fingered a strand of her hair. "I like how you think. Waste not, want not, right?"

"The ever-practical country girl, that's me." She resisted the urge to lick the plate clean. Instead, she crossed her fork and knife in the center.

Deems tapped his fingers on the tablecloth and eyed her. "For your information, I have a fresh supply in my pocket—in case we run out."

We'll use every last one or my name isn't Lauren Howell. She would miss him but wanted him to miss her more, even as he eventually walked down the aisle with a bride on his arm. She sure as hell would remember him and gulped the last of her wine to swallow the sadness creeping into her heart.

A man in a chef's uniform hurried to the table, all smiles. "Deems, so glad to see you. Did you enjoy the meal?"

Deems gestured with a kiss to his fingertips.

"Excellent, Frederic, as always." Then, he kissed Lauren's hand. "Meet Lauren Howell."

The man took her outstretched hand and patted the top and bottom. "You like my place?"

"I love everything, Frederic."

"I'm pleased, mademoiselle." He slapped his hands together. "Well, I won't keep you two apart. Deems, stop by for a drink sometime."

"I will, Frederic. Thanks for seating us on short notice."

"Anytime, my friend."

As Frederic stopped at other tables, she nudged Deems. "If you've only been here once with your parents, how does he know your name?"

A faint smile touched his lips. "When I can, I help small businesses. Frederic needed money, so I lent him some."

"Wow, that's really nice."

He shook his head. "Purely a business arrangement."

The server arrived to remove their empty plates. He used a small hand-held vacuum to suck the loose crumbs on the tablecloth, and then reset the table for coffee and dessert, which followed immediately. "Compliments of Frederic." He grinned and disappeared.

Lauren stared at the huge tower of chocolate. "I'll never get this whatever it is into my stomach!" The dessert was a work of art with curls of chocolate surrounding either a pudding or cake.

"Nonsense. The sugar will give you energy. As for me, looking at you gives me enough stimulus, but I see Frederic gave me his signature custard-filled cake." He took her hand and kissed the fingers before lowering it to his lap.

She gasped at where he placed her hand, for he was hard and ready. She leaned close to his ear. "Are you telling me something?"

His gaze glowed. "That's what you do to me."

"Is that a fact?" She massaged the protrusion.

Eyes widening, he nearly jumped off the seat.

Thank God for the tablecloth.

"Are you ready to leave?"

She almost laughed at the plea in his voice. "I haven't tasted my dessert yet. Does this place provide doggie bags?"

He groaned into his coffee cup. "Maybe I can wolf down a few spoonfuls."

"Good idea. Eat some of the tower." Gaze twinkling, she wiggled her eyebrows. "I don't want you to slacken off tonight."

He exaggerated a gasp with a hand to his chest. "Never!"

Chuckling, she started on her dessert, ever careful to take her time to savor every bite.

He, on the other hand, gobbled his dessert without stopping and then sat back and watched her.

Finished, she dabbed a cloth napkin to her mouth.

Without wasting a second, he leaned close. "Ready?"

"Depends." She shot him a wry grin. "Only if you're ready to experience the vigor of a country girl after you've wined and dined her."

His arm shot into the air to catch the attention of the server.

Chapter Twenty-Two

The next morning, Deems exited the elevator, whistling. He whistled a lot these days. No particular tune. Just a happy-go-lucky tempo because of the woman upstairs. His feet refused to touch the floor, and for the first time in years, he considered canceling an appointment. After all, today was Saturday, a day to sleep in and enjoy the company of a beautiful woman. But he'd agreed to a business breakfast with a prospective high-rise client from Alaska. The meeting should only take a few hours, and Lou called to say he stood ready with the limo at the curb. Since Lauren tested the durability of one too many condoms last night, she should be zonked until mid-afternoon. Once he returned, they'd start all over again. He smiled at the thought.

"Mr. Lambert?"

Robert's voice broke into his reverie. The impeccably-dressed security guard stood behind his counter with a frown creasing his forehead. A brow raised, Deems strolled to the desk. "Yes?"

"You wanted to know if Drummer returned? Last night, he walked in and headed straight for the stairwell. When Johnny stopped him, Drummer demanded to see Ms. Howell, but she just left in a cab." Frown deepening, he crossed his arms over his chest. "Then, he requested to go to her floor and leave a note under the door. Of course, that's not allowed, and he refused to leave the note with Johnny. Apparently, he knew which floor." He shifted the gun holster on his hip.

Deems gave Robert a one-eyed gaze. "Drummer headed for the stairwell?" Heat flushing from his collar, he silently cursed. Jan knew the Stewarts, where they lived, and on what floor. Despite her brother's warning, she told Eric. *How friggin' stupid.* Such a simple slip, and a knot formed in the pit of his stomach. Gritting his teeth, he stepped closer to the desk. "Why didn't Johnny mention the incident when we returned?"

Robert coughed into his hand. "Begging your pardon, sir, but he said you and Ms. Howell were all google-eyed, and his news would spoil your mood."

Deems mentally denied the use of the description, but damn, the woman turned him on without the slightest provocation. He almost took her in the elevator. Like a good boy, he waited until they entered the condo. After that, she was all his. News about Eric most definitely would have killed the mood, so he silently thanked Johnny for his discretion.

"Do you want me to tell Ms. Howell?"

He'd like to move her to his condo with its tighter security, but in doing so, she'd discover everything about him. *And so what?* How could he expect her to stay in New York if he wasn't completely honest? He shook away the question. "No, don't tell Lauren and don't let her leave without calling Lou." He pointed a stiffened finger at Robert. "Make sure you remind her about Lou in case I'm detained longer than I anticipate." He headed for the door and to the waiting limo, his nerves on edge. "A change of plans, Lou.

Take me to the police station."

Hurriedly pushing away from the fender, Lou opened the rear door. "What about your breakfast meeting?"

He scowled. "I'll call and offer my apologies—the usual shit. If he's anxious to sell, he'll meet with me at another time. Otherwise, I don't give a damn." Before stepping into the limo, he stopped and stared down the street. "After the police station, I want you to go to the office. On Betty's desk are the phone numbers for the security firm handling our buildings." Brows tight together, he looked at Lou. "I want a man guarding Lauren day and night. Visible. Sitting in the hallway. Escorting her wherever she goes. I don't want a hair on her head hurt!" He tugged at his collar to release some heat.

Lou cocked a brow. "What happened?"

"I'll explain on the way." He dug into his wallet and extracted Detective Baylor's card. Whipping out his phone, he called the number listed.

"Baylor."

"Good. You're in. I'm swinging by to see you."

"And who might you be, sir?"

His frustration at Eric robbed his brain of logic. For some strange reason, he expected Baylor to recognize his voice. He sucked in a calming breath and released it. "Deems Lambert, Detective. I'm a friend of Lauren Howell. We spoke briefly about the Torres incident. Will you be at the station for a while? I have to talk to you." Baylor would give good advice. *I'll need some before I beat Eric to a pulp.*

"Sure. The front desk can direct you."

"Thank you, sir. I'll see you in twenty." He

disconnected and handed Lou the business card. "Here's the address."

Damn that Eric. Any normal man would take no for an answer and move on, but Eric's behavior bordered on psychotic. And Jan...simple and naïve Jan, engaged to a stalker. She needed a strong dose of maturity or be stuck with this loser forever.

In no time, Deems stood in the precinct's downtown Manhattan lobby where a receptionist directed him to the detective bureau on the second floor. Casting his gaze across dozens of desks, he spotted Baylor with his attention intent on paperwork. His black suit jacket hung on a nearby coat rack, his white tie loosened, and black shirt unbuttoned at the collar. To see him in the same outfit as their prior meeting surprised Deems. Had he no other color clothes? Then again, Deems instantly identified him and hurried toward the detective. Clearing his throat, he extended his hand.

With a lift to his brow, Baylor stood and took the outstretched hand. "What brings you here?" He waved Deems toward the wooden chair alongside his desk.

No pleasantries, which was fine. A cut-to-the-chase man. Unbuttoning his suit jacket, he flopped onto the wooden chair. The damn legs rocked and threatened to collapse beneath him. Grabbing hold of the desk, he expected his ass to hit the floor. When the chair held, he released the desk and explained his visit to the detective. While he had the older man's attention, he mentioned the time span for acquiring a restraining order.

After a heavy sigh, Baylor's hard-lined face relaxed. "I'm homicide, Mr. Lambert. Stalkers are handled by a different team." He leaned back in his chair and promptly created a loud screech. "Yes, I know about the delays with restraining orders, and truthfully, we can't do much without them. If Drummer attempts any physical contact, then yes, we can arrest him on an assault charge. As a cop, I'd like to lock every stalker in a cell, but right now, the law is on their side." He sat forward and leaned on the desk. "How about a bodyguard for Miss Howell?"

"I'm making arrangements. Lauren will have a guard at her door as early as this afternoon."

Nodding, he tugged on his ear. "I'm sorry I couldn't be of more help."

Deems scanned Baylor's cluttered desk. "I'm sorry I wasted your time, but I needed to vent." He slapped his knees and stood. Maybe he wasn't too late to join his client for breakfast. The man said he would eat anyway.

Who was he kidding? How could he possibly think about business? Lauren wasn't safe until something was done about Drummer. Even at the risk of alienating Jan forever, he would do everything in his power to stop Eric. A bribe perhaps, to entice him out of New York and away from Jan and Lauren. He had the resources. The company's legal department, for example. With the right push, they'd obtain a restraining order in no time.

Funny how I haven't considered such an easy route. What the hell was wrong with his brain? He employed one of the best legal departments in the city, and one call to the head honcho would solve all his problems. Early Monday morning, he'd introduce Lauren to his world of finance, take her to see the company lawyers, and push the process through the courts. Enough was enough.

Baylor slipped one of his business cards from the holder on his desk, wrote on the back, and then handed the card to Deems. "Go to the third floor and see if this detective is in. If not, call him on Monday and tell him I sent you. This way, we'll put Drummer's stalking on record."

Deems glanced at the card. "Okay, thanks." He slipped the card into his suit jacket pocket and adjusted his tie. "Any luck with the Torres murder?"

"You mean our backpack thief?" Again, he leaned back then ran all ten fingers through his crew cut before clamping his hands behind his head. "Only that he made a hop, skip, and jump from Columbia to the Bahamas to Florida before landing in New York. Our two-bit smuggler might have gotten in over his head."

Thoughts collided, none good. Deems clamped onto the back of the chair and eyed the detective. "When was he in the Bahamas?"

Creaking forward, Baylor rummaged through the folders on his desk, selected one, and flipped through the pages. "A little less than a month ago. A pass-through. One day."

Deems' jaw tightened. Was his suspicion even possible? But the facts were falling into place, and if the dates coincided… He nodded toward the folder. "What's the date for his stopover?"

Baylor told him and paused, his gaze sharp. "You know something?"

"My sister and Eric Drummer were in the Bahamas on the same date. I don't know if we're looking at a simple happenstance, but Jan told me Eric disappeared for an entire day." Deems groaned aloud then scrubbed both hands over his face. *Dammit to hell.* He mentally kicked himself for not putting two and two together sooner.

Jaw set, Baylor leaned across his desk. "What?"

Deems flopped onto the chair and met the detective's gaze. "The same black sedan that carried away Torres is following Eric. Maybe you should check to see if anything significant happened on Torres' one day in the Bahamas."

Baylor chewed on his inner lip with slate gray eyes alert. "Yes, we have too much of a coincidence. If Torres was after the backpack, then Drummer might be as well. Something is in it."

"But what? You checked the bag."

Baylor grabbed his phone. "Why don't you run to the coffee shop at the corner while I make a few phone calls?" He punched in seven numbers. "Buy me a black, and I'll swing by with my car."

Chest tight, Deems headed toward the elevators. Finally, a possible answer to Eric's obsession with Lauren Howell—her backpack.

Chapter Twenty-Three

Carol Stewart definitely needs a garden-size water jug for her forest.

Lauren refilled the dinky little container for the umpteenth time and still had half the jungle to hydrate. She *should* fill a large bucket with water and simply refill the smaller jug to eliminate the frequent trips to the sink. But for the money going into her pocket, she couldn't ask for a better job. She cooed to every plant and even sang a happy tune to keep up their spirits. The poor things probably missed their mommy. Her hand froze. *Dear Lord, what am I thinking?* She hadn't experienced such a carefree attitude in months. She didn't give a damn about her bleak financial situation. Everything was right with the world...for a few more weeks anyway.

Her one-hundred-and-eighty-degree turn happened because of Deems. Gad, what a wonderful man. Last night, he showered her with so much love, she almost broke down and cried. The man could definitely be persuasive, but as much as he spoke about her remaining in New York, he hadn't once mentioned marriage. Could she even fathom her church-going parents' reaction to hear their daughter lived with a man because he provided great sex? They'd throw themselves on the altar as sacrificial offerings.

Would she stay if he proposed? Pausing at the

kitchen sink, she reflected on her last thought. Yes, she loved him, but marriage? She had so much to learn about his likes and dislikes. His favorite food, for example. Music. Any special activities on his days off? She'd be willing to stay for a while to see where their relationship went but refused to use him to improve her money woes.

A final check to ensure all plants received their food and water, dead buds snipped and disposed…*yeah, all done*. She replaced the little jug under the sink.

She could apply for a New York teaching license, but what were the odds of her acquiring a position in Manhattan? How long before the city stifled her breath and forced her to flee to the countryside? The biggest question of all was, would Deems consider relocating, not necessarily out of New York, but away from Manhattan?

Entering the bedroom, she contemplated the notion and came up with her own answer. He wouldn't relocate, not with multi-billion dollar accounts to supervise. Who was she to ask? A farmer's daughter. *Get real.*

Grabbing her backpack from a side chair, she reached in for her safety goggles with the intention of cleaning the lenses when the strap snagged on the clipped key ring. Like a piece of jewelry stuck on a sweater, she fussed and fumed and got nowhere. Not wishing to break the strap so close to finishing class, she unclipped the ring and successfully untangled the elastic band.

A loud pounding on the front door shot her heart straight into her throat. Losing her grip on the goggles, she whirled toward the bedroom door while clutching her key ring to her chest. No one called from the security desk. Was the building on fire?

More pounding. "Lauren, open up!"

An angry male voice. Definitely not Deems. Who bypassed security? Hurrying toward the living room, she slipped the key ring into her jeans front pocket and cautiously approached the front door. "Who is it?"

"Security. Unlock the door!"

Robert? Gut clenching, she peered through the peephole. Nothing, only an empty hallway. Silent warning bells clanged in her head. "Show yourself."

The pounding continued, startling her to jerk back. Her heart rate skyrocketed, but she returned her eye to the peephole. "I'm not doing anything until you step into view."

Growling, Eric appeared and aimed a gun at the door. "I don't have time for this nonsense."

Holy shit! She leaped to the side as three shots fired in rapid succession, splintering wood and shattering the door around the deadbolt. As pieces flew, she screamed while protecting her face and head with her arms. *What now? How do I fight a gun?* With her heart beat thrashing in her ears, she ran for her phone on the small kitchen table and dialed 9-1-1, not even certain she hit the right numbers.

Eric kicked in the door and flew inside like an animal escaping a cage. His hair slapped his face as he scanned the room with a wild gaze locking onto her. "Put down the phone!"

He waved the gun as if ready to shoot whatever stirred. Namely, her. Every drop of moisture left her mouth, and she froze. A feeling of claustrophobia tightened her chest. She was trapped. Eric stood only twenty feet away, and she stared at a madman, the phone in her hand.

"Touch one finger on that keypad, Lauren, and I'll shoot you dead."

Tossing the phone onto the table, she raised her hands in surrender, hoping—praying—she had connected to the emergency dispatch center. *What the hell should I do?*

Her thoughts flashed through a slew of options, none good. The condo rose four stories above the sidewalk so jumping out a window guaranteed sudden death. The only escape was through the front door, and Eric blocked the way. *If I can slip around him...*

His lip curled into a sneer. "Don't even think about running. I won't hesitate to put a bullet in your head. Where's the pack?"

Dumbstruck, she only stared in answer.

Extending his arm, he aimed the gun at her head. "The backpack, dammit! Where is it?"

What the hell is everyone's obsession over this friggin' bag? With a shaky finger, she pointed. "In the bedroom. Down the hall."

Where were all the neighbors? Wasn't anyone home these days to alert security? What about the cameras in the hall? *Robert, where are you?*

"Let's go." He waved the gun.

And be trapped in a bedroom with this lunatic? *No way, Jose.* Straightening her shoulders, she elevated her chin and glared. "What's so important about the pack?"

"You're carrying something that belongs to me."

Her mind raced through the contents. What was he talking about? Everything belonged to her—just a bunch of inexpensive supplies for art class. She shook her head. "Jan gave me an empty bag, Eric, and I double-checked."

"I don't have all damn day." He kicked over the fern. "Get the pack, Lauren, and I'll prove it. Move!" He jerked the gun in the direction of the hall.

A feverish gaze cut her in two. His finger twitched on the gun's trigger, and his hand shook. He held a nine millimeter, but she didn't know enough about pistols to guess how many bullets were in the clip. Probably one too many. *Shit.* Hands still raised, she edged toward the center of the living room.

"Not that way. Bedroom!"

Her stomach turned into a hard knot, but she lowered her hands and faced him. "No." Even if she maneuvered around him and bolted out the door, she'd catch a bullet in her back running for the stairwell. No way could she possibly outrun such a weapon.

"Don't force me to shoot you dead."

Backpack. Black sedan. Torres. She gasped and stared at this wild-eyed maniac. "You knew Rafael!" She pointed. "He's the one who messed up your face." Eyes wide, her knees weakened, and she staggered. "You killed him!"

Gaze blazing, he approached. "He double-crossed me. I told him the pack was my job, but he went ahead without me. I didn't know he'd been following you until the day I showed at your rooming house. With him gone, I'll have the whole seven mil to myself."

Seven million...dollars? In the pack? She reached to steady herself but nearly toppled an English ivy plant. Snapping back her hand, she locked her knees. "You're crazy!" Damn, her voice squeaked. She coughed. "Look, why don't I hide in the closet? You grab the pack and leave. You made enough noise to wake the dead, you know." But even the dead weren't coming to the rescue. Maybe no one lived across the hall. Maybe the whole damn building was empty.

Gun hand quivering, he crept toward her. "You're coming with me, doll. With seven mil in my pocket, I'll live like a king in a castle."

More like a court jester in a jail cell. She backed away and knocked over the aloe plant. *Dammit.* "What about Jan? Did you hurt her?"

His eyebrows shot halfway into his hairline. "Of course not, but if you believe I'd choose Jan over you, you're wrong. You've got everything I need, babe— looks, sex appeal, and smarts. With my windfall, I can take care of you for a long time."

Probably lock her in a tower somewhere like a fairy-tale princess. *As if I won't try to escape.* She jutted her chin. "I don't want any part of you, Eric."

He narrowed his gaze. "You're my insurance, in case we meet Deems on the way out. Now, get the pack. I won't say it again."

"Good, because I'm tired of hearing you." She shifted her gaze to the front door. With Eric moving toward her, he left a nice opening behind him, but where the hell could she run?

No, she must stall for time. Someone *had* to hear the gunshots. If anything, she'd fight until death rather than be Eric's hostage.

He released a growl, lunged forward, and grabbed her arm, nearly ripping the bone from the socket. A sharp pain shot through her shoulder, and she screamed. *Damn, that hurt.*

Shoving the nuzzle of the gun under her chin, he

jerked her head upward. "We'll go to the bedroom together. Otherwise, I'll blow off your head." He yanked on her arm.

Gun or no gun, she wasn't one to be pushed around. *I'm dead anyway.* Lauren swung a fist toward his head while simultaneously lifting a knee to his groin.

He released a loud oomph and buckled but recovered to swing the gun at her head.

Metal impacted. Bone cracked. The room whirled.

Eric clutched her throat and jammed the gun between her eyes.

The metal felt cold against her skin, and the distinct smell of gun oil hit her nose. Images of her father and brother hunting groundhogs passed through her mind. Strange to think of something so silly when the hand gripping her throat tightened against her airway. Her father would never forgive her if she didn't fight. Pain ignored, she again kneed Eric's groin and buckled him enough to loosen his hold. But she hit the floor, too dizzy to escape. Nausea churned her stomach. She crawled along the floor, struggling to clear her vision. Blood dripped onto the white carpet. *Oh, my God, Mrs. Stewart's rug!*

Eric released a harsh laugh, jerked her to her feet, and struck her jaw with the pistol.

Her head snapped, and a gray glaze covered her vision. She lost all sense of place and time. No sounds registered. No one rushed to the rescue. Eric forced her onto feet that refused to move. *So, this is what it's like to die.*

****

Deems led Baylor into the condo lobby and

stopped with a quick glance in all directions. Robert was not at the desk. Although not unusual for security to be on the upper floors helping a tenant, nevertheless, an uneasy quiver vibrated his gut…especially after what Baylor uncovered. Of course, Robert could be on the fourth floor settling Lauren's personal guard.

Baylor stepped alongside. "Something wrong?"

"No security guard." Deems circled the desk and crunched something beneath his shoe. A broken juice bottle and its liquid contents had spilled onto the floor. He released a sigh of relief. "The mess explains his absence. He's gone for a mop."

Baylor cocked a brow. "Hopefully, not all the way to the discount store." He looked around. "Does this place have a utility closet nearby?" Without waiting for an answer, Baylor walked down the short hall behind the desk where several doors lined the corridor.

Remaining in the lobby, Deems glanced at the blinking red lights on the desk phone. Nine messages waited. Robert had been gone from the desk too long. The uneasy quiver intensified. Then he spotted the smear of blood on the linoleum floor. "Baylor!" He pointed.

With his back to Deems, Baylor waved a hand over his head. "Way ahead of you, Lambert. I'm following a blood trail." He opened the door to the utility closet.

Deems hurried to join Baylor. "The door should be locked." A security infraction. Robert would never slacken with protocol.

Baylor entered and flipped the light switch. "Whoa!"

Gut lurching, Deems froze in the doorway.

A moaning Robert lay sprawled on the floor,

bleeding from a back wound. He looked like death with his eyes closed and face whiter than the paint on the wall. His cell phone was by the door, smashed into pieces.

Baylor knelt alongside and lifted the material on Robert's shirt. "Stab wound near the spleen. Not good. Call 9-1-1—damn!" He locked onto Deems' stare. "Service revolver is gone."

Deems bolted to the security desk as two patrolmen rushed through the double doors, hands on their holstered guns.

One officer held out a hand in a stop gesture. "We received several calls for this location."

"In the utility room." Deems pointed. "Detective Baylor is with him. We need an ambulance." Several calls? And no one bothered to investigate? The poor man might have bled to death.

"I'll handle the ambulance, sir." The officer clicked the button on his shoulder mike. "Ambulance to this location." He looked at Deems with an inquiring lift to his brow.

"Stab wound," Baylor answered as he approached, holding out his badge.

The officer cocked his head. "The calls were for gunshots."

Gunshots? Deems' breath froze. Robert's service revolver!

A female voice crackled on the officer's mike. "You still have an open 9-1-1 line, the one where we heard the struggle."

Robert's phone was smashed into pieces. Who then—

Deems snapped his gaze to the computer screens.

The first four stairwell cameras were out, as was the fourth floor hall camera. Five and up worked. *Holy shit*! He gripped the detective's arm. "Lauren! Hurry!" Adrenaline pumping, Deems ran for the stairwell, vaguely hearing Baylor's instructions for one officer to tend to the security guard. Slamming open the door, Deems raced up the staircase, taking the steps two at a time.

The quiver in his gut grew into a full-blown volcanic eruption. He'd left her alone. Had Eric seen him leave and waited for an opportune moment to ambush Robert?

From five steps behind, Baylor huffed out a breath. "Lambert, we need to go first."

"Like hell!" For Lauren, he'd willingly put himself in harm's way. He prayed she was all right. On the third floor landing, he nearly fell over a man bleeding from a chest wound. Crew cut, no neck. Deems gasped. "He's the man who grabbed Torres!"

Kneeling alongside, Baylor placed his fingers against the man's neck. "He's still alive." He lifted the man's open suit jacket, inspected the wound, and then stood. "Bullet wound." Turning to the officer behind him, the detective withdrew his service revolver. "Call dispatch for another ambulance. Stay here with him. I'll continue with Lambert."

Baylor led the way to the fourth floor and, gun ready, approached Lauren's door only to see the lock splintered from the frame. He used a palm to stop Deems. "Wait here."

Wait? Was he nuts? Not giving a damn if the cop arrested him, Deems followed into the living room and stopped. Chaos stretched before him. Splattered blood stained the white rug and sofa. Toppled plants strewed their dirt everywhere with several stems and flowers crushed from a heavy foot. Not a sound greeted him except for his heart pounding in his chest. *Oh, God, please let her be all right.* "Lauren?" *What if we're too late?* He'd never forgive himself.

While Baylor crept along the hallway to the bedrooms, Deems stepped toward the center of the living room. What if Eric escaped and took Lauren with him? What then? How would he find her?

An ache throbbed in the back of his throat. He couldn't swallow since every ounce of moisture vanished from his mouth. "Lauren?"

A soft moan flowed from the direction of the sunroom. He ran to find her crouched in the far corner between two cabinets, blood smearing her beautiful hair and drenching the left side of her T-shirt. Carol Stewart's prized orchids were scattered all over the floor along with a bag of opened plant food. "Baylor!" Whether the detective heard or not, he didn't give a damn. Deems fell to his knees beside her.

A vacant glaze covered her green eyes—no pain or anger nor any emotion of any kind, despite the whale of a bruise swelling on her left jaw. Cuts and bruises colored her knuckles, and the injury to the side of her head oozed blood. He choked on a sob. "Lauren?"

She turned those vacant eyes on him and gave a wisp of a smile. "He wanted the backpack...and me."

His chest tightened as her lids closed, and she passed out in his arms.

Chapter Twenty-Four

While Deems paced Metropolitan Hospital's crowded waiting area for the nurse to call him, he fought tears building behind his eyes. Lauren's CT scan revealed a slight crack on the left side of her skull but no internal hemorrhaging to the brain. She sustained a hairline fracture on her left jaw, bruises throughout her body, but no internal injuries of any kind, for which Deems was eternally grateful. Purple contusions discolored the knuckles on both her hands, and her left pinkie finger snapped in two with a splint now holding the bones in place. All in all, she put up a good fight. As much as he wanted to remain by her side, he couldn't watch the doctor stitch her head wound. So, he left before he bawled like a baby.

The camera footage covering the lobby showed Eric's premeditated attack on Robert. Knife in hand, he flew at Robert before the guard had a chance to react. Doctors confirmed the blade had penetrated Robert's spleen, and the man underwent emergency surgery with a full recovery anticipated.

To take his mind off the ungodly wait, Deems phoned Lou and explained the situation, canceled Lauren's security detail, and asked Lou to assign Robert's replacement. Normally, he'd ask his assistant, Betty, to do all this stuff, but she left for a weekend trip to Connecticut with her family. After disconnecting from Lou, he phoned the building's maintenance department and told the manager to make haste with the repairs to the Stewarts' condo once the NYPD crime scene crew finished their work. The door, the rugs, and several pieces of furniture needed the best repair available, and he wanted the place spotless before the Stewarts returned. He'd notify Carol and Bill tomorrow to inform them of the 'death' of some of their precious babies.

From the hallway, a plump woman with a head of silver hair gestured with a quick wave of her hand. "Mr. Lambert?"

With his stomach fluttering, he followed her down a row of curtained bays full of moaning and groaning patients. "How's she doing?"

Smiling, she glanced over her shoulder. "Not bad considering. We wheeled her from the trauma room to a bay on the end. She's awake." She led the way around the nurses' station until stopping to swing open a drape. "The doctor is writing her discharge papers."

Deems hesitated. Why, he wasn't sure. He couldn't shake the heavy feeling in his chest nor ease the flutter in his belly.

The nurse nodded toward the opening. "She'll be all right. I'll leave you two in privacy." She retreated to another part of the emergency room.

Deems entered a ten-by-twelve-foot bay with curtains on three sides. A wall with cabinets and sink was to the rear. Over the stretcher hung a monitor showing a heart rate and a bunch of numbers of which he had no clue.

Lauren's eyes were closed. She had a sheet snuggled under her chin with her body curled into a ball. The discoloration to the left side of her jaw was more pronounced against the paleness of her face. A black eye slowly rose to the surface as the blood from her head wound pooled beneath the skin around her left eye socket.

A lump caught in his throat to see her so banged up. Yet, he had to stand still and let the relief sink in. He'd almost lost her and silently cursed Eric, damning him to hell. And Jan… He blamed his sister for all that happened. She'd brought Eric into her life, and Eric nearly took Lauren's. Deems had warned Jan, but, of course, she was love-struck and rejected his advice. At the thought, he gripped the stretcher's handrail.

Lauren touched his hand. Startled, he looked down to see one green eye watching him. The other eye was half-closed from the pooled blood. He leaned over to kiss her swollen lips then tucked a strand of loose hair behind her ear. "I don't think I've ever run up four flights of stairs so fast."

Her lips twitched into a half-grin. "Eric?"

"Escaped. Your backpack is missing so he grabbed what he came for."

A tear formed against the bridge of her nose.

Snapping a tissue from the box behind her, he dabbed her good eye.

She took the tissue and patted the swollen eye. With an effort, she rolled onto her butt and winced before shooting him a pleading gaze. "Deems—"

Somehow, he understood precisely what she wanted. He slipped his hands under her armpits and helped reposition her body on the stretcher.

Grimacing, she mouthed the words, "Thank you." Elevating her left hand, she inspected the splinted pinkie. "I threw Mrs. Stewart's prized orchids at Eric. She'll hate me." A tear rolled down her cheek.

Oh, God, this woman was beaten to hell, and all she worried about were flowers. He slipped his hand under her uninjured one and stroked her skin with his thumb. "You leave everything to me. Your job is to rest and recuperate."

"But the mess—"

He wagged a finger. "I've already notified the proper personnel."

A smile curled one side of her mouth. "You can tell her not to pay me for these last two weeks."

"I'm sure she won't hear of such a request." He fingered a few strands of her hair, damp after a quick rinse to wash out the blood. The doctor shaved her hair to stitch her head wound but left the area uncovered. Cringing, he counted the stitches. *Eight, nine, maybe ten.* "The doctors are releasing you, as long as you go easy for the next few days. You'll miss some class time, but you can return if you promise not to do anything strenuous."

"I promise." She shifted on her butt. "What about Jan? Does she know?"

At the mention of his sister's name, he bristled. All his anger resurfaced, and he swallowed hard. "Baylor called her." *Thankfully.* Otherwise, Deems might strangle his own sister.

Lifting her hand from his, she toyed with his jacket sleeve. Then she opened the suit jacket to inspect his shirt and tie. Another tear fell. "Your clothes are ruined."

Blood smeared every part of his clothing. Her blood. From holding her. "Don't care." She looked so beaten-down and vulnerable, and his throat tightened. He wished he could erase all her pain and wrap her in his arms. Instead, he leaned on the bed rail, reclaimed her hand, and kissed the bruised knuckles. "I have instructions on what you can and cannot do. You're to listen to me, hear?"

"Yes, sir." She yawned and winced than shot him a sheepish glance. "Everything hurts."

He brushed a thumb across her swollen lips. She kissed the tip, and his heart melted. "We'll leave as soon as Lou gets here. In the meantime, they're giving you a pain reliever."

"I can use something." She shifted her butt on the thin gurney pad and then met his gaze. "Are you staying with me?"

"Of course. The doctor stipulated you not be left alone. You know, someone to make sure you don't experience a change in mental status."

The silver-haired nurse entered, holding a filled syringe at the ready and an ice pack. She smiled at Deems. "The needle for her posterior and the ice for her eye."

Clearing his throat, he released Lauren's hand and stepped toward the curtain. "I'll check on Lou." No way could he watch the nurse stick a needle into Lauren's pretty butt.

****

Lauren's headache jarred her awake. The room was nearly dark, or perhaps nearly light. She couldn't tell which. The pain killer had knocked her out, and she had no idea how she arrived wherever she was. She lifted her head and looked around.

A large, unfamiliar bedroom stretched before her.

Propping herself onto one elbow, she winced from the throb of muscles unwilling to cooperate. Then, she nearly poked herself in the eye with her pinkie splint while reaching to hold her pounding head in place. Sighing, she scanned the king-sized bed with a sound-asleep Deems beside her. A digital clock on his nightstand showed five-fifteen. Predawn. She'd been out for a good eleven hours.

Slipping from the covers, she stood shakily with an aim for the nearest bathroom. A draft caught her backside. She glanced down to see herself wearing an oversized T-shirt smelling of musk, no socks, no pants, or underwear. Every part of her body complained with movement, but she shuffled toward a side door and, with luck, discovered the master bath, also large. A cute, little light over the toilet allowed her to see and, thankfully, hid her reflection in the mirror.

Afterward, she re-entered the bedroom and wiggled her toes in the plush carpeting. Floor-to-ceiling draperies stretched the entire length of one wall, the center partially opened to allow the glow of city lights through the glass. Heavy, masculine furniture decorated the room and, even in dim light, showed solid brass hardware. She approached the windows.

Shifting aside the drapes, she experienced a strange sense of disorientation at the view. She rubbed her one good eye and then looked again. The city lights twinkled back, along with headlights from Manhattan's never-ending traffic. But her gaze froze on the sight of the copper-tiled church steeple and the rooftop garden. The same view met her every night from the Stewarts' sunroom. *This scene isn't possible...unless I'm higher in the same building.*

With a shake of her head, she closed her eyes and debated whether she was delusional from the pain medication. Seconds later, she peeked, but the view hadn't changed. Her stomach fluttered.

Releasing the drapes, she turned toward the bed. Deems hadn't stirred. His chest rose and fell with each easy breath, and he looked so peaceful. Could they be in the same building? But really now, how many copper-tiled church steeples rose in Manhattan?

Her thoughts collided. Rubbing her forehead, she willed her headache to ease. Not like she expected the ache to miraculously disappear, but being confused and bewildered only added to the tension. She tiptoed from the bedroom and entered a wide hall. The way led to an open space, wider and longer than a baseball diamond. A combination living room, dining room, entertainment center, and kitchen made for one gigantic room. The layout was similar to the Stewarts' but on a much-larger scale.

The appliances' digital displays provided enough illumination to see, and she spotted her basket of Granny Smith apples on the kitchen counter. With a cracked jaw, apples were definitely off the menu for a while.

In the living room, another set of windows drew her. The floor-to-ceiling draperies were fully retracted to reveal a magnificent view of Central Park and lampposts lighting the asphalt walkways. From this height and in the predawn light, the city took on an enchanted look, beautiful in its own way. She half-expected to see little fairies dancing on the grass.

For the first time since arriving in New York, she had the strongest desire to stay put and not think of the past or future. Between the panoramic setting through the windows combined with the size of his condo, she wanted to enjoy the moment for however long it lasted. If Deems walked into the room and asked her to stay, he'd hear her say "yes" without a second of hesitation. Then, of course, he'd drop from a faint.

"Lauren?"

Holy shit, he really did walk in. She turned to see him wearing only a pair of boxer shorts. His hair was mussed and chest bare, but damn if he didn't look sexy as hell. "You live here?"

"Yes." With both hands, he rubbed his eyes while pulling down on his face in a scrub. "I hadn't meant to show you so soon, but you can't return to the Stewarts' place." Dropping his hands to his sides, he met her gaze. "I hated keeping the secret, Lauren."

Something emptied inside her. She wasn't sure what. Another man hiding a secret, she supposed. Were all men genetically programmed to be so mysterious? Maybe they harbored a superiority complex that warned them not to be honest. Turning away, she stared out the window. "All this time, we've been in the same building." Gut clenched, she faced him. "Why were you afraid to tell me?"

"I had my reasons."

Typical male response. They *always* had their reasons, right or wrong. Her gaze fell onto the far left wall where a metal spiral staircase caught her eye. At the bottom was a lit Exit sign over a door. She followed the spiral upward to another door and pointed. "Where's that go?"

"To the roof."

The roof? That meant...*ohmygod*! Her heart rate

skyrocketed. "We're in the penthouse? But you told me you lived in a company-paid condo." More secrets. What was this, his tell-the-truth time? She licked a pair of dry lips. "You must be a damn good employee."

"I have one of the best territories in the world, Lauren." Lips tight, he crossed his arms over his bare chest and meandered across the carpet. "I don't tell too many women. I never know if they love me or the money."

"You can't hide the fact you earn a decent income, Deems. Your expensive suits are a dead giveaway." She wandered away from the windows toward the art work on the walls. Rembrandt, Picasso, and van Gogh. *Holy crap. The crème de la crème.* She swallowed hard. "Okay, so you have fantastic paintings, live in a company condo, and have a limo at your disposal. You were afraid to tell me, because women notoriously latch onto a man with money, and I'm a woman who is flat broke." Turning toward him, she gave a half-smile. "I understand, Deems."

He approached the windows and placed his hands on his hips while staring out over Central Park. His silhouette against the predawn light with his back straight and legs slightly apart gave her the impression of a man who alone created the City of New York. Her father had the same stance whenever he stood on the high hill and surveyed his orchards.

"I own High-Rise International, Lauren." He shot her a quick glance.

What—wait! Something was wrong with her hearing. Maybe the blow to her head interfered with her auditory sensors. She cleared her throat. "According to the Internet, High-Rise is privately owned." Her gut twisted. "Privately owned by you?"

"Correct."

Every muscle in her body froze. He wasn't just a man with a great job. Hell, he owned a company worth billions. How could he possibly be attracted to a woman struggling to make ends meet? Too stunned to move, she stared.

He ran his hands through his already mussed hair and wandered away from the window. "I rarely let a woman into my world anymore, Lauren. Far too many are self-centered and want nothing more than an easy life." Gaze intense, he approached. "You're the first woman I've met with substance. You work hard and depend on no one." He took her good hand in his and smiled. "I'm hopelessly in love with you, Lauren Howell. I don't give a damn if you spend every penny I have."

Her breath hitched. "You're in love with me?" She choked on her own saliva, coughed, gasped, and stumbled toward the sofa. His hand reached, but she waved him away. Like a blind woman feeling her way, she patted the sofa's armrest and flopped onto the end cushion. Garbled thoughts clouded her brain, and she struggled to make sense out of something incomprehensible. She met his gaze. "Who are you?"

"A wealthy man in love for the first time in my life."

No...hell. Was he for real? Maybe she was still asleep and having a great dream. But his face was so serious. How could she *not* believe him? She stifled a sob. "You've been dating a woman with absolutely no money, Deems. I can't even pay the hospital bill."

"I've already settled the bill." He slipped onto the

sofa beside her and cupped her knee. "I wanted our relationship to build on its own, Lauren. You stressed a friendship, but we both realize we've become much more." With a finger touch, he lifted her chin to force her gaze to meet his. "Stay in New York with me."

Oh, God, now what? Ten minutes ago, she'd have said yes. He was the answer to all her prayers, and she loved him so much. She'd be out of her mind to refuse a lifestyle of luxury. But what kind of lifestyle? A rich man's mistress? Any normal woman would jump into his arms and kiss him senseless. But not Lauren Howell. She wasn't one to sit around and polish her nails. "I'll have to think about this piece of news, Deems. You threw an awful lot at me all at once." She stroked his cheek, and stubbles tickled her fingertips. "I'm not sure I can handle this city as a steady diet." With a heavy heart, she dropped her hands into her lap and stared at her splinted pinkie. "These months with Antonio have been hard. Every day, I feel like the walls are closing in, and I can't breathe."

He frowned, causing a deep crease at the bridge of his nose. "I already told you I can't move the company."

She brushed her palm along his thigh. "I understand, really, I do, but the country is in my blood. Maybe if you came home with me—"

Lips pinched, he shook his head. "Out of the question."

"Not even to visit my folks?" Brows high, she retracted her hand.

Scowling, he drummed his fingers on his knees. "At the moment, I don't see the need."

He answered her question about marriage. He

wasn't interested, and she sure as hell wouldn't mention the subject. "Okay, then, let me think about your offer." She stood.

"Lauren?"

One brow cocked, she met his gaze.

"You never said you loved me back." He shifted on the sofa cushion, his gaze scanning her face. "Do you?"

She brushed a lock of his hair to the side. "I love you more than you imagine, Deems, more than any man before you."

With a satisfied nod, he slapped his knees and stood while sweeping under her legs to lift her into his arms. "That's all that matters. Back to bed."

She threw a thumb over her shoulder toward the windows. "The sun's almost above the horizon."

"Yeah, well, to a country girl, the approaching daylight might mean something, but to me, I've still an hour of sleep left, and I'd like to spend the time holding you. Besides—"

She placed a finger to his lips. "The doctor—"

"I know what the doctor said. No sex for two weeks since such an activity has a tendency to raise blood pressure. I'll live with the disappointment, even if you leave New York without us having another chance to make love. I'm hoping you'll stay."

He entered the bedroom and slipped her onto the bed. Grateful for the softness against her aching body, she threw the covers onto her legs. Without moving, he stared down, his need obvious through his boxer shorts.

"I can offer you so much, Lauren."

Except what she desired the most—marriage and a family. She would not be a rich man's mistress, but the words stuck in her throat. *I must be a friggin' idiot.*

Chapter Twenty-Five

After a long soak in a whirlpool tub, Lauren toweled herself and actually felt human again, despite looking in the mirror to see a woman used as a punching bag. The ache in her head and jaw had eased, and one eye was no longer half-shut from swollen tissue, but the knuckles on both hands were the problem. Her fingers swelled with excess fluid, and the stiffness made normal activities impossible. Like holding a bar of soap. Or closing the zipper to her jeans. The pinkie splint hadn't improved matters. Hell, her entire hand could be splinted with what use her fingers provided.

Earlier, Deems ran to the fourth floor for some of her belongings. While there, he talked to the head of maintenance who received clearance from the NYPD. Repairs to the condo were scheduled to begin immediately. Deems invited her to spend the next few days with him, and of course, she accepted. What woman wouldn't love to live temporarily like a queen? This week, her classes would conclude. Then, in two weeks, the Stewarts would return, and she'd be on her way home to put her life back in order. *And missing Deems terribly.*

She hadn't discussed his offer any further. In her heart, she couldn't be indebted to anyone—not even Deems, especially in the role as mistress. While not adverse to spending more time in New York, she loved the hills of Adams County too much to move permanently. Harrisburg had been a hop, skip, and jump to Arendtsville whenever she wanted to clear the smog and crowds out of her system. *If only Deems agreed to a visit...*

But he was right. His life and business were here, and she hadn't any expectations on a compromise. He was, after all, a self-made billionaire who dictated rules to everyone around him. She didn't belong in his world nor he in hers. End of story.

"Lauren, you have a visitor!"

"Be there in a minute." Truthfully, she wouldn't hurry even if the Queen of England waited.

Barefoot, Lauren left the bedroom to see Jan pacing the living room, looking like a flowing flower in her loose clothing. Deems stood behind the kitchen counter chopping vegetables for their noontime meal. From the way he whacked the knife onto the cutting board, he was none too happy with his sister.

Both brother and sister shifted their gazes onto Lauren.

Throwing a hand over her mouth, Jan cried out and ran to Lauren. Her hands reached but never touched, and her gaze circled Lauren's face. "Oh, Lauren, I'm so sorry. I don't know what got into him." She bit her lip. "Do you hurt?"

"Everywhere but my feet."

Jan stiffened her back, jutted her chin, and glared. "You scared him away."

Wow. Jan transformed from wimpy little co-ed to a woman defending her man. Right or wrong, Lauren gave her credit. Frankly, she didn't give a damn if Jan hated her guts. Whatever Eric wanted from her backpack drove him to desperation. She wandered to the sofa and curled into the corner.

In daylight, the penthouse took on a whole new look. Soft, tan leather sofas faced each other with a round, glass table in between. Two matching chairs sat at opposite ends, gold-stemmed lamps rested on glass tables at all four sofa corners, and accents with orange pillows were placed for color offset. Beautifully decorated by a professional, no doubt.

Deems slammed the knife onto the cutting board, making both women jump. "I warned you about him, Jan. He was no good."

Jan flopped onto the opposite sofa and buried her face in her hands. "No one cares about my fiancé."

How could one argue with such a close-minded mentality? In Jan's eyes, Eric was a saint. She had no clue Eric planned to skip town without her—and drag Lauren along for fun and games.

Lauren glanced at Deems, who stood behind the kitchen counter with his arms crossed over his chest, his right hand yielding his chopping knife. He looked like a Samurai warrior posing for a photo, complete with stern expression. When their gazes met, he smirked, relaxed his stance, and unfolded his arms.

He placed the knife on the counter. "You owe Lauren an apology, Jan."

Straightening, Jan glared at Lauren. "I won't apologize for Eric."

"No, you should apologize for not believing Lauren's side of the story." He clanged a pan onto the stove burner.

"Oh." With a quick glance at Lauren, Jan cringed.

257

"Deems is right. I should apologize. I'm sorry." She leaned forward with elbows on her knees and gaze staring at the rug. "I still don't believe everything you told me, Lauren." She glanced up. "Eric never looked at another woman whenever he was with me."

Lauren stopped her mouth from falling open. *Holy crap.* Jan's naivety reached a whole different dimension. Stifling a retort, she wagged a finger. "You can't keep a man on a leash, Jan. From the moment Eric moved in, his aggression grew progressively worse."

Shifting her gaze, Jan shuffled her sandaled feet on the rug. "I should have told you our plans before springing the news, but I wanted you to stay."

"If I was left alone, I would have stayed, and if he loved you enough, he wouldn't come after me." *Hint, hint.* Like talking to a brick wall.

Deems' condo phone rang—a bright yellow one hanging on the wall in the kitchen.

After a brief conversation, Deems replaced the receiver and approached the sofa. "Detective Baylor just got in the elevator."

Seconds later, a chime echoed through the penthouse. Deems walked over to a set of double doors and opened them to show Detective Baylor standing in the middle of the elevator.

Raising a brow, Lauren turned to Jan. "The elevator opens into the living room?"

Waving her hand, Jan nodded. "Those doors are like a front door. The person in the elevator can't enter without a key." With a quick glance at her brother, she smiled. "I can see you two have something special brewing. I'm glad."

Heaviness settled in the center of Lauren's chest,

and she stared out the wide expanse of windows where a bright, blue sky beckoned. Too bad Deems hadn't proposed. She'd stay in a heartbeat. "I'll leave in two weeks."

Leaning forward, Jan gaped. "He didn't ask you to stay?"

"Yes, he asked."

"Oh." Jan blinked several times then cocked her frizzy head. "You're giving up a lot."

More than she cared to admit.

The two men approached.

Baylor's gaze locked onto Jan. "I'm glad you're here, Ms. Lambert. Has Drummer contacted you?"

Shoulders slumped, Jan shook her head.

Deems waved the detective toward a chair. "Have a seat, Baylor. You look done in."

The detective dropped into a side chair with a grateful sigh. "I haven't stopped moving since yesterday." He glanced at Lauren. "How do you feel?"

Smirking, Lauren toyed with the edging on the sofa cushion. "Like I completed ten rounds in a boxing ring."

A smile touched one side of his mouth. "We have an APB out on Drummer, and two cops positioned to watch the brownstone. If he found what he wanted in the pack, then he's probably long gone."

Deems stood at Lauren's end of the sofa. "Who was the man in the stairwell?"

Frowning, Baylor tugged on his white tie. "An insurance investigator who followed Torres' and Drummer's trail from the Bahamas. He and his partner were out to recover the seven-million-dollar, diamond-studded necklace stolen from a courier." He eyed Jan

259

through slits. "A courier who was murdered not far from your hotel, Ms. Lambert."

Brows fluttering, Jan shifted her gaze from her brother to Lauren then to Baylor. "Don't look at me like I know anything about a courier, and I certainly know nothing about a necklace." Her mouth pinched. "You're accusing my fiancé of murder?"

Deems held up a finger. "You mentioned Eric disappeared for a whole day, Jan."

Mouth twisting to the side, she waved aside the comment. "I thought he got lost or something."

Baylor coughed. "According to our information, your fiancé tucked the necklace inside the lining of your backpack, Ms. Lambert. *You* carried the bag through customs."

Eyes wide, Jan stared.

Lauren shook her head. "I found no necklace in the pack, Detective. You examined the lining yourself."

He turned a sharp gaze onto her. "How do we know, Ms. Howell? According to the Arendtsville PD, your financial situation is bleak. Finding a valuable piece of jewelry can be tempting."

Great. First, the Harrisburg cops accused her of being in cahoots with Jo-Jo's embezzlement scheme. Now, jewelry theft. Sighing, she glanced at Deems, at a loss for a defense. "I didn't steal anything."

Sitting on the arm of the sofa, Deems patted her shoulder while directing his attention toward Baylor. "By chance, was this insurance investigator driving a black sedan with tinted windows?"

Using a hand, Baylor stifled a yawn then gave a quick nod. "The same one. His partner was still sitting in the driver's seat when all the hoopla started. He provided us with a lot of details about the robbery." He crossed his legs. "Since the necklace was no longer in the pack, why was your fiancé so desperate to retrieve it, Ms. Lambert?"

Avoiding eye contact, Jan shifted on the seat cushion. "I don't know."

"I understand the pack was originally yours. He had to tell you something."

She shook her head. "He told me nothing."

Jan's voice spoke volumes. Like most men, Eric kept secrets. He wouldn't dare brag about a seven-million-dollar heist to a woman with Jan's innocence, especially if he had every intention of leaving her behind. Catching the detective's gaze, Lauren pursed her lips. "You know, the day Jan and Eric returned from the Bahamas, Eric received a phone call and left with the pack. You remember, Jan?"

Her brows lifted. "Yeah. He had to dump the dirty laundry, but he never explained why he ran out."

The detective slapped his knees and stood. "Well, if anyone thinks of anything else, please let me know. As much as I'd like to sit here, I've a ton of paperwork to do." He turned to Lauren with a slight bow. "Ms. Howell, if possible, I'd like you to come to the station tomorrow for an official statement." He turned to Jan. "As for you, Ms. Lambert, I'm afraid you're coming with me."

"Wait a minute!" Deems' hand tensed on Lauren's shoulder before he jumped from the sofa arm and approached Jan's side. "Why should she go with you?"

With an appreciative gaze on her brother, Jan released a long sigh. Her face reflected her adoration, and Deems responded with a reassuring pat on the top of her head.

Baylor rubbed his stubbled chin as his gaze locked onto Deems. "So far, she's guilty by association. Not a chargeable offense, but I need a detailed statement. If I uncover her lying to protect Drummer, then I'll press accessory after the fact charges."

Standing, Jan straightened her flowery clothes and faced her brother. "I'll go and tell him anything he wants to know, but Eric kept me in the dark." Stretching on tiptoe, she kissed his cheek. "I think I should have a lawyer by my side."

"I'll see you have the best."

Jan turned to Lauren. "I'm really sorry."

As if mere words eased the pains of broken bones. Lauren simply shrugged and toyed with her shirt hem, unable to meet Jan's gaze. For a while, their friendship stood on solid ground. They even talked about meeting in Harrisburg so Lauren could show her apple country. She inwardly sighed. Too bad Deems wasn't interested in a similar tour.

Chapter Twenty-Six

After the elevator descended with Jan and Baylor on board, Deems extracted his cell phone from his pocket and punched in a series of numbers.

Lauren watched him in silence and marveled how he so easily commanded attention. From the gist of his conversation, he arranged for Jan's legal counsel. Finished, he replaced his phone and stood stationary, head bent, hands stuffed into his trouser pockets. Her heart tumbled in her chest, for the man looked so defeated. "Jan's a grown woman, Deems, making her own choices in life. She'll live through the embarrassment of being associated with Eric, just as I have with Jo-Jo."

Grunting, he returned to the kitchen to resume chopping.

Her cell phone chirped indicating a text message. She slipped the device from her jeans back pocket. Brows high, she glanced up at Deems. "I've a message from my mom. In yesterday's mail, a letter arrived from one of our home town banks. An account has been opened in my name by Mark Jordan."

The chopping stopped, and he narrowed his gaze. "How much?"

"She doesn't say. I'm to contact the bank officer in person before access will be granted." She grunted. "He listened to you."

Deems gave a crisp nod. "He has no choice, Lauren. If he rights all the wrongs, he'll retain his job with the company. He's still a damn good salesman."

And an even better liar. Jo-Jo had fooled everyone, and she wouldn't be a bit surprised if strings were attached to the bank account. Her phone rang in her hand. She rolled her eyes at the insistent shrill and glanced at caller ID. "This is Mr. Stewart." Cringing, she answered.

"Ms. Howell, are you all right? Deems called this morning and explained everything."

She stole a quick peek at Deems. "I'm so sorry about Mrs. Stewart's orchids."

"Don't worry about them. She'll buy more. Frankly, dear, you did me a favor by having a few plants destroyed. Hopefully, you cut down on the garden-store look. Please, don't replace anything and tell Deems, too."

"I will. Thank you, Mr. Stewart."

"We'll be home Friday."

So soon? "You're not cutting your trip short for me, are you?"

"No, no. My son called from New Jersey. His wife is in premature labor with their second child. Carol promised to be there."

"Well, congratulations then. I'll see you Friday." *Rats.* Since her art class ended on Thursday, she had hoped to spend an entire week in total luxury and simply enjoy her time with Deems. *Not to be, dammit.*

Heart sinking, she disconnected and stood from the sofa, but thoughts collided all at once. Mouth agape, she whirled toward Deems. "Ohmygosh, they're coming home. Will the repairs to the condo be done?"

He gave her a lopsided grin. "The head honcho assured me everything will be perfect in a day or two. You have time."

Her posture relaxed, and she approached the counter. "I should have told Mr. Stewart not to pay me since I messed up the place." She slid the phone onto the counter while easing her butt onto a stool. Her gaze scanned the cutting board. Onions, green peppers, and mushrooms were chopped into tiny pieces. "What are you making?"

"Omelets. No chewing involved." Reaching for the stove, he turned on the burner under a pan.

His thoughtfulness formed a lump in her throat. Amazing how this man gripped her heart in all the right ways. He was perhaps the kindest and most considerate man she'd ever met. She cleared her throat. "Can I help?"

"No. You sit and watch. I'll have your meal ready in no time." He broke the eggs into a bowl, added salt and pepper, and beat them with a fork before dumping in half of the vegetables, and then pouring the mixture into the heated pan.

She smiled at his skill. "For a billionaire, you're handy in the kitchen."

"I wasn't always rich, my dear. Besides, cooking is a nice way to relax."

A man of many surprises. A beautiful condo, a prestigious job, money in the bank—all right, *a lot* of money in the bank. He probably had a bevy of women at his beck and call.

The vision depressed her. She hardly had the sophistication for a billionaire's world. Her country roots ran deep inside her veins. She enjoyed driving the tractor during apple harvest time and sneaking the first taste of cider from the apple press machine. Even her field trips with her art students were a joy as they learned the details of painting a pasture or waterfall.

"Something on your mind?"

She snapped from her trance to acknowledge the steaming food in front of her. "This omelet smells wonderful." The combined aromas of the vegetables made her salivate.

He inserted a corkscrew into a wine bottle and popped the cork. "You might be eating eggs for a while. The doctor said soft food for ten days before you try something more solid." He poured white wine into two glasses and set them on the counter before walking around with his plate to sit alongside her. "You seem reflective."

Using her fork, she toyed with the egg. "The first night we spent together, did you really run out for condoms or run here?"

He sipped his wine. "I ran here." With two fingers, he guided her chin to rotate her head, his gaze searching her face. "I don't make a habit of jumping into bed with any woman, Lauren. I can't even tell you the last time I had a date."

Again, her cell phone rang. She growled under her breath. "Why am I so popular all of a sudden?" She wanted to open a window and toss the phone to the street below. A fifteen-story drop should shatter the device into a thousand pieces. Except she had no money to replace the damn thing. She sighed heavily and stared at the caller ID. "I don't know this number."

Glancing at the phone, Deems nudged her arm. "I do. That's Mark Jordan. You should answer."

Her spine stiffened. "Why? I've nothing to say."

"But he does. Just talk to him."

To right the wrongs. Lauren glanced at Deems who flashed an encouraging smile. She pursed her lips. "All right, but I'm doing this for you, not him." Sighing, she picked up the phone and hit the *Accept* button.

"Lauren? It's Jo-Jo. Please, listen."

At the sound of his voice, she gripped the phone and resisted the temptation to hurl the device across the room. Memories flooded her mind. His betrayal. All his lies. "What do you want?"

"We need to talk. Can we meet somewhere?"

Yeah, on a mountainside so I can push you over the cliff. "I don't want to talk. We're done."

"Please, Lauren. A quick cup of coffee at a small cafe at Sixty-Ninth and Madison. Okay?"

She tightened her grip on the phone. "I'm not interested."

"I need to make amends. Please."

She closed her eyes and leaned her elbows on the counter while rubbing her forehead with her fingers. She damn near poked out her eye with the splinted pinkie.

"Please, honey, one last request."

"Don't call me honey, dammit." She should tell him to go stuff an egg. "What about your mom and sister?"

"I put them on the train this morning. They give you their love."

Oh, gee, how friggin' nice. Like I believe them. Where the hell was a dropped phone call when she needed one? She gritted her teeth and immediately felt the twinge in her jaw. "Not today, Jo-Jo. How about

267

tomorrow, say around eleven?"

"Today, Lauren. I'm on limited time."

"Tomorrow or not at all." She didn't give a damn if he were dying.

Silence. "Okay. I'll text you the address. Thanks, honey."

Honey, my ass. Wincing at the endearment, she disconnected and stared at her phone. "Somehow, I get the feeling Jo-Jo will screw me all over again."

****

She and Deems spent a wonderful night together—in bed and without sex. They talked, watched some television, and enjoyed a few laughs. She couldn't believe she was in bed with a billionaire. Not that his money made any difference. Even if he butchered beef for a living, he'd still be the same Deems—without the pricey suits. Then, he held her while she slept. She was so much in love she could cry.

In the morning, Lou drove Deems to the office then returned for her trip to the cafe. Deems refused to hear of her taking a cab, so she relented. After all, she looked like a used and abused punching bag. No acute pain today. Just a steady throb everywhere. If she had an ounce of common sense, she'd force Jo-Jo to meet her in Arendtsville, but urgency strangled her. She wanted him out of her life, and the sooner the better.

As she stood outside the condo entrance waiting for Lou, she let her gaze follow the traffic while she sucked in the cool air. The day was beautiful with clear skies and the scent of forsythias blowing from the park. Johnny, the security guard now on day shift, stood beside her. He had direct orders from Deems to glue himself to her side until Lou arrived. Since Eric still remained on the loose, he might return and make good on his promise to take her with him.

Lou glided the limo to the curb and, acknowledging to Johnny with a nod, hurried to open her door. As if she was incapable. But Lou was so sweet, gently taking her elbow like she was a frail, little old lady. He drove with hardly a sway, and a short drive later, he slowed the limo and pulled over to the curb.

With a quick glance into the rearview mirror, he waved toward the front windshield. "This area is notorious for poor parking, so I'll drop you here. When you're done, just text me."

Traffic was too heavy for Lou to run around to her door so she grabbed the handle. "That's fine, Lou. Thank you." She alighted and waited for him to drive off before continuing toward the cafe. She had absolutely no desire to share a cup of coffee with Jo-Jo. If truth be told, she'd rather have all her teeth extracted. But since her ex made the effort under the pretense of keeping his job, he'd have to carry out one hell of a sales pitch for her to believe him. Nearing the cafe, she drew in a deep breath, slowly released, then squared her shoulders and opened the door.

The coffee shop was simply called Mom and Pop's Coffee Nook, a cute, little place with small round tables big enough for a cup of coffee and bagel and not much else. One wall had square tables with people staring into open laptops, oblivious to everything except the contents on their screen.

Jo-Jo sat at a table by the window, sipping from the standard paper cup.

Her gut clenched at the sight of him as anger threatened to explode, and she purposely splayed her fingers to prevent fists from forming.

Catching her entrance, he raised a hand then froze as his blue eyes grew wide. "What happened to your face?" He stood to pull out her chair. Within seconds, fire burned in his gaze. "Did Lambert hurt you?"

"Good Lord, no." She flopped onto the seat. "Long story." His display of concern touched her but too little too late.

He reclaimed his seat and slid a covered cup of coffee her way. "French vanilla, the way you like it."

She popped the plastic lid and sipped. Delicious. He hadn't changed much. Same wavy blond hair, pale eyebrows, and sky-blue eyes. A classic California look that captured her attention the second he walked into the school cafeteria. For as long as she remembered, she listened to his dreams of one day being the town big shot with his own business and tons of money. She hadn't doubted his success either, except she preferred he'd achieve his goals in a different way. "Why'd you keep your interview with High-Rise a secret?"

"Aw—" He rubbed his palms on his thighs, his gaze intent on the passing foot traffic by the window. "I wasn't sure they'd hire me."

She leaned across the small table. "We were engaged, Jo-Jo. You should have said *something*, but obviously, you planned to skip town without me." Gad, how she wished she could get up and leave. Why the hell should she listen to his sorry excuses just so he could keep his job? She owed him nothing, dammit.

A strong sense of power filled her chest. She'd never seen him so nervous, and with good reason. She held the key to his future…assuming she had a vindictive bone in her body. If anything, watching him squirm brought her enough pleasure. She cocked her head and smirked. "You didn't expect me to come here all forgiveness, I hope. You left me so broke, I had to borrow money in order to survive."

He met her gaze. "But you hit pay dirt, Lauren. How'd you meet Mr. Lambert?"

"I happened to be living with his sister."

Shifting forward, he cocked his head. "Lambert's face glowed when you walked through the door the other night. The man's definitely in love."

"And I'm in love with him."

He smiled. "He's a very wealthy man. He'll buy you anything, even the art studio you've always wanted."

As if money mattered. She sneered. "I haven't agreed to our meeting for a lecture on my love life." She tilted her head forward and lowered her voice. "Why'd you take my clothes and art supplies?"

While swirling the contents, he stared into his coffee. "I told the movers to pack everything. They cleared the apartment in under two hours."

If she hadn't stopped to see her mother, she'd have walked in and spoiled his plans. How fortunate for him. "What made you so desperate? I know damn well you don't have creditors breathing down your neck. Why weren't you brave enough to tell me you wanted out?"

He shifted his gaze toward the window. "I had to make a clean break, Lauren." He met her gaze. "No more of this small-town stuff. I wanted a bigger life, and High-Rise International gave me the opportunity to finally leave my roots." He gulped a large amount of coffee and wiped his mouth with the back of his hand. "I also needed a lot of cash to start a new life. I knew you'd be all right."

If her knuckles weren't so damn bruised, she'd strangle him right here in the cafe. *And to think we were engaged.* Friggin' fool. Her blood hot, she seethed. "Well, I wasn't okay. You left me with rent due, no clothes to wear, and no money for either." She wiggled her left hand's fingers in his face. "In case you're wondering where the engagement ring went, I sold it to pay the back rent."

He reached across the table to touch her hand.

She retracted her arm and lowered both hands to her lap.

Sighing, he tugged on his shirt collar. "Look, Lauren, I told Mr. Lambert I had heavy debts because I had to say something. Don't spoil my chances with the company. I intend to repay every dime stolen."

"Commendable." Not like she believed a word. She twiddled her thumbs under the table. "You still haven't explained why the necessity for a clean break."

Shrugging, he draped an arm over the back of his chair. "You told me from the get-go about your brother inheriting the farm, but I never truly expected your parents to follow through." He stared out the window. "In my opinion, you and your brother should have received an equal split, and then, I planned to convince you to sell your half." Dropping his arm, he sat forward and wrapped both hands around his cup, his gaze intent on the contents. "To make matters worse, you got laid off. With Antonio's class delaying your job search, another school year would pass before you found work." Avoiding eye contact, he shook his head. "I couldn't afford to wait."

Her muscles tightened. *Dear Lord, give me*

strength. She narrowed her gaze. "That's why you left, because I didn't inherit part of the farm and lost a good-paying job?" She wanted to kill him or toss him into a vat of used coffee grounds so he could choke to death. How had she fallen in love with this asshole? She obviously missed all the clues—whatever the hell they were.

Drumming all ten fingers on the cup, he glanced her way. "Don't you see, Lauren? Your unemployment set us back a few years. I applied for this job, hoping to put us on track again."

She placed her palms flat on the table, nearly ready to lunge. "But we had the money for a sizable down payment on a house, yet you delayed—" Eyes wide, she gasped. "You purposely waited to see what my parents did with the farm! Jo-Jo, how could you?" Chest tight, she scraped her chair across the linoleum and stood.

He reached for her arm but stopped. "Keep this between us, Lauren. I don't see any purpose in telling Mr. Lambert. If I make good on all the trouble I caused, I've a cushy job waiting in South America. If you don't want to stay with Lambert, come with me."

Staggering from his words, she clutched the chair for support. The man had a way of taking away her breath and not in a good sense either. "Are you out of your mind?" She leaned close. "I was yours, Jo-Jo, but you tossed me to the wolves." She turned to leave then whirled back and glared. "If you're planning on retribution, don't forget my family. They loved you, and you hurt them as much as you hurt me." Too hell with his self-centered attitude. She fully intended to tell Deems verbatim about this eye-opening conversation.

Chapter Twenty-Seven

Lauren rushed through the coffeehouse doors as if the place was on fire. She couldn't get the hell out fast enough. She felt smothered and desperately needed fresh air. "Come back with me," Jo-Jo said. *Of all the gall!* To think she'd drop everything and pretend nothing happened.

Growing up, he was the one boy in class who skillfully talked his way out of a situation and threw the bullshit like no tomorrow. She should have realized he'd eventually throw the crap her way. More likely, he'd been throwing her shit all along, and she wore blinders. From the beginning, his sweet-talking attitude made for a successful salesman, and he had a good career ahead—with the emphasis on *had*. Unfortunately, he followed her out the door. *Aggh!*

Arms outstretched, he jumped ahead and walked backwards. "Lauren, please don't go away mad. I'm doing what Mr. Lambert requested."

She couldn't give a crap anymore about Jo-Jo's future with the company. Snarling, she faced him. "I seriously doubt he wanted you and me to couple-up again."

"Well, no. I blurted that, because I still love you."

More bullshit. *Do I have 'sap' stenciled to my forehead?* While sending a quick text to Lou, she scooted around him and headed down the street. Her muscles revolted from the stress and threatened to incite an analgesic overdose. When would this friggin' nightmare end? She glanced over her shoulder to find him following like a puppy on a leash. "Leave me alone. Do what you must to keep your job, but don't ever call me again. We're through, Jo-Jo."

Silence followed. Maybe he fell down an open manhole. When she arrived at the street corner, she looked over her shoulder, but Jo-Jo disappeared. Like a puff of smoke. Poof. *Good.*

Her hands hurt. She held out her palms to see nail indentations imbedded into the skin. All she wanted was to get the hell away and return to Deems. She'd fall into his arms and tell him everything and not give a damn whether he fired Jo-Jo. She owed her ex absolutely nothing.

Rotating her head, she scanned the busy thoroughfare. Lou wasn't in sight yet. With traffic being so heavy, he probably circled the block just to keep moving. She stepped closer to the corner store building to wait.

Why must her life be so complicated? Despite her dire circumstances, she thought she was doing quite well. Now, Jo-Jo re-entered to bring back all the anger and hurt. She wouldn't trust him even if he solved world peace.

A strong grip on her arm slammed her against the brick wall. Gasping at the roughness, she met Eric's wild-eyed gaze. He had a black eye and a cut lip, but his snarl sounded more like an animal than a man.

Jutting his face close, he jammed a hard object against her ribs. "I want the keys."

Well, his appearance just about makes my day.

Pursing her lips, she squirmed against his grip. "Let go of me."

"Not until you give me the keys. They weren't in the pack."

The keys? Why did he want her keys? The last she remembered she stuffed them into her jeans' pocket before she answered the door. Now, where the hell were they? "I don't have them, Eric. I'm not even sure they came home with me from the hospital."

His growl deepened. "I need those keys, Lauren." He twisted his grip.

The man was bound and determined to bruise every inch on her body. Damn him. "I can't make them materialize out of thin air, Eric." She tensed her muscles and yanked her arm free. Whirling, she shoved on Eric's measly chest. "What the hell do you want? You plan on shooting me right here on the street corner?" *Lou, where are you*?

Several passing people heard the tone of her voice and turned to stare. Of course, no one stopped. Heaven forbid anyone should get involved. If Eric confronted her on the streets of Arendtsville, he'd be strong-armed to the ground by a cluster of farmers.

Shoving the gun into his jacket pocket, Eric growled close to her ear. "I need those keys, Lauren. One of them is mine."

"And the key unlocks your precious necklace. Yes, I know all about your heist, Eric. Every cop in the city is looking for you." She adjusted her jacket sleeve. "Why don't you surrender?"

Shifting his gaze up and down the street, he jammed her against the wall. "Keep your damn voice down."

Like hell. Gun or not, she had her limits. Lifting her knee, she hit him dead center in the crotch. He buckled and put his face in a perfect position for another knee jerk. Swinging hard, she caught his nose, and blood spouted. Not finished yet, she clamped her hands together to form a tight fist and struck the side of his head, shattering her pinkie splint in two. *Ouch.* She shook her hand to ease the pain.

Eric hit the pavement with a thud.

Feeling like a prize fighter who just won the golden belt, she swung a foot into his rib cage. "That's payback, Eric, for damn near killing me Saturday."

A crowd gathered. Cell phone cameras clicked away so she suspected she'd be on the six o'clock news. Slightly breathless, she faced them. "Is someone calling the police?"

With a phone to her ear, one woman held up her hand.

Before long, two patrol cars arrived followed by a silver limo. All three vehicles blocked traffic on Madison Avenue. The cops immediately cuffed Eric.

Lou jumped out and ran toward her. "You okay, miss? I circled the block as fast as I could."

"I'm fine, Lou. I got him good." She beamed at the groaning Eric. Hauling bushels of apples finally paid off.

****

Deems met her at the police station, and all her fears and anger at Eric dissipated. The man's arms were magic, and his embrace eased every tight muscle, including the sore knuckles on both hands. Medics re-splinted her pinkie and stopped Eric's bleeding nose, but she was proud to watch Eric's right eye swell to match his left. The man resembled a raccoon.

She joined Baylor, Jan, Eric, and Deems in a small conference room, along with Jan's female attorney and a male police officer who stood directly behind Eric's chair. Deems sat by Lauren's side, holding her hand. Jan sat opposite, biting her lip and stealing glances at Eric who paid her no mind. Baylor had his chair closest to the handcuffed Eric, who grumbled obscenities throughout.

Opening a folder, Baylor spread papers across the table and read. "Eric Drummer, you are being charged with aggravated assault on Lauren Howell, attempted murder on the security guard, Robert Hecker, and second-degree murder of Carl Morris, the insurance investigator." He glanced at Deems and Lauren. "Mr. Morris died three hours ago." He leaned toward Eric. "Want to confess to the murder of Rafael Torres? All I need do is match your DNA to the wounds on his corpse along with blood traces on your knife."

Eric answered with another string of obscenities.

Obviously, the man had no desire to make Baylor's job easier. Lauren cleared her throat. "Eric confessed to murdering Rafael to me, Detective."

"He wanted to cut me off," Eric growled. "He shouldn't have been so damn greedy."

Baylor grinned. "I'll take your statement as a confession. Where's the necklace, Drummer?"

"I ain't telling you nothing."

"The necklace is locked up," Lauren said. "He wanted my keys." *Come to think of them...* She turned to Deems and jerked back to see his fire-and-brimstone glare directed at his sister. She patted his thigh to break his focus. "My key ring was in my jeans pocket. Do you know where they are?"

Snapping his focus onto her, Deems softened his gaze and nodded. Standing, he extracted her key ring from his trouser pocket. "For some reason, I grabbed them along with my keys before leaving for work." He dangled the ring.

Baylor held out his hand. "I'll take them, Mr. Lambert." He slammed the keys on the table in front of Eric. "Which one?"

"I want a lawyer." Eric snarled at Jan. "I'll beat this wrap, honey. Don't you worry." He winked at the woman behind Jan. "How about lending me that pretty lawyer of yours?"

Deems coughed into his hand. "Mrs. Carmichael works for me, Eric, and she will not take your case."

Frowning, Baylor motioned to the officer behind Drummer. "Lock him up and notify the public defender's office."

Scraping his chair as he stood, Eric cussed all the way out the door.

The man definitely had a limited vocabulary today. Lauren glanced at Baylor. "Well, that was fun. What now?"

Sliding the key ring toward her, Baylor pointed. "One of the keys belongs to him. For the sake of procedure, please identify each key out loud, Ms. Howell."

Taking the ring, Lauren separated two keys from the others. "These belong to my parents' house—front and rear doors. This next one is for my room over the garage. This one is for the storage shed where I keep my paintings and important papers." Frowning, she paused to hold up the two remaining keys. "These two are identical in size and shape." She showed them to Baylor. "One belongs to our apple warehouse. My dad recently changed the lock so the key looks as new as the other one."

Baylor took the keys off the ring. "They're for cylinder locks, usually for a heavy-duty door." He looked at Jan. "Any ideas, Ms. Lambert?"

Still biting her lip, Jan shook her head and shot a quick glance at her brother who sat with arms folded across his chest, watching Baylor.

Lauren rested her arms on the table and wagged a finger. "You know, Detective, one morning, I received a call from the landlord, Mr. O'Reilly. He wanted the twenty bucks Eric owed him, or he'd toss his stuff to the curb. I'll bet Eric is renting the storage locker in the basement. That has a heavy metal door."

Jan leaned forward. "How do you know what's in the basement?"

The poor girl was so ga-ga over her lousy fiancé, she never noticed how often Lauren stopped to talk to the landlord before heading to the apartment. Hell, Lauren even had coffee one night with Mrs. Gleisberg, the tenant on the second floor. Lauren shrugged. "I helped Mr. O'Reilly carry a bunch of old bicycles from the basement. I noticed the locker then." She'd bet any amount of money Eric stashed more than a necklace.

****

A regular parade flowed from the conference room and down to the street. While Jan and her lawyer stepped into Baylor's car with a uniformed officer, Deems guided Lauren toward the limo. He had better ways of spending a busy Monday morning, and a quick glance at his watch told him he just wasted an awful lot of time. So much waited at the office and required his attention, but he dropped everything when Lou called. Finally, Jan's friggin' fiancé was behind bars. Lauren would be safe to walk without fear. Unfortunately, Lauren caught him checking his watch.

She jerked her head in Baylor's direction. "I can go with them."

"No. I'd like to see the whole matter resolved. This way, I can concentrate on work without worrying about you."

She shot him a look he didn't understand, but he was too aggravated to question her. He waved her into the limo.

Arriving at the brownstone, Lauren led the way to the front door.

She lacked her usual springy step and even glanced over her shoulder as if in apology. She'd taken quite a beating Saturday, and all the money in the world wouldn't erase her bruises. She needed only time. He winked with what he hoped gave her reassurance.

Approaching the side door on the first floor, Lauren knocked.

Seconds later, Mr. O'Reilly answered, chewing. His brows shot upward. "Ms. Howell? What happened to you?"

She waved aside the comment. "Long story." She introduced Detective Baylor. "Is Eric renting your old storage locker?"

With a brow cocked, he glanced from one face to the other. "Well, yeah, but Drummer is the only one with a key—his stipulation, not mine. But I haven't seen him in a few days." A nod toward Jan. "She should know his whereabouts."

Baylor stepped forward. "We have the key, Mr. O'Reilly. Can we have a look?"

"Sure, hold on." Pulling on a retractable cord attached to his belt, he extended a key ring then gestured for them to follow. "I keep the door to the basement locked. Anyone who goes down has to notify me first, including Drummer." Leading them to a door under the stairwell, he unbolted the lock and flipped on a light. Then, he stepped aside with a wave. "All yours. Let me know when you're done."

Deems followed Lauren down a set of wooden stairs with a metal tube railing attached to the wall for support. The others descended like a herd of cattle clomping on the stairs. The finished basement had a concrete floor and white-painted cinder block walls, but like most basements, the space became a catch-all for junk. If he hadn't invested in high-rises at an early age, he'd have purchased every storage facility in the country. People just refused to throw out their treasures, opting instead to store worthless crap at exorbitant prices.

Maneuvering around piled boxes, Lauren led the way toward the rear to a metal door.

Deems recognized the style and shape as one of the many bomb shelters built in the 1960s when the threat of the Cuban missile crisis loomed.

Taking the two keys from his pocket, Baylor tried one key then the other. The second key fit perfectly and turned the cylinder. He opened the door and flipped a light switch.

The small four-by-eight room held junk piled to the ceiling. Boxes, small pieces of furniture, car parts, and sporting equipment—some of which still dangled a price tag.

"This stuff is from his apartment," Jan said with a catch in her throat.

Baylor rubbed the nape of his neck. "We might be here a while."

Probably all day, Deems thought with a frown. Like looking for a needle in a haystack.

Stepping toward the detective, Lauren wagged a finger. "Eric probably tossed the necklace's box, but I'm sure he wasn't stupid enough to leave a seven-million-dollar piece of jewelry unprotected. A velvet cloth bag, for example."

Throughout the shifting of the contents, Deems spotted the moisture building at the base of Jan's eyes. What would she do now with her young heart broken? Did she still love Eric despite his murderous rampage? Hopefully, she wouldn't visit him in prison and cause Mom and Dad a stroke.

Deems glanced at Lauren who helped Baylor shift through the boxes. Nothing stopped this woman from dirtying her hands, and a sense of pride swelled within his chest. Even with sore hands and a splinted pinkie, she rifled through Eric's junk when most women would be afraid of breaking their nails.

With a grunt, Baylor hauled out a small suitcase and set it on a box. Releasing the latches, he threw open the lid and uncovered a black velvet bag.

While everyone's attention centered on Baylor's find, Deems rechecked his watch. If he hadn't received the phone call this morning about trouble brewing in Salt Lake City, he'd be more patient with the slow process. Hell, even Lauren repeatedly glanced back with a brow raised, but she'd have to deal with his constant interruptions in order to understand a wealthy man's world.

Baylor stretched a thin draw string and tilted the opening toward his palm. A brilliant sapphire and diamond-studded necklace sparkled from the overhead light.

Jan gasped. The detective whistled, and Lauren merely stared in awe.

Finally, Deems could return to the office and find out what the hell happened in Salt Lake City.

Chapter Twenty-Eight

Wow. The necklace was the most gorgeous piece of jewelry she'd ever seen. The diamonds alone were maybe three to four carats and surrounded six brilliant sapphires with one blue gem hanging low enough to grace a woman's cleavage. Not that she'd wear such a piece. She'd need a wardrobe to match, and right now, she owned one very expensive black dress.

While talking on his cell phone, Baylor led the way up the staircase. Solemn Jan followed her attorney, and taking up the rear was Lauren and Deems. Midway, Lauren gave a quick glance over her shoulder to see Deems again looking at his watch. For some reason, her heart sank. A reminder of their disparities, she supposed. A man too busy to stop and smell the roses.

Once out of the basement and walking the short hall toward the front door, Jan caught her arm. "Lauren, I am truly sorry."

Yeah, well. At a loss for words, Lauren simply nodded and patted Jan's hand.

Saying goodbye to everyone, Jan and her lawyer climbed the stairs to Jan's third floor apartment.

Still on his phone, Baylor headed for the police cruiser while Deems took Lauren's elbow and led her toward the limo. Again, Deems checked his watch. What the hell was he doing, counting the minutes?

His cell phone rang. Excusing himself, he stepped

off to the side.

Forcing a smile, Lauren approached Lou who held open the limo's rear door. With one foot in the door, she shot another quick peek at Deems. He paced the sidewalk, phone to his ear, and a frown creasing his forehead. Sighing, she met Lou's gaze. "Something's bothering him."

"He's a busy man."

Too busy, probably. How much time would they spend together once the sexual novelty wore off? Shaking her head, she stepped into the limo.

A minute later, Deems slipped onto the seat. "I'm returning to the office, Lauren. I've an emergency."

His face had changed to stone with a gaze full of fire. She hoped to spend the rest of the day with Deems cuddled in his arms while he consoled her over her second brush with Eric. Not to be. She was in her last week for everything. Thursday, Antonio's class would end with an Italian feast prepared by his lovely wife, Carmela, and the Stewarts were scheduled to return Friday afternoon. She'd love to spend the weekend with Deems before returning to Arendtsville on Sunday and maybe discuss their relationship. He asked her several times to stay, but she was so damn undecided. Tonight perhaps, she'd sit him down and have a frank discussion about their relationship.

As the limo rolled alongside the condo building's curb, Deems grabbed her hand and pressed the penthouse key onto her palm. "Make yourself at home. I don't know how long I'll be." He kissed her lightly then shook a finger in her face, his expression stern. "The doctor said to rest. You've had enough excitement for a while."

A while? More like a lifetime. Feeling abandoned at the curb, Lauren sighed as the limo drove away. Deems hadn't asked about her meeting with Jo-Jo. In fact, he hardly said two words from the moment he arrived at the station. She attributed the silence to anger toward his sister, but now, she wasn't so sure. Whatever happened to foul his mood must be a doozy.

Opening her palm, she stared at the key thrust so hastily into her hand. The key was a simple symbolic gesture. A necessity in a man's point of view—to open then lock a door with ease. To a woman, the key meant home and a place to belong. She should feel happy Deems trusted her with the use of his penthouse, but the doubts rolling around inside her heart were enough to make her cry. She entered the condo building.

Johnny stood with a big smile stretching onto his thin lips. "The Stewarts' place will be ready by Wednesday at the latest, Ms. Howell. I understand you'll be in the penthouse for a while? If you need anything, just call the desk."

"Thanks, Johnny. Any news on Robert?"

"He's doing fine, ma'am, and scheduled to be released from the hospital day after tomorrow. But we don't expect him on duty for a couple of weeks. Night shift security will be handled by Lester. Good man."

Lauren stepped into the penthouse elevator and inserted the key. Since she was alone and heading to Deems' luxurious condo, she took stock of the opulence, starting with the elevator. Marble walls and floor surrounded her and only one key slot so no stopping at the fourth floor to check on the Stewarts' condo. Brass handle bars lined the perimeter and matched the brass-covered doors. When the elevator stopped and its doors opened, she stared at the black walnut entrance with its strange keyhole. *Funny what money can buy.* With the same key, she unlocked the door and stepped into the living room.

Huge wasn't the appropriate word to describe the place. Enormous maybe. She'd never seen anything so big in her life. Hands down, the room beat the size of her father's apple warehouse.

Approaching the center, she ran her fingers along the sofa's plush upholstery then onward to the glass end tables, the silk lampshades, and the dining room table with its beautiful dark cherry suite.

A powerful wave of awe hit. She felt like a queen inspecting her castle, ready to snap her fingers to request a new picture on the wall or to rearrange the furniture. She wouldn't do either, of course. Everything was perfect...absolutely perfect.

As she strolled in the direction of the bedroom, she opened the first side door to see a corner office surrounded by windows. On entering the master bedroom, she caught sight of the red rose resting on her pillow. Lifting the stem with two fingers, she sniffed the fragrant petals and smiled. When had he the time to get a single red rose? The man was so damn sweet. Laying the rose onto the night table, she refreshed herself in the bathroom and retraced her steps to the living room.

Beyond the two sofas, three doors led to three more bedrooms, each with its own bath. Another door opened to a hall bathroom for guests, and a fourth room—a vacant corner room—contained an impressive array of windows. *Great lighting for canvas painting.* She entered the empty room and stood before the windows.

The view faced Central Park, and her breath caught at the sight. Fifteen stories above the city with a breathtaking view. Although…

Leaving the room, she headed for the spiral staircase leading to the roof. After ensuring an unlocked door behind her, she walked into bright sunlight and stopped. The roof resembled a huge patio with square stones for a floor, lounge chairs and tables, a small flower garden, and a canvas-covered barbecue grill. A wrought-iron rail prevented any drunken guests from falling to their death, and toward this, she ambled.

Her breath caught at the bird's-eye view of the city. From this height, the sounds of traffic and people had a muted quality, and she distinctly smelled the park with its trees and cut grass. Tears filled her eyes. This view, more than anything, could convince her to stay, but without legal ties, their relationship might end with a snap of his fingers. She'd be in the same situation as now—no job and no money. She'd love to experience this type of life for a little while, but she knew herself. She wasn't a woman who lounged around and polished her nails. Work was inbred, and she seriously doubted a billionaire's mistress/wife/girlfriend worked for a living. On the other hand, she refused to be a man's sex toy. *Damn, I don't know what to do.*

Chapter Twenty-Nine

From the moment he stepped into his limo, Deems answered one phone call after another. Apparently, the trouble brewing in Salt Lake City required his immediate attention, and his physical presence could be the dam to stop the flood of lawsuits. After a quick call to Lauren and hearing her disappointed voice, he almost told his legal team to go to the airport without him, but he always handled every crisis personally. Lauren needed to understand the importance of the company's reputation. So, grabbing an already packed suitcase from his office closet, he and his team boarded his private jet bound for Utah.

By Thursday, three whole days away from Lauren, Deems returned to his office, ranting and raving at anyone brave enough to step in his path. The trip to Salt Lake was a total disaster with the company facing one building code violation after another, and all because the Utah manager acted like a slumlord instead of following the company's maintenance guidelines. Deems fired the man on the spot. For the next forty-eight hours, he and his legal team worked on a game plan to combat the multi-million-dollar lawsuits accumulating by the day.

He'd spent endless meetings with code inspectors, politicians, and lawyers, one after the other, and each with their own demands. With every blessed hour, he wondered why the hell he came in the first place when he'd rather be with Lauren. He missed her terribly— more than he ever believed possible, missed her beautiful smile, and the sparkle in her green eyes. Every time he dialed her phone number, another call interrupted. Hell, he hardly had a chance to sleep, let alone talk to the woman who only had a few days left in New York.

His assistant, Betty, poked her head through the partially opened door. "Has the fire died yet?"

He'd been pacing before the large windows like an animal trapped in a cage, desk phone glued to his ear, and barking one command after another. He barely ended one call and prepared to make another when she interrupted. With chest tight and head throbbing, if he wasn't careful, he'd have a stroke and find himself flat on the floor gurgling like an idiot. *A solid week of high blood pressure.* He desperately needed the comfort of Lauren's arms. Had she decided to stay? After her taste of the good life, what sensible woman could refuse? All her problems would be his, and he'd love to come home every night to see her smile and hear her lovely voice.

Carefully placing the phone onto its cradle, he sucked in a deep breath and slowly released. He gave Betty a half-grin. "I'm sorry. You won't believe what our Utah manager did." He stared at the silent phone and sighed. "I need to take a breather." He flopped into his leather chair.

Stepping inside, she stood, holding the door like a shield. "I've heard some of the gossip, and most made my skin crawl. You open for visitors?"

"Depends. Who's out there?"

"Mark Jordan. He came to say goodbye."

"Oh—yes. Send him in and hold my calls." Mark's visit afforded a much-needed break. Something different to think about besides this friggin' Salt Lake problem.

Betty waved Mark into the office and quietly closed the door.

In full suit and tie, Mark stood in the center of the room like a soldier ready to face the firing squad. Since Deems hadn't talked to Lauren, he had no idea what transpired at their meeting. He should have told everyone else to go to hell and called her. But one problem after another required his immediate attention. When the dust cleared, he'd make some serious changes to the demands on his time. He leaned back in his chair and swiveled. "You have your work cut out for you, Mark."

"Yes, sir, I do." He inched forward, his posture rigid. "So, I'm not fired?"

Mark sounded like a little boy waiting for punishment. Deems wagged a finger. "As long as you clean up your act, I'll give you another try. You still have an impressive evaluation from Dan."

With slow steps, Mark approached one of the chairs facing the desk and ran his hand along the top of the leather backrest. "Excuse me, sir, but do I have any guarantees about returning?" He grimaced. "I might serve time, and the company policy—"

Deems waved aside the comment. "Yes, I know, no criminal records. I'll connect you with one of our lawyers. Maybe he can swing a deal, you know, like community service—provided you rectify all the trouble you've caused." He sat forward and hit the intercom button. "Betty, see if Taylor is in his office. I want Mark to pay him a visit."

"Yes, sir."

Again, he leaned back. "Stan Taylor is our local go-to man for problems. He'll find you the right lawyer in Pennsylvania."

His stance relaxing, Mark released a large breath. "Thank you, sir. I'd have bet money Lauren turned you against me."

"Don't be ridiculous." He stood, walked around the desk, and rested his butt on the corner, one leg dangling. "Truthfully, I haven't had a chance to call her. This crisis in Salt Lake took all my time."

One blond brow cocked. "You didn't talk?"

"Regretfully, no." He tugged on his ear. Saying the words out loud sounded so damn feeble.

Mark's brow twitched. "Then, you don't know."

Head snapping, Deems narrowed his gaze. "What?"

"We're returning to Arendtsville together." Mark shot him a sideways glance. "We had a long discussion and discovered we still love each other." He pulled on his necktie. "I explained everything, sir, about the debts and why I left in a hurry. She understood and forgave me."

Mark could have swung a sledgehammer into Deems' chest. The pain cut so deep, his balls retracted. *What the hell is happening here*? Yes, they had been engaged and presumably in love, but Mark screwed her big time. How could she forgive him so easily?

Words eluded him. He had no idea what to say or how to feel. Anger, yes. Shock, disbelief, but the heaviness in his chest was new. Was Lauren's loyalty to Mark stronger than her professed love for Deems

Lambert? Or worse, had she agreed to support Mark and then expect to come back to New York as if she never left? *Does she take me for a fool?*

He returned to his chair behind his desk but couldn't sit. Instead, he gripped the backrest and avoided eye contact.

Mark cleared his throat and stepped toward the desk. "I can't believe she agreed to return with me, but I'm sure glad she is. She'll give me some much-needed moral support." With a shaky palm, he smoothed the front of his tie. "I realize I'm jeopardizing my career with High-Rise, but she means a lot to me, sir. I'll gladly make the sacrifices to win her back."

Something flickered in Mark's gaze, and just a hint of a smile touched the corner of his lip. Deems didn't like the look at all, especially for a man about to hit the unemployment line.

Mark's expression grew shuttered. "Her art class ends today. We leave for Harrisburg in the morning, and we'll head straight to the police station." He shifted from one foot to the other. "She knows I'm here with you and told me to say goodbye."

Heat rising, Deems contemplated sweeping the contents of his desktop onto the floor. A fine how-do-you-do after spending the happiest two months of his life. She had the gall to dismiss him as if he was a passing fling. Hell, she resided in his penthouse, living the life of a queen. If he discovered she and Mark slept in his bed…

Mark squared his shoulders. "Look, Mr. Lambert. Lauren and I have known each other for a long time. I'll never get through my trial without her. So, please don't give her any grief."

"I wouldn't dare interfere." He'd barely kept from biting off his own tongue. He squeezed the back of his chair. "You can use the company charge card for transportation home, but the card expires Friday night. Make sure you pay for Lauren's ticket." Truthfully, he didn't give a damn if the two of them fell into a bottomless pit. He turned toward the window, dismissing Mark. Come Monday, he'd have Human Resources officially terminate the bastard.

Once alone, Deems hadn't any idea what to do first. He had a dozen phone calls to make before the conference video with the crisis team in Utah. Instead, lead bones weighed him down. He wanted to shut out the world and be alone, but hell, so much depended on his interaction. Chest too tight to take in a decent breath, he flopped into his chair and stared at the wall.

He considered himself an astute man—one who analyzed people with a quick sweep of his gaze. Bankers kissed his feet. Politicians gushed, but the one achievement he'd yet to accomplish was a wife and family, a woman who loved *him* and not his money. He thought he found such a woman with Lauren, and now, even his money couldn't hold her. All right, she'd verbalized her unease with city life, but how could she conceivably return to Mark Jordan? *I'll never understand women.*

"Mr. Lambert?"

He jumped at the sound of Betty's voice on the intercom. Leaning toward the desk, he clicked the button. "Yes?"

"Lauren Howell is on the phone. Shall I patch her through? She's been trying your cell."

Like an omen, he had entered his office, and his

cell phone died. He hadn't thought twice about a recharge. "No, Betty. Tell her I'm busy and to have a good trip. I won't be home until late, but if the Stewarts' condo is done, she should return."

Mark probably called her to say Deems had given his blessing. *What a crock of shit.*

****

Heart thumping, Lauren stared at the phone in her hand, her mind blank. *Have a nice trip?* He'd said goodbye through his assistant plus requested her return to the fourth floor. Why? What the hell happened in Salt Lake?

She'd gone a whole week wishing he'd walk through the door so they could discuss options to continue their relationship, but for some unfathomable reason, he said goodbye without explanation. Was he tired of her already, or was this common rich-man's behavior?

Just as well. He'd never agree to her suggestions. Deems was a self-made billionaire with his own set of priorities. She had no experience with wealth and should cut her losses. *All right—I guess. I'm a big girl. I'll deal with the rejection and cry later.* But hot eyes and cheeks burned as she packed. She had the strange feeling of being expendable. *What the hell is wrong with me?* Was she a big sap to let men use her until discarded, like a dirty dish rag?

For the second time in her life, she racked her brain for answers. Where had she and Deems gone wrong? While in Salt Lake, he hadn't called, and she dared not bother him. Unlike his first trip where they talked every night, this time, they'd exchanged only quick text messages with the wish-you-were-here crap.

Was Salt Lake the beginning of his cold send-off? Because he believed she refused to stay? *Why do men grow bitter whenever they don't get their way?* As if a woman should bow before a man in humble worship. She debated leaving Deems a scathing note about his behavior, but the gesture would be an exercise in futility. Perhaps he'd met someone else on his trip and decided she was more worthy of his world. *So be it. Life goes on.*

Luggage in hand, Lauren approached the elevator and took one last look around the penthouse. Her memory of this suite would last forever—as would Deems. With her heart shrinking, she stepped into the elevator and inserted the key, but on the way down, a fire burned in her gut. Deems hadn't any right to cast her aside as if she was some two-bit floozy he picked off the street. After switching elevators on the first floor and then dropping her bags at the Stewarts' condo, she whipped out his business card for the High-Rise International address, hurried past Johnny with a wave, and stepped outside to hail a cab.

The taxi dropped her off at—naturally—another high-rise. The interior had a more business-like decor without marble and gold sparkling everywhere. A much larger security desk stopped everyone from walking straight to the elevators. The man behind the desk acted more like a traffic cop for people with no clue about why they wandered through the revolving door. Foreigners maybe, thinking they stepped into the Empire State building. After telling the guard her destination, she entered the elevator and punched the button for the eighteenth floor. Seconds later, she exited into a reception area where a young woman glanced away from her computer, her round eyes growing larger at the sight of Lauren's bruised face.

"Can I help you?"

"Mr. Lambert, please."

She gestured over her shoulder. "Head down the hall to the end. His assistant will help you."

The "hall" was a long corridor with partitioned cubicles on the left and offices encased in glass on the right. Curious gazes followed her as she passed.

Some of her bruises had faded, but instead of looking like a woman who survived a beating, she resembled a person with an unknown discoloration disease. Nearing the end of the hall, Lauren squared her shoulders and marched directly to the woman sitting at a desk near a door marked Private.

The woman's eyes widened. "Can I help you?"

"Is this Mr. Lambert's office?" She pointed at the door.

"Yes, but he's busy."

"Is he with someone?"

"No, he's—"

Without waiting for permission, Lauren barged into the office.

Deems stood behind his desk with a phone to his ear and his suit jacket draped over the back of a large leather chair.

He looked tired with dark circles around both eyes, and her heart almost weakened…until he met her gaze and glared.

The assistant rushed ahead. "I'm sorry, Mr. Lambert. She just let herself in."

He tossed his phone onto the desk. "That's okay, Betty. Leave us." He waited for the assistant to close the door then frowned. "What are you doing here?"

His gaze cut through her like a laser. What the hell happened in Salt Lake for him to hate her so much? "I'm here to return your damn key." Pulse pounding wildly, she approached the desk and slammed the key onto the blotter. "You aren't even brave enough to tell me to my face."

"Under the circumstances—"

"What circumstances?" Her arms flared. "You never called to see if I dropped dead. I should have taken the hint then." Tears welled in her eyes. *Dammit, I will not cry.* Sniffing, she jutted her chin. "May you have a wonderful life." She turned toward the door.

"Lauren."

Refusing to face him, she paused with her hand on the knob.

"I wish you and Mark all the best."

Her heart thudded. She whirled, jaw tight. "What?"

"He told me." He stuffed his hands into his trouser pockets, his hot gaze steady on her face.

She narrowed her gaze. "Told you what?"

"About your plans to stand by his side."

Her mouth dropped, and she fell against the door. "You believed him without questioning me?"

For a few brief seconds, she got lightheaded and was thankful she leaned against the door. She *knew* Jo-Jo would somehow screw her again. Since he took everything else she had, he had to take away Deems. But why couldn't Deems see the obvious? Was Jo-Jo *that* important to the company?

She cleared her throat. "Jo-Jo is notorious for vengeance, Deems. You and I being together probably ate him alive." She squared her shoulders, chin high.

"For your information, he left me because my brother inherited the farm. He had counted on the money from me selling my half. If you choose to believe I will *ever* return to him, then you don't know me at all." She blinked away the moisture accumulating in her eyes. "You trusted a thief and a liar more than me." She sucked in a shuddering breath. "Yes, we're done." Throat tight, she gripped the door knob and glared. "For the second time in my life, I've made a complete fool of myself. I've fallen in love." Throwing the door open with a bang, she stormed from the office.

Chapter Thirty

For the past two days, Deems grumbled at everything. At the office, the computer wasn't fast enough, or his cell phone crackled from poor reception. Then, at home, the smoked bacon tasted like shoe leather, or too many birds pooped on his penthouse window. No appetite, no sleep, and no humor. All because of Lauren's comment about falling in love. She had expressed her love earlier. He believed her then. Why not now?

While washing his coffee cup, he pondered the question. If he hadn't been so angry at the Salt Lake calamity, would he have taken the time to talk to Lauren? Instead, he accepted Mark Jordan's declaration of their undying love and brushed off Lauren as another unworthy female with his mind closed to any explanation. Deep down, he wanted no more problems and, in retrospect, caused a colossal one of his own. Mark took the easy path to riches and embezzled money from a boss who trusted him with the books. Knowing Mark's background, how the hell had he ignored such a blatant act of disloyalty? He really should have his head examined. Turning off the faucet, he sighed. *Too late now.*

The penthouse phone rang. He turned from the kitchen sink and, before grabbing the receiver, wiped his hands on a towel. "Yes, Johnny?"

"Your sister is here. Shall I send her up?"

"By all means."

Not like he wanted company. He'd been moping around all morning, and here, the day was half gone, and he wasted a sunny Saturday because he couldn't screw his brain in right.

Jan arrived a minute later with her flower-power clothes flashier than usual. He hugged her and smelled the strong, citrus scent in her hair. "So, what's new with your criminal status?"

Smirking, she tossed her canvas bag on a side chair. "The District Attorney will not press charges. Eric convinced him I knew nothing of his activities."

"That's good." The man finally did one decent thing in his life. He headed for the kitchen. "Want something to drink?"

"Bottled water, if you have some." She followed and leaned on the counter.

Deems reached into the refrigerator, slid aside the casserole Lauren left with heating instructions, and grabbed two bottles of water. He lobbed one to his sister.

After opening her bottle, Jan pointed to the basket of green apples at the end of the counter. "I see Lauren left her supply."

Lauren couldn't eat the apples, not with a crack in her jaw. She planned on making apple sauce. He pursed his lips. "I should throw them out. I'll never eat them." The casserole, too. Both were a reminder he didn't need.

Smacking her lips after a long swig from her water bottle, Jan wandered toward the living room. "So, what's with you and Lauren? Why'd you toss her out?"

Deems paused with the water bottle halfway to his mouth. "How did you know?"

"I stopped by last night to see how she was doing only to collide into her as she walked onto the street with her luggage." She curled into a side chair and tucked her legs beneath her butt. "She told me you ended the relationship but was rather vague with details."

"I'm not surprised since the whole damn matter is bizarre." He sipped his water. "According to Mark Jordan, she's standing by his side, one of those through-thick-and-thin deals. They still love each other." He choked on a laugh. "She denied every word."

Jan shrugged. "So, what's the problem? Don't tell me you believe Mark?" Eyes widening, she gasped. "You *do* believe him! How could you, Deems?"

Hell, he didn't understand his own actions let alone explain them. He combed his fingers through his hair, not giving a damn if every strand stood on end.

His sister shook her head. "Mark's playing you." She took a swig of water then looked his way. "What else did he say?"

He stared at his bottle. "They were returning to Arendtsville together." Glancing up, he frowned. "Yesterday morning, in fact." Just saying the words gnawed at his gut. He joined her in the living room.

"But yesterday *night* was when I ran into her. So obviously, she didn't leave on the morning train." Covering her mouth with her hand, she stifled a yawn. "By the time Carol and Bill returned, Lauren had nowhere to sleep except a bench at the train station. I convinced her to come home with me."

Deems stopped mid-swallow and faced her. "I

don't understand. Mark had a hotel room."

"If she was going with him, you mean. He probably didn't know Lauren was condo sitting and had to wait for Carol and Bill. I bumped into her around eight o'clock, and her luck finding a hotel room on a Friday night was nil, especially with opening day for the Yankees today." Squinting, she cocked her head. "Where'd you expect her to go at that hour?"

A sour taste covered his tongue. Not even a swig of water helped. How could he have forgotten about Carol and Bill? Lauren would never leave without assuring their arrival. *What a friggin' ass*! Deems turned to the windows and stared at the green of the park, a beautiful green, like Lauren's eyes. Clenching his jaw, he spun from the window. No use tormenting himself.

Jan pointed to his cell phone vibrating on the coffee table. "Since when aren't you answering your calls?"

He glared at the phone. If he hadn't been so damned focused on Salt Lake… "I need a break from all the friggin' calls."

"What if the call is Lauren?"

He shook his head. "She won't call, not after what I said." Besides, he assigned her a special ringtone, which he had yet to remove.

"She told me you hadn't called once while in Salt Lake. Was the building ready to collapse? Were you in charge of physically removing people to save their lives?" She wagged a finger. "I know you, big brother. You're too hands-on. All this rigmarole could have been avoided." She studied her nails. "If you ask me, Mark took a big chance saying what he did. Maybe he couldn't stand to see you and Lauren together and risked losing his job just to keep you separated."

Deems' gut twisted. Lauren had stated Mark's need for vengeance. What had Mark hoped to gain? *Besides separate us.* Dread filled his heart and turned the vessel into a lead ball. What a fool.

Jan held her water bottle to the light. "I had high hopes for you and Lauren. She made you forget business for a while."

"No one makes me forget business." Actually, every time they were together, Lauren clouded his thoughts with wonder. Last night, he tossed and turned, because she would not get out of his mind. Today, he had no intention of concentrating on business. All right, she definitely distracted him from business.

Sighing, Jan clutched both hands around her water bottle. "This morning, I went with Lauren to the train station. She had a twelve-thirty ticket. Do you know her eyes change to a deep green when she cries?" She took a sip. "And yes, she boarded the train alone."

A damn headache threatened to explode his brain matter. Deems finished the last of his water, crushed the lightweight plastic, and tossed the container toward the kitchen, not giving a damn where the bottle landed. "My relationship with Lauren was over anyway, Jan. She hates New York. I'm sure she was thrilled to leave."

Jan shook her frizzy head. "I can't believe you gave up so willingly. She wasn't going back with Mark, and somewhere in your thick skull, you know I'm right. Yet, here you are, moping around while the woman of your dreams is on a train to Harrisburg." She studied him. "Sometimes, you can be so stupid. Like how you expect Lauren to make all the sacrifices."

Lips tight, he whirled to face her. "What sacrifices? I had everything to give her."

"Except your time. You're too busy making money and running all over the country."

Gaze narrowed, he studied his sister. "Money's keeping you comfortable."

"I'm not saying your money is a bad thing. You have more than enough and should be concentrating on settling down. Lauren was perfect. But you're right. The union won't work. You'd ask her to leave her family and friends to live in a luxurious condo alone while you work off your butt to make more money." She fussed with her pant leg then shot him a quick glance. "Have you considered a compromise?"

He looked at her, one brow raised. "What do you mean? I asked Lauren to stay. Nothing more."

Dropping the bottle to her lap, she widened her gaze. "That's it?"

"What the hell else do you expect?" He paced behind the sofa. "I don't have options, Jan. I'm tied to this city."

"Like a prisoner." Twisting her mouth to the side, Jan frowned. "I've news for you, brother. Last night, Lauren told me she planned to stay for a little while, but you took Mark's side and tossed her to the wolves."

Deems stopped pacing and stared. "She never said anything to me."

"How could she? You ended your affair." She finished her water and stood, walked toward the kitchen, retrieved his crushed bottle, and dropped both into the recycle bin. She stopped, head bent. "What am I hearing?"

The hum of a running machine echoed behind his

closed office door. "That's my fax. I'm not in the mood to work." He wasn't in the mood to do anything. In fact, he wanted to be alone…then he didn't. Jan had helped dispel his wallowing-in-self-pity feeling, but the strange tightness remained in his chest. He gave his sister a sideways glance. "What should I do?"

Jan grabbed her canvas bag and hoisted the strap onto her shoulder. "You had your chance to keep her in New York. I'm not sure what you can do to win her back." With an unfocused gaze, she stared at the far wall. "Proposing might help." She met his gaze. "Lauren isn't the type of woman who'll be happy living as a mistress."

The statement struck him like a blow to the gut. His sister was right. Lauren grew up with church-going parents. How long would she stay without a legal commitment?

Nearing his side, Jan stood on tiptoe to kiss his cheek. "I'm leaving, big brother. I know I'm younger with a lot less experience, but I'm a woman, and I know a woman in love when I see one. Lauren loves you very much. Her ex is definitely not in the picture. Whatever he told you was for his own selfish purpose." She placed a hand on his arm. "Don't let Lauren go. Trust her enough to know she will never reconcile with a man who stiffed her." She hugged him before heading for the elevator. After opening the door, she paused and gave him a sideways look. "Being married to your job will become lonely, Deems." She entered the elevator and then faced him. "Here's another detail to consider. Do you realize you and I followed the same pattern with our mates? I believed Eric's word and disregarded Lauren's warning, and here, you took Mark's announcement as gospel without allowing Lauren a chance to explain."

Holy shit. Jan was right. How could he have been so stupid? He stared at his sister, all frizzy hair and flower clothes, wiser than he ever expected. He inserted the elevator key and waved as the doors closed.

Throat tight, he wandered about the living room, not at all sure what to do. *What the hell is wrong with me?* He chastised Jan for ignoring the advice of a mature woman, but when confronted with the same voice of reason, he dismissed Lauren without a second thought. How in thunder had he made a fortune with such a closed-minded attitude?

Once again, the fax machine hummed. The lawyers were still in Salt Lake and promised to keep him updated regarding the fines and civil suits. Thanks to the inept manager, the building required a massive overhaul, and the company's reputation in the area sank to an all-time low. *So much work ahead.* At least, High-Rise International was a private corporation without a board of directors breathing down his neck.

With his muscles in knots, he swung his arms in wide circles to loosen the cannon-ball effect in his chest and then headed for the office. After grabbing the papers from the fax machine, he skimmed through the sheets. The majority came from Salt Lake. One, however, caught his eye. Dan Williams, Mark's boss, sent a fax from Buenos Aires in Argentina.

Mr. Lambert, what gives with Mark Jordan? Did you fire him? He sent a fax from Belize, saying he won't return and stated you and he had insurmountable differences. He wrote of some cockamamie bull about self-

preservation. I should think I'd be informed of your decision, and to be honest, I'm confused. I sent an impressive evaluation of the man. I'd appreciate some type of explanation. Yours truly, Dan Williams.

With heat flushing into his cheeks, Deems read and re-read the fax. Mark never had any intention of turning himself in to the authorities. *What a friggin' idiot.* Crushing the paper within his fist, he wanted to kick the damn fax machine right out the window. All this time, Mark played him for a fool, and billionaire, Deems Lambert, fell for the oldest trick in the book. But Mark's statement about self-preservation hit a little too close to home. Deems had gone to Salt Lake to preserve the reputation of the company and, in doing so, ignored the woman who'd made him happier than he'd ever been. He had his team of lawyers along. They performed all the work. He stood by as a figurehead. Why go at all when he had competent people on his payroll? Wasn't it high time to stop?

Compromise.

Funny how the word never entered his mind where women were concerned. He certainly had a give-and-take attitude with potential clients, mostly men. But compromise how? The company was too big to move, and his international operations used New York as its central hub. *What the hell can I do?*

He yanked his office phone from the receiver and dialed. "Jan, get your ass back here. I need help!"

Chapter Thirty-One

Lauren dragged her feet as if she wore iron clogs, complete with ball and chain strapped around her ankles. Finding a food server job was the easy part, but for the past month, she lived with the smell of muscle rub. Damn, she was tired. With a vengeance, tourist season hit Gettysburg, Pennsylvania, and the influx of morning patrons into the restaurant flowed through the doors like Greta's Restaurant was the only place in town. Of the seven food servers, each waited on ten tables. She'd bet her measly bank account she'd gotten the crankiest and the can't-pull-it-together-without-coffee crowd. No sooner had she cleared a table when another group slipped in to keep the seats warm.

She'd signed on for the breakfast shift to allow time to run over to her parents and use her brother's computer. Every week, she sent resumes to school districts, but with budget cuts across the state, she had little hope of remaining in Pennsylvania.

After working seven days a week since she started, she finally accumulated enough cash to move out of her parents' garage and into a cheap apartment in the heart of Arendtsville. She had no furniture yet. Just a mattress and frame with some sheets, a few of her mother's old pots and pans, some leftover dishes, glasses, and utensils, and a used coffee maker. Life couldn't be better.

Jo-Jo's so-called effort to return her money amounted to an account opened with the minimum balance of fifty bucks, a token gesture to appease his boss. He made no further deposits. To maintain her sanity, she forced her New York adventure out of her mind. Hard as hell, of course. The image of one particular man would be imbedded into her memory forever.

While happiness filled her to be home and on familiar ground, she always struggled with a lump in her throat whenever her thoughts drifted to Deems. She missed him so much, and then, she'd remember how they ended. Master salesman Jo-Jo successfully screwed her one final time, and Deems believed him. That realization, more than anything, hurt the most.

"Lauren!"

She had just slid her employee badge through the time clock when her boss waved her toward the kitchen. *Please don't tell me you have a call-out.* Her feet were killing her now, and she couldn't possibly cover another shift.

With her purse swung over her shoulder, Lauren approached Big Greta, a rotund woman who tasted one too many of her dishes. The poor woman was so obese, she'd be dead from a heart attack or stroke within two years, but Greta's Restaurant was the place to stop if one had a hearty appetite. She fed her patrons until they exploded.

The establishment had an excellent location off the main drag leading into the heart of Gettysburg and sat in the middle of a large complex with two hotels flanking both sides. Since neither of the hotels had their own restaurant, the breakfast crowd consisted mainly of foot traffic. The majority of the lunch and dinner patrons drove in as they took breaks from sightseeing.

Greta stood before the stove, stirring a large pot of soup for the coming lunch crowd. Grunting softly, she glanced at Lauren. "One of your patrons left an extra large tip at the register. I've authorized Cindy to give you the money before you leave." She used a small spoon to taste the soup and immediately crinkled her nose then turned to the soup chef. "Put in more salt." She tossed the spoon into the wash bin and faced Lauren. "What'd you do that was so special?"

"I don't know which patron, Greta. Any hints?"

"Nay. See if Cindy knows."

Lauren welcomed any tip, large or small. Extra large probably meant five bucks. The usual for the breakfast crowd was maybe one or two dollars. From the kitchen, she returned to the dining area and approached the cash register.

After finishing with a couple's tab, Cindy waved goodbye then turned to Lauren. "The tip amount will blow your mind, dear. He paid in cash, and I almost dropped into a faint." Opening the register, she extracted a clipped wad of bills from the cash drawer. "When he first walked in, he requested you as his server and actually waited for one of your tables." After removing the clip, she handed over the bills. "I've heard of people leaving tips because of a sob story but never this much."

Counting quickly, Lauren stared at the wad in her hand and gaped. Gripping the counter for support, she shifted her gaze from the money to Cindy. "Fifteen hundred dollars!"

"That's what he left, dear. He paid cash and said to

be sure you received the full amount. He was adamant." She pointed at the bills. "I checked them for counterfeit."

Lauren wouldn't know a fake bill unless Abe Lincoln wore sunglasses. Shaking herself, she stared at Cindy. "What did he look like?"

Cindy smirked. "A mousy-looking guy. Small. Thick glasses. Dressed like a tourist in Bermuda shorts and T-shirt. I didn't get the impression he rolled in dough."

The French toast and eggs-over-easy guy? Eyes wide, she jerked back. "He hardly said two words to me. I figured he wasn't awake yet."

"Well, the money's yours, hon. Enjoy."

A man eating alone sometimes left a larger-than-normal tip, but large gratuities came from the dinner crowds at the higher-end restaurants where booze flowed like water. Greta's was more a family environment with black coffee as the strongest brew. Stunned beyond explanation, she thanked Cindy and exited the restaurant, burying the money deep into her purse.

Wow. Truly an unreal morning. Maybe she was dreaming, but her grip on her car door handle snapped her to reality. The metal was hot as hell from the overhead July sun.

If she wasn't so dog-tired, she'd do her usual routine and head to her parents' house to use the computer, check on any responses to teaching jobs, and send out another resume to keep the flow going. But not today. She wanted to put up her feet and rest, maybe paint a little, and revel in a man's generous tip. She hopped into her SUV and headed for home.

Millie and Phil Costanzo lived in their seventy-year-old colonial situated right in the middle of the main drag in Arendtsville. They rebuilt their attic into a two-bedroom, income-producing apartment with its own entrance and advertised for a tenant to replace the one who vacated.

The place was small with angled ceilings in every room, but Lauren couldn't beat the price nor the location. She supported herself again, and such a simple accomplishment created a tremendous sense of pride. Now, with fifteen hundred bucks in her hand, maybe she should go out tomorrow and buy some furniture. She stopped for a red light.

Traffic was its usual horrible gridlock. Tourists visited from around the country to see the battlefields of Gettysburg where America's Civil War fought its biggest battle in the town's backyard. To reach Arendtsville, she had to pass through the heart of Gettysburg, crawl around the town square where people on foot created more gridlock, until finally driving beyond all the tourist shops, eateries, and hotels. On a good day, the ride took twenty minutes.

A short time later, she glided her car into her usual spot in the Costanzo's driveway and cut the engine. A metal staircase at the rear of the house led to her apartment door. She started toward it when Millie stepped from her backdoor and hailed.

Her landlady was a short, little woman, always in a flowered dress covered by an apron. Her husband, Phil, wasn't any taller, but they were the nicest couple—old farmers who'd sold their forty-acre cornfield to retire in town.

Millie approached with a smile. "I have your mail.

Came early today."

She handed over several envelopes and also a folded sheet of paper.

Curious about the paper with no envelope, Lauren tapped the sheet. "What's this one?"

"Read and enjoy."

Cocking a brow, Lauren opened the letter and read. Her mouth fell open, and she stared at Millie.

Millie's grin stretched across her face. "Your rent's been paid for the rest of the year." She slipped her hands into her apron pockets. "Some guy stopped by today and gave us a check plus interest. Can't tell you who he was."

First, a fifteen-hundred-dollar tip and now a year of fully paid rent. Coincidences of this magnitude didn't happen every day. "Can you describe him?"

"Oh, sure. Small guy, thick glasses, kinda mousy-looking. No taller than Phil." She tapped the letter in Lauren's hand. "He paid with a cashier's check from a Harrisburg bank."

Only one man had money to throw around, and he certainly wasn't Jo-Jo. Heart thundering, she refolded the letter. The man *had* to work for Deems. Why would Deems make her life easier when he wanted nothing more to do with her? Shaking aside the thought, she looked at her landlady and smiled. "Thank you, Millie. If he comes around again, please call me." She ran up the metal flight of stairs to her door.

With confusion flooding her brain, she entered the kitchen and threw her purse and the rest of the mail on the metal card table where she ate her meals. Re-opening the letter, she reread. *Yup, the rent's paid all the way to January.* She refolded the letter and clutched it to her chest. She should feel anger at a man paying her bills, but she'd been up to her eyeballs with debt for so long, she felt a flood of relief. Why, though? That question was the big one. After placing the letter onto the kitchen table, she headed to her bedroom.

The rest of the mail could wait. The first order of business was to open every window and allow the scant breeze a chance to circulate. The apartment had no air conditioning, and being an attic, the temperatures reached uncomfortable levels by late afternoon. When sleeping, she used a small fan, but now, she had the cash to buy a window air conditioner at the home improvement store. *Damn, what a lucky break.* She kicked off her shoes and let them fly.

Returning to the kitchen, she sorted through the rest of the mail. *Well, what do you know.* Her first credit card finally arrived. The limit wasn't high but sufficient to reestablish a credit score. A mural project helped repay her parents' loan, and the earned tips from Greta's finalized a few outstanding bills. So, except what she owed the church, she had slowly reduced her debt to a manageable level. Because every prospective employer completed a credit check these days, her chances of being hired by a school district were nil without an impressive financial background. Somehow in today's screwed-up society, credit had become more important than qualifications.

She opened a handwritten envelope from the church. *Probably an update on my balance owed.* Reading quickly, she felt her heart stop, and she flopped onto a metal chair. Her largest loan had been paid in full plus a generous donation to cover the planned expansion project! For the first time since the breakup of her engagement, she was totally debt-free. The weight of so many torturous months was gone. She could concentrate on her art and teaching career and bank whatever money she accumulated.

To control a mounting sob, she sucked in a hard breath and stood to retrieve a bottle of water from her small refrigerator. What she really needed was a bottle of wine, but until this moment, wine was an extravagance she couldn't afford. Closing the fridge, she unscrewed the water bottle and took a long swig.

Should she call Deems and thank him? But why would he bother? He hadn't made any attempt to contact her. More than likely, he hopped on his jet to handle another crisis and wouldn't take her call anyway. *Oh, hell.* Time to relax and slip out of her work attire of black slacks and white shirt, but first... She loosened the hair band holding her hair off her shoulders—a work requirement—and leaned forward to shake and scratch her head.

"I like your hair loose," a male voice said.

With her stomach jumping into her throat, she jerked to an upright position and stared at Deems on the opposite side of the kitchen's screen door. She blinked several times to ascertain whether he was real. Heart thundering, she never imagined she'd see him again, and there he stood in khaki pants and open collar summer shirt looking as handsome as ever. She couldn't breathe. Hell, she couldn't even acknowledge him behind the screens, so she simply stared. Then, she smelled his musk scent blowing with the faint breeze, and her knees wobbled. Every whiff was torture and triggered memories she'd rather forget.

"Can I come in?"

Suppressing the urge to run to the door, she waved with as nonchalant an air as possible. "Screen door's unlocked."

Deems stepped inside, carrying a large fruit basket wrapped in clear yellow cellophane. He pointed. "On the table?"

She swallowed hard. "Sure."

Tilting his head upward, he glanced at the angled ceiling barely a foot from the edge of the table. Anyone rising too fast would put their skull through the roof, but with limited choices, the spot was the best position for the table.

She steeled herself against the feelings he stirred. She still loved him and to see him again tore her gut into shreds. Her heart said he'd come to apologize, but what changed his mind? They had countless differences to resolve—of which none were discussed. "How did you find me?"

"Private investigator." He turned the basket so the big yellow bow faced outward.

Her gaze narrowed. "Does he happen to resemble a mousy-looking man with thick glasses?"

He chuckled. "He's my head of accounting, Lauren. He said he always wanted to see Gettysburg."

"You made me debt-free," she'd said the words so softly she barely heard herself.

He stepped away from the table. "Yes. I hope you don't mind."

From the beginning, he'd taken care of her, always in subtle ways, and she appreciated every effort, but he had no further need to continue. He'd wiped his hands of her clearly enough. Straightening her shoulders, she lifted her chin. "Why?"

"I'd say the answer is fairly obvious." His gaze steady on her face, he slipped his hands into his trouser pockets.

He appeared ominous with the light from the door behind his back. The kitchen was way too small for a man of his size, and she suddenly felt trapped, like she wasn't safe in the same room with him. If he so much as touched her, she'd melt into a puddle of goo.

"I'm here to apologize, Lauren. I was wrong." With an unwavering gaze, he stepped forward. "Mark traveled straight to Belize."

"I'm not surprised." A flood of emotions ripped through her and hit so fast she wasn't sure what else to say or do. None of the confusion had anything to do with her ex. Just Deems. She hurt too much to look at him, but his gaze had her mesmerized. He fixated on her face as if to see if anything changed. All her bruises were gone. Her skull and jaw were healed, and she only recently ate her first green apple.

He stepped around the table toward her side.

She backed away, not sure why since she had no place to go except against the sink. With her emotions on edge, she had this overwhelming urge to jump onto the sink and propel herself out the window, but she'd only fall into a large brier bush. *Oh, God, what can I do?* He smelled of musk and sunshine and, in her book, a deadly combination. She wanted so much to hold and love him but was afraid her love for him ran deeper than what he felt for her.

His brow cocked, but he nodded and stopped by the refrigerator. "I discovered something very important about my life, Lauren. You and I could have spent your remaining week together if I wasn't so obsessed with doing everything myself. *You* were the first person I should have seen on my return from Salt Lake—not my assistant, not Mark, but you."

He leaned against the refrigerator door, but the appliance rocked on its broken feet. Jumping away, he shot a quick glance in her direction.

Her lips curled into a half smile. "The fridge came with the place. I keep forgetting to ask my landlord for a block of wood to level it." She waved an open palm at a metal chair. "Do you want to sit?"

"Not yet." He replaced his hands into his pockets. "I don't know if we can regain what we had, Lauren, but I'd like to find out. Over these past few weeks, I realized what a fool I've been. How much money I have or how many buildings I own doesn't matter. I don't have you." He ran a hand through his hair then met her gaze. "Jan told me you planned to stay."

Heart hammering to escape, she shrugged. "For a little while, but I wasn't in complete agreement with your terms."

"A mistress, you mean?"

Smirking, she nodded. "Yeah…mistress. I hoped to discuss some options, but…" She stared at the floor.

He took a step toward her then stopped. "I love you, Lauren Howell, and am willing to make some drastic changes. I have the money to bring our two different worlds together, but I'll need your help." He swept his hands up and down his clothes. "Starting with suits. Do I look okay?"

Oh, God. He looked absolutely wonderful—casual and sexy, his hair slightly windblown, and a hint of color to his cheeks. She smiled. "I love your clothes, Deems."

Sweeping his gaze over her face, he stepped closer. "I told you earlier of my plans to give up the North American territory. I have since appointed a man for the job. I've also redirected business calls away from my cell phone. This way, my calls to you won't be interrupted." He took another step closer. "I want a family, Lauren, with children as beautiful as you."

Her breath hitched. Emotions slammed together like a tidal wave against a brick wall. All the love she felt for this man returned with one big whoosh. She went mute, too stunned to speak.

He stared down the hall leading to the apartment's two bedrooms. "I'll still need to travel, but I want you with me every step of the way. We'll make a compromise of sorts. Time here and time in New York." He cocked his head. "Are you willing?"

Somehow, she found her voice. "I'm not sure." She searched his face. He still hadn't said the words she wanted to hear. Technically, she'd be the mother of his children and nothing else. *That arrangement will go over big with my parents.* She cleared her throat. "Deems, I—"

Stepping toward her, he pressed a finger against her lips.

Oh, dammit! His touch instantly melted her bones. Fighting a powerful urge to wrap her arms around his neck, she plastered her hands to her thighs. How could she be so friggin' in love with him after all this time?

His lips stretched into a gentle smile. "Unwrap the basket."

Anything to move away from him. She ripped the cellophane to expose red, green, and yellow apples. Nestled in the center stood a little black box. A ring box definitely. But what kind of ring was the question. Fingers shaking, she lifted the box and flipped the lid. Her breath caught. A gorgeous, diamond-studded engagement ring sparkled against a black-velvet backdrop. She dropped her jaw and threw him a questioning gaze.

He slid his hands up and down her arms. "I've missed you so much, Lauren. I thought I'd never again see your beautiful smile or hear your laughter. Please, marry me. I knew you were the one the moment we met in Jan's apartment, but I've taken too long to say the words to keep you in New York." His fingers caressed her arms. "Maybe I can convince you not to teach and stay home to raise our children, but you will always have an art studio and all the supplies you need. All I want is to hear you say you'll be my wife." He dropped his hands to his sides. "You can think about your answer."

Think? What the hell had she to think about? He was handsome, rich, and she loved him so much. He was as necessary as her next breath, and she'd be a fool to let him go. "Deems—" Her voice failed her.

Doubt clouded his gaze. He cocked his head and waited.

"Please, kiss me."

His honey-colored eyes sparkled as he wrapped his arms around her in a tender embrace and slid his lips over hers.

The memory of their New York time together flooded her soul, and tears welled in her eyes. She had her own happily-ever-after story straight out of a movie. Slipping her arms around his neck, she lifted her head to gaze into his beautiful eyes. "I'd love to be your wife." She choked on a sob.

Again, his lips connected, and a groan escaped from his throat.

She kissed him with all the pent-up love she'd held in since their last encounter. He belonged to her, and she would love him until the day she died. Sniffing, she released his neck and stared at the ring still in its box. "I can't believe I'm marrying a billionaire." Suppressing a grin, she tapped a palm on his chest. "If you want, you can have a cheap rate for three-D murals in all your buildings."

He laughed heartily and squeezed her tight. After releasing her, he took the ring box and slipped the diamond onto her left hand. "You are the country girl I cannot give up, Lauren."

Hand extended, she stared at the beautifully cut stone. "I feel like I've entered another dimension." She positioned her hand to catch the light from the open door. "The setting is perfect, Deems." Her heart filled to overflowing with a love she could no longer contain, and the tears rolled down her cheeks. Oh, God, how she adored this man. She placed a palm against his cheek. "I love you so much." She sniffed then smiled. "If you're willing, we can run out for a pizza and some wine—assuming you don't mind sleeping in an apartment without air conditioning."

Gaze sparkling, he used both thumbs to wipe the tears from her cheeks. "With you by my side, I'll sleep anywhere, but—" He lifted her chin and waved a finger in her face. "Here is our first compromise. How about pizza and beer? After a hot day like today, I need to guzzle a few pints. And while we're out, let's buy a window unit to keep us cool."

Laughing, she wrapped her arms around his neck. "All right. Pizza, beer, and love on cool sheets." But not necessarily in that order.

A word about the author...

With a growing backlist of books, Jane Drager continues to write mysteries with a strong romantic element, always with a happily-ever-after theme. An avid reader as well as writer, Jane has lived her life as diverse as her stories. She was a journalist, sports editor, office manager, firefighter, ambulance captain, caterer's assistant, but retired from her long career as a Respiratory Therapist and instructor. She's married to a wonderful organic farmer who keeps her busy with canning and freezing.

Visit her website at www.janedrager.com

Other Titles

Ask Nothing in Return
Infinite Choices
Secrets and Assumptions
Secrets by Necessity
The Riddle Key

Thank you for purchasing
this publication of The Wild Rose Press, Inc.

For questions or more information
contact us at
info@thewildrosepress.com.

The Wild Rose Press, Inc.
www.thewildrosepress.com

To visit with authors of
The Wild Rose Press, Inc.
join our yahoo loop at
http://groups.yahoo.com/group/thewildrosepress/